GOAL Suck

GABRIELLE DELACOURT

Goal-Suck Book One of The PuckHead Series Copyright © 2022 by Gabrielle Delacourt
First Edition | Paperback Publication Date:
ISBN: 979-8-9856984-0-4

All rights reserved. No part of this book may be reproduced, distributed or transmitted in any form or by any means, including information storage and retrieval systems, without written permission from the author except for the use of brief quotations in a review. This is a work of fiction. All characters, names, and events in this book are products of the author's imagination. Any resemblance to any place or person is simply coincidental.
Copy Editing by: RaeAnne @Lavenderprose.editing and Colby @colby_bettley
Paperback formatting by: Books & Moods Internal
Cover design by: Gabrielle Negrillo
Published by Gabrielle Delacourt

*To my girl group, I love y'all endlessly.
Reminder: Don't suck... Swallow. ;)*

Goal suck

a derogatory ice hockey slang word for a player who loiters near the net in hopes of doing minimal work to score. Origins: Goal + Suck
("Self-pitying person")

PLAYLIST

Green Eyes- Jake Scott
Hands on you- Austin George
Homebody- Valley
Bedhead-Shoffy
Maybe- Jake Scott
Do you believe- Ali Gatie, Marshmello & Ty Dolla $ign
How do you love- Cheat Codes, Lee Brice and Lindsey Ell
Fireaway- New Rules
Cotton Candy- Nic D
I Told You- Haywood, Loote, Petey Martin
CWJBHN- Jake Scott
Growing Pains- AJ Mitchell
Naked- Jake Scott
All 4 Nothing (I'm so in love)- Lauv
Waves- Miguel ft. Kacey Musgraves
Pull Me- KAYDEN
Under the Influence- Chris Brown
up again- mike.
Love me from a distance- Emily Vaughn
Where's That Girl?- Abigail Barlow
GIRL- Maren Morris
Lost- Noak Hellsing
this is how you fall in love- Jeremy Zucker
Slow- SHY Martin
Cinderella's dead- EMELINE
She- Jake Scott
One of the Good Ones- KAYDEN
The Bones- Maren Morris, Hozier
Like No One Does- Jake Scott

AUTHOR'S NOTE

Hello lovely readers!

Thank you so much for picking up this book and for taking a chance on me as an author.

Before we get into the fun of *Goal-Suck*, I want to make a note here about possible Trigger Warnings.

This book includes mentions of physical abuse by a partner. Although there is no abuse on page, there are heavy discussion of the after effects of abuse.

If this makes you uncomfortable, I will not be offended if you pass on reading this.

Not every book in this series will have dark themes like this, but Dakota had an incredible story to tell that I couldn't pass on.

In addition to these things, myself and both of my editors are only human. If you find any errors which are likely to happen, please feel free to email me at gabrielledelacourtauthor@gmail.com. I ask that you don't report them to Amazon, as it can result in the book being taken down.

If you enjoy this story, be sure to follow me on social media!

Instagram- @Gabbiesshelf

Join my Facebook group- https://www.facebook.com/groups/477448663802475/

I hope you love Dakota and Wyatt as much as I do.

xx Gabbie D

CHAPTER 1
Dakota

I think I'm broken. Or at the very least, I'm a freak of nature.

I hate hockey. I absolutely loathe the game. I hate the cocky men who walk around like their shit doesn't stink, and I hate the fans of the game. Okay, I hate most of the fans. My best friend in the entire world just so happens to be an avid hockey fan, and I can't hate her for it because I love her.

My hatred for hockey *may* stem from negative experiences I've had in the past. Maybe it's immature of me to judge all hockey players, but I feel it's safer to generalize than to take the time to trust someone again and wind up getting hurt.

Growing up in Toronto, people eat, sleep, and breathe hockey. It's serious business. The fans, the players—everyone *loves* hockey. They didn't care that I'd been hurt by one. Thousands of psychotic hockey fans surrounded me at every waking moment. My dad and brother are easily some of the biggest Thunder fans. Even my mother—that traitor—loves hockey. I can't fault them, though. Even they don't know of the pain I went through. I don't know if they ever will, but for now, I'll hold on to my hate and keep it close to me.

After college, my best friend and I took the first flight out and landed ourselves a cozy little apartment in Boston. And guess what? There are hockey lovers here too. There are literally hockey fans everywhere I go.

A tug on my denim jacket brings me back to the present.

"Koda, I see that look on your face, and I promise it won't be that bad." Sterling's gray eyes bore into mine, that brief note of humor swirling within them. She's enjoying this. I mumble profanities under my breath, and she chuckles, tugging me toward the concession stand.

One of my clients gifted me with tickets to see the Boston Yellow Jackets. I've lived in Boston for years now and I've avoided TD Garden like the plague. Sterling, on the other hand, takes every opportunity to pester me about going. I tried desperately to get out of going tonight, but here I am.

"Just try to enjoy yourself. For me? Pretty please." She holds her hands in front of her chest, bouncing a little on the balls of her feet. A beat of wariness rolls through me. She must see it because she's quick to assure me, "I checked. It's the Yellow Jackets and the Sharks only."

I sigh, relief flowing through me. I roll my eyes before replying.

"Fine, but only because I love you."

She smiles widely at that, her nose wrinkling as her face scrunches in happiness.

We order food and drinks before making our way toward the doors that lead to the rink.

"Tickets," the security guard says. I pull out my phone and show him the barcode for our tickets. He promptly scans them, calling someone over to lead us towards our seats. Sterling gasps at my side as

GOAL *Suck*

we walk down and right behind the penalty box.

"How the hell did he get these tickets and why did he give them away to *you?*" She squeals, making a show of looking around dramatically. The man points, directing us to the two seats next to a slouchy fan with his face hidden behind a baseball cap. Sterling goes first, leaving me to sit next to the *stranger*. I almost glare at her again, but think the better of it because I *promised* I would behave.

I sit down a moment before Sterling places a Yellow-Jacket-colored toque on my head.

"Really, Silver?" I narrow my eyes at her, and she smiles wide.

"You need to fit in," she says, her voice growing louder as more people file in. She's wearing her hair natural today; the fluffy curls rest around her face and neck, her toque keeping it in place. Her dark hair only makes her light eyes more striking.

"What if I don't want to fit in? My whole vibe is about not fitting in, Silly." I kick my Doc Marten boots up on the railing, pushing back into the seat.

She eyes me curiously, her eyes flicking behind me to the man at my side. I try to ignore his presence, but it's weird being so close to someone I don't even know.

"One day, Koda, I'll get you to admit that you actually like hockey. Men ain't shit, but hockey is *still* an amazing sport. It's my life's mission to hear those words muttered from your mouth."

I snort, closing my eyes and resting before the game starts.

Music blares through the speakers, fans going crazy as soon as the announcer starts the countdown.

Chills rush through me as the lights dim, a video playing on the large screens above us. I drop my feet to the ground, my leg bouncing as I watch. I try my best to look bored, but I know it'll be short-lived. The excitement in the atmosphere is like a drug, and I almost feel myself giving way to it. The screams that sound around us are deafening.

From the corner of my eye, I see the stranger lift his cap a bit, revealing some of his face. I catch sight of his incredible jawline, peppered lightly with stubble. From what I can tell, he's quite attractive, and that makes me nervous.

I look back up at the screen, the dramatic music booming all around us. A shark swims across the screen, and the crowd boos. The Yellow Jackets are facing St. Louis today, and it appears Boston is not a fan. Blue lights fill up the space on the ice, almost like water. I barely have time to blink before the ice goes white again, then cracks, leaving the two mascots skating on small slabs of ice with massive sharks swimming around them.

Sterling grips my leg, her eyes locked on the scene before us. My heart pounds in my chest. I take a breath, then arrange my features back into that bored face it was before. Sterling leans forward to get a better look, and I follow her. The massive shark swims back in and then jumps out of the water, sending Sterling and I back into our seats, laughing lightly. She looks over at me, her eyes amused. I roll mine back at her, and she laughs.

The stadium goes dark, then all at once, lights fly around us as players file out onto the ice. Sterling screams at my side, and I can't help but smile. I'm glad she's enjoying this.

They go through the introductions of the players, Sterling telling me which are her favorites. I can barely keep up as she lists out stats and numbers of each player. Before I know it, the game starts. I'm barely keeping up. I look over at the man on my side again. He seems almost as uninterested as I am. Taking a calculated risk, I look over to Sterling, unable to hold my shit-talking in any longer.

"You realize this whole thing is incredibly stupid, right? It's a bunch of full-grown men playing with their sticks." I poke her side when she doesn't respond.

"Huh? Sorry, I was watching a bunch of hot men playing with their sticks." She smirks, and I swear I hear a snort come from my right.

"How much do you wanna bet all of their teeth are fake?"

"Dakota, do you want me to punch you? I will." She turns her head back to the ice, her leg bouncing anxiously as the players skate across the ice.

Two massive men come barreling to our side of the ice, the puck flying across it to another Boston player a moment before number eleven is smashed into glass. A moment later, Boston scores, and the crowd goes wild.

"If I wanted to watch men beat the shit out of each other, I'd watch MMA," I say under my breath. I see the corners of the man's mouth rise, his full lips visible from this angle.

Sterling leans over me, her face getting closer to the stranger. "I am *so* sorry about her. She's a hater because everyone loves hockey but her. Please feel free to tell her to shut up at any moment."

The man's brow shoots up, a small smirk replacing the bored expression that was there a moment ago. I can see his face fully now. The moment our eyes meet, the breath is nearly knocked out of me, my heart fluttering. I hope the blush doesn't show on my face. I drop my eyes to the floor, then look up at him again. Butterflies rush through me like a storm. His icy blue eyes bounce between Silver and me. His full lips and stubble compliment his light eyes that seem to look only at me now. He's incredibly handsome, and I half regret my shit-talking.

I purse my lips. "Silver," I hiss.

She smiles, reaching her hand across me to offer it to the man.

"Sterling," she says. He takes her hand and shakes it. "But people I like call me Silver. And this grump is Dakota. She's not always a bitch. She's very pleasant to be around, usually."

I toss my head back, groaning. *Please don't embarrass me in front of the hot stranger.*

"Silver," I say again, my voice lower, more embarrassed than irritated this time. I look at her, and she just smirks. Sterling *Silver* is currently on my shit list. When I look back, his hand is still there, his eyes looking at me curiously. He quirks an eyebrow again, and I begrudgingly decide to extend my hand and shake. I want to yank my hand back the moment our hands connect. Is it possible to feel electricity run through your body because of a simple touch?

"Wyatt," he says. His voice is rich and deep, like expensive chocolate. It sends a shiver down my spine. "And I don't mind. I'm quite enjoying myself." His eyes twinkle with something I can't quite place.

Sterling looks at the man for a moment, her cheeks rounding with a smile. There's some sort of unspoken thing happening between them.

"Oh, Wyatt. Don't say that. She'll never shut up now." She flicks the ball on top of my toque and leans back into her chair.

"I mean, how *do* you even watch this game when you can barely see the puck?" I pose the question to Sterling, mostly.

Right. Shit-talking will help me breathe properly again.

"Oh, Koda. Will you ever learn? Hot men, remember?"

"The hockey players I knew were *not* hot. Well, most of them, and they were complete assholes."

This piques Wyatt's interest.

"Well, maybe you're just meeting the wrong ones," he says.

"Nah I don't think so," I challenge. "They've got those massive egos and hardly any redeeming qualities."

And horrible tempers. And anger issues. And hands that cause pain. The list goes on. I cross and uncross my leg, turning to face him.

Sterling shoots to her feet, screaming obscenities as the Sharks score.

It's one-to-one.

"Koda, you don't know every hockey player to exist. Plus, you were hopping on the hockey train back then."

I clench my teeth, my temper flaring slightly. She *knows* why I don't like hockey. I've got a personal vendetta against one player in particular.

"You're right, I don't." I fold my hands across my lap, my eyes trained forward. I see Sterling's face soften in my peripheral. She sighs. Her hand comes to my wrist, and I relax slightly.

"I'm waiting for the day that you meet one that's got a dick good enough to make you speechless."

I know she says it to lighten the mood again. Sterling cocks her head, and Wyatt snorts at my side.

I open my mouth, then close it.

"Silver, you're going to be the death of me."

"Just you wait. God forbid you meet a hockey player you actually like." She winks at Wyatt behind her, then tucks her foot under her butt.

"What was that?" I ask her.

She smiles at me innocently.

"Oh, nothing."

"Want to take bets on it?" Wyatt deadpans, waiting for Sterling's response.

"Most definitely."

"What are the stakes?" he asks.

"If she's not enjoying herself by the end of the game, you're taking us out for drinks tonight." Her eyes twinkle, and I feel my jaw clenching.

"Uh, don't I get a say in this?"

"No," they say at the same time.

I roll my eyes and sit back in my seat, my eyes watching the ice again.

"And if she is enjoying herself?" Wyatt presses. I look at him without turning my head. That was a mistake because I see that he's watching me. A flutter takes over my belly, and I flick my eyes back to the ice.

"If she is enjoying herself in the presence of hockey players, I will…" She moves her hands to her lip, thinking.

I don't think before I speak. The words just spill out of my mouth. "If the two of you can get me to enjoy myself by the end of this game, I will give you a free tattoo."

Sterling's eyes shoot to mine, her expression dancing with amusement again.

Fuck.

"A free tattoo," Wyatt says.

"Koda here is a tattoo artist. The best, if I do say so myself." She peels up her sweatshirt, revealing the rib piece I did for her a couple of years ago. It's a snake wrapped around a skull surrounded by a myriad of florals. Some of my best work, I think. Only the best for my bestie.

Wyatt examines her tattoo, seeming to come to an agreement.

"Deal," he says. They shake on it, and I purse my lips, my heart beating a bit faster. If he wins, that means I get to see him again.

Over the next two hours, the two of them take turns pestering me. Sterling is *such* a cheat. History is my weakness. As soon as she started spewing historical facts about the game, it was almost impossible to hide my interest. That doesn't mean I will find myself frequenting hockey games any time soon, but maybe, just maybe, I don't hate it as much as I thought. Boston is winning, three-to-one.

Wyatt's tactic includes pulling out his phone and giving me an up-close-and-personal experience with each player on the ice. Number eleven's name is Jaiden, and he's a left winger. Number twenty-three is Roman, and he's a right defenseman. With each player, he brings up a picture and points them out on the ice. The way he talks about them is as if he knows them. I've never considered myself to be a fangirl, not for hockey, so taking time out of my day to learn about people I'll probably never meet sounds like a waste.

I'm surprised I'm able to pay as much attention as I have. Each time Wyatt speaks, he leans into me, his leg brushing mine, and *every* time, my heart beats a little faster.

As Wyatt and Sterling continue, bouncing off each other like a sounding board, I take a moment to look at him. From here, I can tell that he is tall. His legs are stretched wide in a man spread, his knees nearly hitting the wall of the penalty box. When he adjusts the cap on his head, I get a glimpse of his dark brown hair.

The voices grow loud around us again, and I look up to see a player walking into the penalty box. It's number eleven. I dive back through my memory for his name.

"That one's Jaiden, right?" I lean into Wyatt so that he can hear me.

"Yes." When he speaks, I can feel his breath against my ear. He smells like mint and magic, if magic had a smell. As if Jaiden's ears were ringing, he looks back at us. He nods his head, then turns back to the ice. Sterling smiles wide, her eyebrows raised.

"Oh, this is gonna be so good," she says, laughing.

"What?" I say, feeling like I'm missing something. She just smiles.

The timer counts down, the last few seconds stirring an excited sort of anxiety within me. I watch as the players skate across the ice with such ease.

With five seconds left on the clock, Boston scores again, and the crowd springs to their feet. I shamelessly join them, my voice breaking as I cheer. Like a bucket of ice water, I'm suddenly aware of the fact that I'm the only one cheering out of the three of us. Both Wyatt and Sterling are staring at me. Wyatt looks down at me, his eyes smirking—if that's even possible. He's so damn tall. I feel puny next to him.

"Oh, shit," I say, my cheeks reddening.

"Looks like you owe me a tattoo," he says. "And I'm taking you out for drinks."

Sterling jumps, throwing her bag over her shoulder. "Great. Onward!"

And that is how we end up at a random bar in Boston with a *really* hot stranger we met at a Yellow Jackets game.

CHAPTER 2
Wyatt

October is one of my favorite months. Not only because it's the start of the regular season, but also because the weather is just so damn nice. This is one of the few times I can enjoy Boston weather before the season picks up.

Dakota brushes by me as she takes a seat at the table. She removes her jacket, laying it across the back of her chair, and shoves her beanie into her bag. The movement causes her long-sleeve to rise up a bit, giving me a view of what appears to be a floral tattoo wrapping around her wrist. I can't help but watch her as she piles her long blonde hair into a messy bun at the top of her head, tying it with a scrunchie.

She's incredible. Not to wax poetic, but *damn*. She's got a body sculpted by God himself and big green eyes that make my mouth water. And those lips.

I shake my head as the server comes with our drinks, setting each one down gently in front of us. I take a sip of my beer, letting the slightly sour taste coat my tongue and then disappear.

Dakota watches me, her gaze looking slightly defeated. I can't help but smirk. The moment she started talking shit, I knew that I liked her. She wasn't going to be one of those girls who throw themselves at me because of my name or because of who I am. It's hard to trust people when your name is well known. I never truly know if someone wants to use me only for my status. Dakota is a breath of fresh air.

I want to keep her.

Sterling knows, though, and I like that she's keeping it quiet. I don't want to embarrass Dakota, but when she finds out, I know that I will have hell to pay.

Sterling sits across from us, her eyes gleaming with triumph. "Isn't this so nice, Koda?" She sips her drink, an eyebrow quirking in her direction. I can practically feel Dakota roll her eyes.

"Yeah, whatever. I guess I'm *mildly* a hockey fan now. The sport, not the men." The way she says it has absolutely zero conviction, and that makes me laugh. She looks over at me, her eyebrows drawn together, eyes narrowed. "You didn't look much like a hockey fan either, Wyatt." She hisses my name, but I just want her to say it over and over again.

"And why would you assume that?"

"Oh, would you like me to make a list for you?" She holds her hand up, ticking off a finger for each one. "You were sitting there like you were half asleep, all the fans have at least some sort of team color or jersey on and you had neither, and you were just going to let me keep talking shit during the game."

"Maybe I'm just polite. And I don't need to sport black and yellow to be a fan. But I never said I was a Boston fan." I look at her, my lips pursed to keep the smile at bay.

"Oh? Then why were you at a Boston game, behind the penalty box?"

I ponder her question, wondering how much to say. I open my mouth to speak when two burly men come barreling through the door. I see Jaiden immediately, his toothy grin and unruly brown hair staples of his.

"Wyatt! My man. Why didn't you wait for us at the stadium?" Jaiden walks closer, and I feel Dakota still beside me. Her eyes go wide when I rise from the table, grabbing his hand and tossing my other around his back, landing a hearty smack there. When we pull apart, Roman sidles up beside Jaiden and pulls me into a hug. "Who are these lovely ladies?"

I look over at Sterling and Dakota. Sterling is grinning from ear to ear, whereas Dakota is frowning, her face pink. Sterling extends her hand to Jaiden.

"Sterling. Nice to meet you. Big fan, by the way." They shake hands and then trade places as Roman steps forward, doing the same.

"I've seen you before," Roman says. "You've done photos for us, right? I've never looked better than in the photos you took of me." Sterling smiles, her hand coming to her chest.

"I'm glad to be of service. I'd love to get some photos of the both of you in action one day."

Jaiden and Roman exchange a look. "I'll see what I can do," he says, smacking Jaiden on the arm. "We might know some people." He winks.

Roman shifts, his gaze on Dakota now. He looks her over, and a part of me wants to wrap my arm on the back of her chair or growl, just something to say hands off. I do neither of those things.

"I didn't catch your name," he says, extending his hand.

"Uh, Dakota." She looks at me. "How do you know them?"

"We all went to Boston University before this one here left us like a traitor." Roman slaps me on the back, pulling a chair from a neighboring table and sitting to the left of Dakota. Jaiden takes the seat next to Sterling.

"Left you like a traitor," she says, her voice low. Roman looks at me curiously. I don't know whether to drop the bomb now or let it keep going. Roman decides for me.

"Yeah. He left us for the fucking Riders. Damn traitor." He smirks, enjoying the rivalry.

"The Riders," she says, still mulling it over. Sterling laughs, folding her hands across the table.

"So how did y'all meet?" Jaiden flags down a server, ordering a beer for the two of them.

"Ms Easton here was shit-talking hockey in front of Wyatt, so I told him to shut her up at any point." Sterling smiles innocently.

"Woah, woah, Dakota. What's wrong with hockey?"

"The men," Sterling says. "She thinks they're all cocky jerks."

"Silver," she seethes. "Shut up."

"Wait, I thought your name was Sterling," Jaiden says with a serious look on his face. I burst out laughing, and Roman smacks the table.

"Jaiden, dude," Roman wheezes. "Sterling silver. It's a clever nickname, really."

Dakota smiles, but it doesn't quite reach her eyes.

"You left them for the Riders?" she asks again.

"Yeah, he's the best defenseman they got," Roman says. I watch her as the gears turn in her head. I can see the way she runs through the information I shared with her earlier and how she puts all the pieces together. When it finally clicks, her head snaps to me.

GOAL *Suck*

"You ass," she says. Her face has turned crimson. "You let me shit-talk your sport for nearly an hour and said nothing? I insulted basically every hockey player and you didn't even try to defend yourself." She looks at Sterling, who's now trying really hard to look innocent. "You knew?"

She finally loses it, a snort escaping her nose. "Koda, hockey is my life. Of course, I knew. That's what made it so great."

"But why would you do that? This is so embarrassing," she says, holding her hands up to her face and shaking her head. "Why?" she moans.

The table bursts out laughing, Dakota shrinking further into her shell. I don't laugh, though. I watch her, my stomach in knots. I hadn't anticipated a reaction that would make me want to pull her into my arms to make it better. I'd expected her to laugh it off, then move on.

"Wait, she didn't know you played hockey?" Jaiden asks.

"Dude, catch up." Roman shoots him a look, and Jaiden scowls.

"Koda," Sterling says. "It's all in good fun. You went to a hockey game with me, shit-talked, and it just so happened to be next to an NHL player in hiding, Wyatt Alexander *fucking* Lane. It was too good an opportunity to pass up."

Roman looks at me. I'm watching her intently, but even so, I can see him observing me. I finally look away from Dakota to look at Roman. He leans back in his chair, seeing my intentions on my face. *Mine.* He backs off, his eyebrow raised at me and a hint of amusement on his face. She may not be mine now, but I certainly won't allow my best friend to shoot his shot at her. I won't risk it.

He doesn't even need to say it, I already know. I have a feeling that this girl is going to turn my world upside down.

Dakota appears to be over her embarrassment. She's in a heated argument with Roman over the right way to eat your pizza. He's demonstrated a taco-like fold twice now to argue that it's best to compress before eating.

"That is so wrong," she says, laughing. She sips her drink, then puts a fry in her mouth. "Maybe not *all* hockey players are bad after all."

"Oh? What was that I just heard?" Sterling places her hand around her ear.

"You bitch. You know what I said, and you'll be lucky if I admit I don't hate the game again after tonight." Dakota laughs, tossing a fry toward Sterling. I enjoy watching them together.

"How long are you in Boston?" Roman asks me.

"I leave tomorrow. We've got a game on Thursday." Roman hums something, then joins the conversation that Jaiden is having with Sterling. Dakota is sitting quietly; listening or watching, I wouldn't know. I hope she doesn't notice me watching her.

I'd like to get to know her, to explore every piece of her, the way her body feels against mine and what she looks like beneath me. Her eyes glance in my direction, and I hold her gaze for a moment. They flutter, hiding behind that fan of lashes. I miss those beautiful green eyes already.

"I'm sorry," she says. Her voice is quiet and subdued. "For talking so much shit at the game, I mean. I hope you didn't take it personally."

"Hey. You don't need to apologize. You should hear some of the other shit I hear on a daily basis. That was mild in comparison."

A ping sounds, and Dakota pulls out her phone from her jacket. She scrolls through the notifications on her screen. I try to look away to give her privacy. She holds it slack in her right hand as she looks up to Sterling.

"Girl, we've gotta run. I've got a client tomorrow." I don't process her words right away. Instead, I take my chance and slip the phone from her hands and punch my number into her contacts. She turns her head to look at me. "What are you doing?"

"Giving you my number," I say.

"Are you ladies from Boston?" Roman asks.

"Canada, actually, but yes, we live locally," Sterling answers for both of them. I can see Dakota shoot her a look from across the table. My brain runs through this new information. I want to see her again. I'm suddenly thankful for my friends in Boston.

"I'm sure we'll see you ladies around, then," Jaiden says as he eyes Sterling. I know that look. It takes me back to college days when he coined them as *hungry eyes*.

Dakota shoves back from the table, pulling her jacket off the back of her chair. The others stand with her. She tries to shake hands with the guys, but they pull her in for bear hugs. She practically disappears within their arms. I see her shaking with laughter as she pulls away, and I can't help but smile. She looks at me, smiling lightly as we follow her outside.

I want to touch her, but instead I shove my hands into my pockets and follow behind her, giving myself a view of her ass.

The chill of the air hits us immediately as we step out into the street. The bright street lights illuminate her face as she turns to me. Sterling and the others have walked down a bit, giving us a moment to talk. She doesn't meet my eyes right away, but then she looks up at me fully and I never want to forget this moment. I mentally take a picture of the beautiful girl I met in Boston.

Leaning forward, I pull her into my arms. Her arms move to my back, and I still. She fits perfectly within my grasp.

"I liked that you didn't know who I was." I say it into her ear so that only she can hear. Her breath is warm against my cheek. "And I didn't need to defend myself. I'll prove you wrong eventually. We're not all cocky assholes." I pause, taking a moment to appreciate how her breathing hitches as she takes in my words. "Make sure you use that number. You still owe me a tattoo. And if you're ever in Raleigh, call me." I wink at her as I pull away.

Her cheeks are pink, probably more from the cold. She blinks at me, her hands now tucked into the pockets of her jacket. She looks absolutely beautiful, and I suddenly have the urge to kiss her. I shove the urge away.

"Yeah, yeah," she says, a small smile filling up her face. "Later… Wyatt Alexander Lane." She walks off, Sterling gripping her arm as they walk. I wonder if I'll ever get the pleasure of looking into the beautiful eyes of Dakota Easton again.

CHAPTER 3
Wyatt

My mind wanders back to reality when Coach calls for a break. Any time I'm on the ice, I let my mind go blank, allowing muscle memory to take over and drive. I skate to the side, grabbing my water and squirting a mouthful before spitting it onto the ice. Sweat drips down my face as the longer bits of my hair drape in front of my eyes. I'm in desperate need of a shower, but we still have another hour of practice.

After today, we'll be on the road for several days. We're only two weeks into the regular season, but every single one of us is taking this season more seriously than the rest. We've got a killer team this year, and I'm confident that it could take us right to the finals.

Skating back into position, I look over and wink at Damian. His eyes narrow at me, then he shakes his head, rolling his eyes and focusing back on the ice.

The last hour moves quickly. I hardly notice how long it's been until Coach steps back onto the ice, blowing his whistle and skating in front of us.

"I'm calling it," Coach yells across the ice. "Hit the showers."

Damian skates up beside me, slapping a hand across my back.

"You coming out with us tonight?"

"Nah," I say. "I'm meeting Roman and his li'l girl at some play palace for her birthday."

I pull off my sweaty practice jersey and lower myself to the bench.

"Shame. Liam's invited some puck bunnies to come along."

I cringe at his words. I know their plans to divvy up the women, seeing which ones will end up going home with them tonight. I have no desire to participate. If he'd asked a few weeks ago, my answer may have been different.

"Not my thing, man." I pull off my skates and the rest of my gear, tossing a towel over my shoulder and padding to the showers. Damian follows behind me, stepping into the stall beside mine. Liam takes the one on my right.

"You feeling sick or something, dude?" Liam flicks water onto my side, and I roll my eyes.

"I'm perfectly fine." I step under the steaming water, scrubbing at my face and rinsing out my hair.

"Out with it, then. Who is she?" It's Damian who speaks this time. I ignore him.

"Leave him alone," Hudson, our captain, says from a distance. "Not everyone is interested in taking a new puck bunny home every night of the week." They grumble in response, continuing a conversation with each other. I step out of the shower, a towel wrapped around my waist.

Damian strips down at my side, his longer hair dripping down his

GOAL *Suck*

back. "You seriously don't want to come out with us?" He runs his hair through his towel and then throws it up in a bun at the top of his head.

"Nah. Like I said, I'm meeting the guys for Lily's birthday."

"What's got you looking all mopey, then?" He looks at me from the corner of his eyes. My wet hair blocks my vision slightly as I reach into my bag and pull out my clothes. I don't know what to tell him. I'm moping around because the woman of my dreams has my number but won't use it.

"I think that I'm losing my edge," I say

"How so?"

"I met a woman last weekend and she's...*fuck*." I run my hand through my beard. "She's unlike anyone I've ever met."

"But?" Damian urges.

"But I gave her my number and she hasn't used it. She made it clear that she's not a fan of hockey players, and I have no idea why." Damian gives me a look of disbelief. I narrow my eyes at him, and he laughs.

"Don't be such a goal-suck, man. If you want the girl, you gotta do the fucking work." He stands, landing a slap on my back. "Get to it." He leaves me with a renewed sense of determination. I've become accustomed to the puck bunnies and the women who make it easy for me. I'm rarely wrong about my judgments of character, and Dakota is someone who radiates authenticity and kindness. She's the furthest thing from what I'm used to.

I rush to get dressed, ruffling my hair in the mirror, and then slinging my duffle over my shoulder as I walk out of the door.

Jaiden is standing by my Bronco when I walk up. He pats the door a couple times, smirking at me.

"Nice ride," he says.

"Thanks. Bought it myself." I hit the remote start, the sound of my car coming to life bringing a smile to Jaiden's face. "I'd offer to take you for a ride, but I don't want to waste gas." I smirk at him, pulling open the driver's side door and sliding into the seat.

"Asshole," he mutters, walking to his Jeep Wrangler and hoisting himself inside. I laugh, closing the door and shifting the car into reverse.

Jaiden follows me to the Princess Palace, where Roman and Lily are already waiting. The moment we walk through the door, I can feel several sets of eyes on us. Every mom in the place is watching us like hawks. I imagine us through their eyes, two giant men looking very out of place. Lily spots me from across the room, releasing a loud squeal and running toward me. I lower myself to her level and feel the impact of a tiny human a moment later. Her hair flies in all directions, some almost going into my mouth.

"Uncle Wyatt," she says, her voice pitched higher in excitement. "I missed you!"

"I missed you too, kiddo." I grab her waist and lift her into the air, spinning us around. "Look at you! You're almost full grown. How old are you now? Twenty-five?"

She giggles, her feet touching the ground again.

"No, Uncle Wyatt. I'm five, silly!" She throws herself into Jaiden's arms, saying hello to him as well. I step past them, giving Roman a hug, then turning around to watch.

"Anything from Sarah?" I ask.

Roman grunts, shoving his hands into his pockets.

"No. I doubt she even remembered her daughter's birthday."

I say no more. If Sarah had wanted to be a part of her daughter's life, she'd be making an effort. The thought makes me angry on Lily's behalf. That little girl is perfect in every way. I don't see how anyone could abandon her. I feel my jaw clench.

Roman watches me.

"What?" I snap.

"I'm angry, too," he says. "She doesn't understand fully, but I know it hurts her as well. She's just lucky to have us."

"That woman makes me violent." I clench my hands into fists, releasing them when Lily and Jaiden walk over to us, hand in hand. She grabs for my hand, pulling us toward the back room where there is a wall lined with hangers upon hangers of dress-up materials.

"I want to make you all beautiful," she says.

"Lily, are you trying to tell me that I'm not already beautiful?" Jaiden gasps, his free hand flying to his mouth. Lily giggles.

"Uncle Jai, you *know* that's not what I meant." She points to three different pairs of wings, Roman reaching to grab them off the wall and handing them to his daughter. She hands each of us a pair, instructing us to put them on. We dare not argue with the birthday girl.

An hour later, the three of us are dressed up as fairy princes. I've got glitter on my face somewhere, and both Jai and Roman have hearts drawn on their cheeks with pink lipstick. I can't help the laugh that spills out of my mouth when I look over at Jaiden. He's got butterfly clips holding his hair up in two mini ponytails at the top of his head. Lily walks over to Roman, placing a kiss on his nose and smearing a bit of glitter on his cheeks.

"Because I love you the most, Daddy." She smiles wide, then instructs us to stand. We walk over to the photobooth, a woman standing in front of a wall decorated as a castle. Lily holds her arms up to me, and I lift her, propping her on my hip.

"Say 'princess,'" the woman says, laughing lightly.

"Princess," Lily says, her smile the brightest in this room.

Jaiden walks up, handing the woman his phone. "Would you be able to take some on my phone? I need this for blackmail purposes."

She laughs, nodding her head, then snaps a few photos when Jaiden is back in place. When he takes his phone back, he releases a deep laugh, his head falling forward as he wheezes.

"We"—*wheeze*—"look"—*wheeze*— "ridiculous. I'm sending this to Sterling."

I barely register what he's saying before I'm running toward him with Lily still in my arms.

"No!" I try to grab for the phone, but it's too late.

"Already sent, bro." He smirks at me. Lily laughs, asking me to run again, and I have half a thought to deck Jai, but I don't. "Trust me. She'll think it's hot." I know he's not talking about Sterling now. I groan, running in the opposite direction, spinning around in circles and tossing Lily around in the air. Her happy cheers of glee make my heart swell.

"Again! Again!" Lily chants.

"Maybe later, squirt. Uncle Wyatt is gonna pass out if he spins again."

Roman takes Lily from my arms and walks us to the dinner table. There are four places set up surrounded by two pizzas. Roman pulls out a slice of cheese for Lily and then one for himself.

I shove a slice into my mouth, chewing as I slip my phone from my back pocket. I scroll through the notifications. I navigate to social media, typing Dakota's name into the search bar. I immediately find her business account.

Her work is incredible. She creates a lot of pieces that look to be right out of a fantasy novel. She showcases everything from script tattoos to a Medusa portrait. She has a very particular style, and I can't quite say that I mind it.

I pull up her DMs, taking another bite of pizza, but as I start typing, my phone buzzes with a new message.

GOAL *Suck*

I hold my pizza in my mouth as I scroll through my messages. It's an unknown number, but I know immediately who it belongs to.

> **Dakota: Hey. It's Dakota. Now you have my number, too. It's only fair.**

My fingers fly over the keys, typing out a message back to her.

> **Me: Glad you're one for fairness. How's the tattoo business?**
> **Dakota: Lovely, actually.**

As I read that message, a new one comes through.

> **Dakota: Nice wings.**

I look up to glare at Jaiden, but realize that everyone at the table is watching Lily talk animatedly about her field trip last week. I type out a quick message, then shove my phone back into my pocket and turn my attention back to Lily. When my phone vibrates in my pocket, it takes a few minutes for me to pull it back out and glance at the screen.

> **Me: Thanks. I've got glitter highlight too. Does that make me earn points?**
> **Dakota: Maybe a few.**
> **Me: A few?**
> **Dakota: Like ten. Maybe more, maybe less.**

I let the small smile I was hiding break free. When I look up, Jaiden is grinning at me.

"The photo worked, then?"

"You're an as—a brat." I shoot apologetic eyes toward Roman, then continue. "But yes, it did work. I got a text, and that is a step in the right direction."

"We'll have to buy them for you, then." Roman nudges me with his elbow, smirking.

"Uncle Wyatt wants to keep his wings?" Lily looks up at her dad, little giggles escaping when he tickles her.

"Yes, little one. Uncle Wyatt is trying to impress a girl." She gasps, eyes growing wide.

"Daddy says I'm not allowed to date until I'm thirty. When can I meet her?" She flaps her arms in excitement. I see Jaiden's eyes dancing with glee, his grin nearly taking over his face.

"I don't think it will be for a while yet, kiddo." I give her a little pout, and her face drops.

"Oh," she says. "But I want to meet her." She sounds so disappointed, and I immediately want to rectify it.

"I'll tell you what." I wave my hand, signaling her to come closer like it's a secret. "I'm trying to win this pretty girl over. If it goes well, I'll let you meet her. You need to approve, so you get to tell me if you like her or not." Her nose scrunches as she giggles, and it makes my heart swell.

"That's a lot of pressure, Uncle Wyatt, but okay."

"Great. Then it's settled." We shake hands, and she quickly moves on, babbling about school.

It's nearly nine by the time we're leaving the palace. Lily and Jaiden are in a heated argument over puppies. She's been begging Roman to get her a puppy since she could speak. He never said anything about getting a puppy this year with certainty, but that won't stop the arguments on what *kind* of puppy she wants.

"I want a wiener dog," she whines, jumping in little circles. I snort, looking at Roman. He shrugs his shoulders, shaking his head.

"All right, Bug, say your goodbyes." Lily nearly jumps into my arms, her little arms just barely wrapping around my neck.

"I'm going to miss you, Uncle Wyatt, but don't worry, I'm coming to see you play on the ice soon." She squeezes, giving me a little peck on the cheek, then drops her arms.

"I'll miss you too, little one. Take care of your dad for me, okay?"

"Okay," she says, grabbing her dad's hand and walking toward the car.

"What about me?" Jaiden says, offended. Lily giggles.

"Uncle Jai! You're coming back to the hotel with us, silly."

"Oh, you're right," he says with a chuckle.

I give both Jaiden and Roman hugs, then walk back toward my car. When I'm buckled in, I pull out my phone and stare at the screen.

Under normal circumstances, I would have joined the guys at the bar, but I have no desire to participate tonight.

I know what I want. My sights are set on Dakota, and I'd like to make her mine.

After typing a message back to Dakota, I throw my truck into reverse.

> **Me: I'll take any points I can get as long as you agree to a date with me.**

This woman is going to be the death of me. She's got me feeling unlike anything I've felt before. She doesn't care that I'm a professional hockey player, and something about that makes my dick hard. I may have just stumbled upon a once-in-a-lifetime opportunity. I want Dakota to be mine. She hates hockey players? I'll show her just how wrong she is.

Let the games begin.

CHAPTER 4
Dakota

I've had crushes before. I've experienced infatuation and I've felt that grow into something more. Trusting someone, especially in a romantic relationship, is something that I did once and haven't been able to do again, at least not yet. Unfortunately, the online dating world isn't for me. Almost every guy is looking for some sort of hookup or a free tattoo once they find out what I do. My picker is broken, and that is exactly why I'm hesitant to answer Wyatt's text from last night.

I'll take any points I can get as long as you agree to a date with me.

What am I supposed to say to that? We've known each other less than a few days and he wants to take me out. We also live states apart. It could never work. It's probably best if I just let him down easily or blow him off. Maybe I could even ghost him?

I groan into my hands, my eyes squeezing shut. Why does the

thought of ghosting Wyatt send my stomach into a fit of anxious flutters? There's almost a battle of fight or flight happening in my head right now, and I'm *ba da ba ba ba*, not lovin' it. *Freaking Wyatt Lane.*

Plans. My life consists of plans, carefully crafted plans. He is not one of them, yet suddenly, I want him to be. *Holy hell. Make up your damn mind.*

"What's got your panties in a wad?" Sterling waltzes into my room, lowering herself onto my bed and pulling her legs into her chest.

"Wyatt wants to take me out on a date." I don't look over at Sterling right away because I know what I'll see. I slowly slip my eyes toward her and—oh, look—I was right. She's barely holding onto her squeal.

"He what?" she says, her voice higher than normal. "Wyatt Lane asked you out?" She jumps off the bed and does a little excited dance.

"Yeah, kinda."

"What do you mean 'kinda?'" She stops moving, her arm coming to her hip as she stares at me. I shrug my shoulders and hand her my phone. She scrolls through the couple of messages and then looks at me. "Dakota, that's not a kinda. He asked you out. You *have* to say yes." She hands the phone back to me as she sits back on the bed.

"I don't know if I'm ready to date again, Silver. Plus, he lives in freaking Raleigh. That's almost a thousand miles apart."

"So?" Silver challenges. "You dated Tanner from here, which is also hundreds of miles apart." I roll my eyes, but I also know she's right. I made it work with Tanner because I wanted to—emphasis on *I*. He was the one who gave me the out I so desperately needed to be free of him. The distance between us was only one freedom.

"At least think about it," Silver says. "I think he could be good for you, Koda. You may not see it now, but I saw the way you were with him."

"Okay, fine." I glare at her. She smiles wide, her hands clapping with victory.

"Can I ask you a question?"

I nod.

"Do you even want to start dating again?"

I ponder her question for a moment. Honestly, I've been thinking about jumping back into the dating scene for a while. It's been two years since I freed myself from my ex, and I'm finally back in a place where I feel stable enough to entertain the idea of dating again. I've got a business here, and I can travel when and where I want. I hadn't anticipated someone like Wyatt walking into my life and changing up my carefully constructed plans.

"I downloaded that app again last week," I tell her.

"Is that a yes?"

"Yes. It is." I rub my palm nervously with my thumb.

"So then why can't that start with Wyatt? He's hot," she says, and I laugh. She's right. He is hot. He's one of the most attractive men I've laid eyes on. He puts the other men in my past to shame. His icy blue eyes send flutters through my body, and I can't quite get that feeling out of my head.

"I will *think* about it," I say again. "You know how I am, calculated risk and all that."

She smirks at me.

"I'll hold you to that, Koda."

"Great. Now let's get to work where I'll most definitely be harassed by Lani too."

I jog at a casual pace down our main street. Lani, my receptionist and the third musketeer, is at my side. She looks over at me and smirks. I see our destination down the street. I already know what she has planned. It's what we always do. We jog from my apartment complex to this street, then race the rest of the way.

Only Lani and Sterling know the true scope of my competitive nature. I love them for nurturing it so often.

I burst out laughing as we race down the street, coming to an abrupt halt at the gate of the coffee shop. Lani hunches over, her hands bracing herself on her knees. When she looks up at me, I laugh, shaking my head as I pant.

"Good one," she huffs, waving her hand up at me. We catch our breath for a moment before walking into the homey coffee shop. She tosses her orange hair over her shoulder, her hand rubbing up her neck as we approach the counter.

"Hi, ladies!" The barista waves at us. "I don't understand why y'all frequent my shop when you have your own." She winks at us, and I laugh.

"I like to support local businesses. My tattoo studio may double as a bookstore and coffee shop, but you still have the *best* lattes." I say as I take my coffee from the counter.

She laughs, shaking her head with a smile. "Well, you know I always appreciate that!"

Lani and I sit at a table in the shade on the patio. I settle into my seat, taking a sip of my coffee.

"So how was the game?" she asks. There's a twinkle in her eyes, which tells me that Sterling spilled the beans on our weekend already.

"Good," I say, my hands tightening on my coffee cup. I can see her smile grow, an eyebrow rising.

"Just good?"

"It was mildly life-altering. I *enjoyed* a hockey game." Lani wrinkles her nose and then laughs with me.

"Oh, what a shame. It's not like hockey is literally the sport for almost all the adonis men." She waves her hand, then fakes a yawn. "So…when are you seeing him again?" She pauses, typing something into her phone and then looking up at me again. "You *are* seeing him again, right?"

Sterling, that snitch.

"I don't know," I say. Lani watches me like she's waiting for me to continue, and when I don't, she speaks.

"What are you afraid of? And before you ask, I know you well enough to know you have your reservations." I laugh. She's right, I do.

"I really don't want a repeat of my experience with Tanner. I'm scared to trust someone again and get hurt."

"Is it just because he's a hockey player? Tanner was—is—-a douchey hockey player, but he also wasn't a decent guy." She makes a solid point. Tanner was a horrible person in general, and I knew that. Well, I found that out with time.

"I don't know enough about *him* to say he is a decent guy, but he did say he'd prove me wrong." *I'll prove you wrong eventually. We're not all cocky assholes.*

"Then let him," she says. "Let him woo you, take you out on fancy dates, and then decide." She's got a twinkle in her eyes.

"Maybe," I say. "I don't even know if that's what he wants. I'm not the kind of girl who's just another notch in someone's bed post. When I let someone in, I fall hard and fast, and I don't want to do that with someone who doesn't want the same things."

"There's only one way to find out." She taps her phone. "Text him. You're going to Raleigh soon. If he's home, he'd be a fool not to agree to see you."

I mull the idea over in my head. I've got a convention in Raleigh in a couple weeks. The beauty of running my own business is that I can schedule in extra time for play if I want to.

"Can I make a confession?" I ask.

Lani raises a brow, a curious expression taking over her face. "Always."

I hide my face as I speak. "I internet stalked him. I spent nearly two *hours* watching YouTube videos of him playing hockey and his interviews. And get this"—I throw my hands up for dramatic effect—"he's a damn good player too. I know nothing about stats, but he's incredibly fast and a force to be reckoned with on the ice. And I know nothing about the logistics of hockey, so that says a lot."

Lani looks at me stunned, then laughs so hard she almost falls off her chair.

"Girl, that's a li'l crazy. I love it." She slaps her thigh, smiling at me.

"I know." I groan. "I don't even know if he'll want to see me again. And I don't know if this could go anywhere. My brain's all jumbled." She looks at me through her lashes.

"Not to mention he's in Raleigh. Long-distance relationships never work. But it's too early to think about this stuff." I throw my hands over my face. "I can't be talking about long-distance relationships when I don't even know if he'd want to date me. Would *I* even want that?"

"It's not." She stands from her chair, walking toward me. "Let me tell you this: If it's meant to be, it will be. Just get to know him and don't jump into anything right away." She sits on the stool at the next station.

I purse my lips, mulling her words over again in my head. *The* Wyatt Alexander Lane is a famous hockey player who is bound to be photographed while out doing everyday people things. Is that something I want to subject myself to? My heart flutters.

One day at a time.

"Text him," she says, eyebrow raised.

I want to, I really do, but I don't think I'm ready to open up the door for a date just yet.

One day at a time.

The steam from the hot shower fills the small bathroom quickly. I sit on the toilet, scrolling through my phone instead of getting ready for work.

I mindlessly scroll through social media until I stop on a photo of Sterling and Jaiden. I don't know when they took this photo, but it's cute. She's got her hands clasped together, leaning on his shoulder with her hip jutted out. Jaiden's got a big toothy grin, his backwards baseball cap in the middle of being placed on her head. According to her, they've been texting back and forth the past couple days. *Good for her.*

I exit the app, navigating to my contacts. Scrolling down, I find Wyatt's name immediately. He's named himself "Not Wyatt Alexander," and I can't help but laugh. Pink rises to my cheeks. I replay the embarrassment from the night I met him. I felt like a fool. Of course, I didn't know who he was, but my embarrassment was short-lived after I saw the way he looked at me. He didn't care that I didn't know. That was comforting.

I sigh as I shut off my phone and place it on the counter before I climb into the shower and wash off the sweat from my run.

Going through the motions of getting ready is easy. It takes me a solid thirty minutes to get ready for the day. I put a tiny bit of makeup on to make me look less tired, then throw my hair into a chunky braid.

GOAL Suck

Today, I've decided on a more girly look. I pair my black floral skirt with a graphic tee and a body harness. I throw my leather jacket over because we're at that time of the year where it's chilly in the mornings and blazing hot during the day. My heeled booties and my black, wide-brim fedora are the last pieces to complete my look.

Before I started my own business, I would have never dressed like this. My clothing is a form of armor and a way to express myself. I worked hard to be a respected artist, and I've learned that I need to look the part in order to be taken seriously. *This* Dakota is a badass, brave and unwilling to take shit from anyone, but I haven't always been this girl.

When I started in this industry, it was easy to feel unsure of everything I created. My career depended on the approval of my mentor and those around me. My lack of confidence was a result of taking all the ugly words that have been thrown at me and believing them as truth.

Ugly.
No talent.
You'll never make it as a successful tattoo artist.
This is a man's world, and you're just living in it.

Looking in the mirror, I remind myself of who I am and all that I've accomplished. I give her a wink, then toss my bag over my shoulder and walk out the door.

My hands grip the cool handle of the shop door, sending a shiver through me. I walk into the studio, flicking on all the lights and turning on the air. The smell of coffee and baked treats waft through the room. I breathe deeply, enjoying the smell before I walk up the stairs into the bookstore/coffee shop portion of my studio.

Julia is already here, the espresso machine whirring as I step into view. She smiles wide at me as she pulls the metal cup from the frother. "Perfect timing," she says, handing me a latte. She slides a little plate across the counter. I look down at it and smile. "I'm trying my hand at scones. They're blueberry, your favorite."

I grin at her, shoving my nose into the treat and breathing in deeply. "It smells delicious. Thank you."

"Will Silver be joining us today?" Julia flips a towel over her shoulder, her teal ponytail swishing with the movement. I take a bite of my scone, moaning at the sugary goodness.

"I believe so. She's gonna be helping with the bookstore for a bit, just until we can find someone else." I say it all around a bite of food, hoping I don't look like a complete animal.

"That girl is going to spread herself too thin one day," she says with a laugh. "I appreciate it all the same." She glides behind the counter, pouring a double-double for herself, then turning to face me again.

Sterling is a photographer who specializes in sports photography. After working her ass off to get into journalism, none of the big sports agencies wanted to take her on. She's spent her whole life learning the ins and outs of just about every sport possible, yet they treated her as though she was underqualified and a dreamer. Sterling is *really* bad at taking no for an answer. When someone tells her that she can't do something, she'll laugh in their face and prove them wrong. And that is *exactly* what she did.

Sterling started her own website where she posts her photography. Once that took off, it started with certain players reaching out to her, and then entire teams were reaching out to Sterling for her photos. It's shifted to hockey mostly, which I know she doesn't mind. Traveling with her this past weekend was nice. She's often gone on her own adventures, so any time we can take a trip together, I enjoy the time with my best friend.

I take another bite of my scone, thanking Julia, then bound down the stairs to the tattoo studio. This was my dream, to open a tattoo studio that doubled as a coffee shop and a bookstore. As a book lover myself, I'd lose myself in books and then get the itch for a tattoo, or even just the community of people who understood my desire for bookish ink. I'd consider my speciality to be fine line tattoos. Bookworms frequent my shop, grabbing a coffee and bringing down their favorite book to help me design their next tattoo.

My mind wanders to Wyatt and the kind of tattoo that he would ask for. I wonder if he would look me up, find my art on social media, and decide to write me off. I shake him out of my head and set up my space. The jingle of the bell catches my attention, and I look up from my station to see Sterling walking through the door, my receptionist, Lani, close behind.

"'Sup, bitch," Sterling says, walking over to my station and swiping through my iPad. She stops on a design of a book stack surrounded by flowers. "This one is going to be beautiful. I can't wait to see it." She grins at me, then plucks my scone from the plate and takes a large bite before rushing up the stairs to the bookstore.

"Thanks for that," I call after her. She just waves her hand, disappearing around the corner a moment later.

Lani chuckles, setting her purse behind the desk and powering on her laptop.

"You had some changes to your schedule this week, babe." Lani waves me over to the computer. I toss my bag under the front desk and slide into the chair next to her.

"Thanks, love. I'll take a look at it in a bit."

When Lani walks away, there's a pep in her step that wasn't there before. I smile at her back, loving my cheery friend.

The day goes by smoothly, each appointment filling me creatively. Doing what I love every day is all that I could have ever asked for.

The shop is quiet as I sit on my desk, my sketchbook open in front of me and my hands already smeared with pencil. I lean my head down to sketch in some of the finer details of this piece I've been working on for weeks.

When footsteps approach, I don't look up until a coffee mug is placed on the desk. Lani stands there with her own coffee in hand, her head tilted as she looks over my sketch.

"That's beautiful," she says.

I smile, grabbing the coffee and taking a sip. "Thank you. I've always wanted to do something like this." When my mug hits the desk again, I look up at her, my head shaking. "Shit. I forgot to look at the schedule."

I swipe through the schedule, immediately seeing a three-hour block.

"What did they want to do?" I ask.

She looks to the door and then back to me. My eyes narrow slightly at her, and she blinks innocently. "They're planning a sleeve or something."

"This is three hours, though."

"Oh. Well, maybe you can take a long lunch," she says with a wink.

Something about this doesn't feel right, so I click on the details, my heart stopping when I see one name on the schedule.

"When did this happen?" I try to keep the anxiety from my voice.

"Just before you got here. You had a cancellation, and I scheduled it in the car."

"I don't even have anything drawn." I panic. He's coming. Here. And I need to design a tattoo for him on the fly.

"Don't panic," she says. "You'll do just fine."

I spend the rest of my day doing exactly what she said not to do. I panic, panic, and panic some more until the bell on the door rings. I look up, my heart stopping once again.

"Can I help you?" Lani says. I immediately look back down at the piece I'm working on. I've got a few minutes left on this piece, but I'm only delaying the inevitable.

"I'm here for an appointment with Dakota," he says. His voice sends shivers through my body.

My heart stutters. When it starts up again, it's hammering so hard it feels like it's trying to come out of my chest. I bite my lip, keeping my focus on my current client.

I shade in the last bit, ignoring the feeling of being watched. From this spot, he may not be able to see me yet, and I'm banking on that to keep the blush that comes to my skin a secret.

I take a deep breath when my client sits up, the fresh piece cleaned and protected.

"Keep that on for twenty-four hours. Lani will give you the take-home instructions on your way out."

"Thank you so much, Dakota," she says. "I love it so much." She smiles, turning on her heels and walking toward the front desk.

I close my eyes and breathe deeply before taking a step forward and into view of the front desk.

He stands when he spots me. My eyes rake over him. He's even more stunning than the last time I saw him. *This* man asked me on a date. This adonis wants to take me out, and a piece of me feels insecure and doubtful that he'd truly want me.

"Dakota," he says, a dimple forming on his cheek when he smiles at me. If it were appropriate to whimper at a time like this, I'd be on the floor in a puddle. *Please help me get through this appointment.*

"Wyatt," I say, plastering a smile on my face. "Nice to see you again."

"You look beautiful," he says. Lani is practically radiating joy from the desk, and I shoot her a look. She just shrugs, giving me a wicked smile.

"Thank you." I didn't expect a compliment, so I wrinkle my nose as I sit down beside him with my iPad. "What can I do for you today?"

"I'm not here for my free tattoo," he says. "I'd like to plan a sleeve with you." I stare at him, and my surprise must show on my face because he laughs.

"Okay, what are you thinking?" I pull up my sketch pad, ready to write as he talks.

"I was actually thinking of letting you do whatever you wanted."

"So, uh, I don't know if you'd want that." I bite my lip as I look up at him. His eyes linger there. I feel almost greedy for his attention. I don't want him to look away.

"Why not?" He raises his eyebrows at me.

"I specialized in fine line work, mainly florals and book-related tattoos. I prefer black and white, but I also do watercolor. I don't know if that's your style or not, and I wouldn't want to put something on you that you hate," I ramble, feeling uncomfortable. I want to keep this professional, but the way he speaks to me lights my body on fire.

He follows me to my station, and I'm very aware of his presence. He watches me as I clean, but then he moves to my desk, his eyes stopping on my open sketch book.

"Oh—-uh, don't mind that," I say quickly. "It's just something I've been working on for a long time."

"It's beautiful, Dakota. Are you designing it for anyone?"

GOAL Suck

I shake my head. "It's just something I've always wanted to do. I have this obsession with Greek mythology. I read a lot of retellings, and the mythology always intrigues me."

"I want this," he says, his fingers tapping the page.

"Uh, I can design something for you. You don't have to do that." My heart pounds. We're supposed to be planning a sleeve. I was *not* prepared to tattoo him today.

I shove my hands into my pockets to keep from shaking. When he looks up at me, his eyes are filled with a certain intensity.

"I want this. We can still plan for other pieces, but I really like this, Dakota." He sits on the chair in the corner, his face filled with nothing but sincerity.

"I didn't even ask. Do you have any tattoos?"

"I do." He pulls off his denim jacket, then reaches over his head to pull off his hoodie. When he sets them aside, he rolls up his sleeve to reveal his bicep. I stand, walking around to the other side of the bench. I kneel next to him, my fingers tracing the lines of his tattoo. The beat of my heart is probably audible now. I don't often believe in fate, but it feels like the picture in my sketchbook was made for him.

"Ares?" I ask, dragging my eyes from the ink and back up to his face.

"The god of war. My grandma always called me her little warrior. It was fitting."

"If you like the Greek gods theme, we could do this piece today and plan for others later." I trace his arm again, and I swear I hear his breath catch.

"I trust you. And I'm aware of the kind of work you do." His eyes smile as he speaks, and I feel the desire to stare into them forever. His words register to me a moment later, and I feel myself smile as I speak to him.

"Wyatt Alexander, did you internet stalk me?"

"Guilty."

"That's okay. So did I." I stand, gesturing for him to follow me to the back.

"What did you find out?"

"You're a decent skater." I smirk over my shoulder at him, and his eyebrow rises. "A force to be reckoned with, really. Not half bad. Your stats look good too. I found some articles labeling you as one of the most sought-after players in the NHL. Oh, and you're number three on the NHL's hottest players." This feels awfully like crossing the line into flirting.

"Really did your research, didn't you? Who's number one on that list?"

I stop at my station, placing my iPad down on the desk. Crossing my arms over my chest, I look at him again, my face blank.

"Your coach," I deadpan. He throws his head back on a laugh, the nerves from earlier suddenly melting away.

"Of course, he's number one. That bastard." He sits in the chair as I sketch something on my pad.

"Do you have any requests? I have an idea if you're willing to roll with it."

"Go for it. I trust you." He taps his fingers on the table. I smile, my eyes slipping back to my iPad. I draw for a bit, my mind already planning what I'd like to create. I'm keeping it a secret until I can place the stencil. I desperately hope he doesn't hate it.

"Have you thought any more about my offer?" I hadn't realized that I'd been silent for a while. It's easy to do when I'm drawing. Usually, I would have left him at the front while I sketch, but something had me inviting him back.

"Which one?" I ask through lowered lashes. "The offer to prove me wrong or to take me out?"

"Oh, proving you wrong wasn't an offer, it was a promise. I meant the offer for a date."

"I'd like to think about it. I'm not in a place where I've considered jumping back into the dating world yet." The lie tastes like pennies. I don't know why I lie, but maybe it's because he threatens to disrupt this perfect peace I have going for me.

"Fair, but I'll keep asking, even if it's until I get a no." The way he says it is as though it were a challenge. I doubt that people often tell Wyatt Lane no. I find myself struggling to resist his charm already.

I stand, printing off my design onto the stencil paper. "On your arm?" I ask. He nods his head. I go through the motions of applying the stencil. When I direct him to the mirror, he stands, twisting in the mirror to get a good look. The piece I drew wraps around his arm, melding into his Ares tattoo. It's a portrait of Icarus, his wings spread wide, and his body bent like he's falling from the sky. It reminds me of the cover of a novel I read about a fallen angel as a teen.

My heart beats as I watch him look it over. I hold my hands behind my back to keep from fidgeting. Under normal circumstances, I would be confident in my work. I know that I'm a talented artist, but I want to impress Wyatt.

He clicks his tongue, his head nodding. "You're incredibly talented, Dakota."

I snort. "I haven't even tattooed you yet, Wyatt."

He comes back to sit on the chair, his arm resting comfortably now. I fire up my tattoo gun.

"You sure about this?" He just nods his head, and I take a deep breath before the first stroke against his skin.

"How did his tattoo turn out?" Silver asks as we walk down the sidewalk toward the park. Today we're doing goat yoga, which has been a dream of ours for years. It's not often that the weather is beautiful enough to do outdoor yoga. In October, the weather fluctuates from cool to warm. It's one of those months where you're cold in the morning and hot during the day but quickly cold again in the night. We got lucky, and I can't complain.

"I think it's one of my best pieces," I say. "He told me that he was going to post it on social media, and I can't say that I'm not nervous for the impact it may have. I tattooed Wyatt freaking Lane."

"Yeah, you did." Silver smirks at me, walking onto the grass toward the group of women gathered in the middle.

"Did you see the pictures?"

"I did. It was so good. I'm going to need you to tattoo me again because I don't think we can say that mine is your best work anymore." I know it's a tease, but the competitor in me treats it as a challenge.

"So I did something while you went upstairs to handle the coffee-shop situation." Silver runs her hands through her dark hair, those big doe eyes blinking at me innocently.

"What did you do?"

"Wyatt's in town for a few more hours, so I invited him to go to goat yoga with us this morning." The words spill out of her mouth so quickly that I almost don't catch them.

"You did *what*?"

"We gotta go soon, so hurry up." She walks out of my room so fast, my head is spinning.

"I'm not going," I yell after her. "What if I fart or something embarrassing?" She doesn't answer me. "Silver," I yell. This time, her laugh echoes through the hall. I rub my hands on my face. *Fuck my life.*

GOAT *Suck*

"Welcome, everyone," the teacher says over the noise in the park. "Please grab a mat and make yourself comfortable."

Silver and I grab our mats from the supply pile and lay them next to each other. We sit down and take in the group of people who've come out for this class. The baby goats aren't here yet, and my heart is anxious to see them... and someone else.

"I hope that one jumps on my back," Silver says at my side, and I smile.

"Me too, honestly." We laugh, the noise level increasing around us.

My stomach has been in knots since we left the apartment. I run my fingers over my palms, the sweaty feeling making me more anxious.

"Sterling, what if I slip and fall on my face?" I whisper yell.

"You'll be fine. You're one of the best yogis I know." She smiles at me, and I frown in return. Her smile is quickly replaced by a smirk. She grabs her phone from her bag and scrolls. I can't focus, so I pick at blades of grass around my mat, tying them into little knots and tossing them aside.

After a few minutes, the noise level increases. It sounds like everyone is talking all at once until it goes dead silent. I don't notice it right away; I'm picking at the blades of grass when I finally notice the silence. "Are the baby goats here?" I mumble, my hands still picking at the grass.

"No, just me."

Each time I hear his voice, my body reacts stronger than the time before. It's like that feeling I get when I listen to a really great song.

The feeling of goosebumps pimpling my skin as a euphoric chill rushes through me. It's delectable. *That* is exactly how my body reacts to the deep, sultry voice that speaks.

A mat slaps down next to me, and I hold my breath. My spine snaps straight and I slowly lift my head, sucking in quiet yet deep breaths. I'd known he was coming, but that doesn't stop the surprise I feel at actually seeing him.

"Dakota," he says. "Nice to see you again." He smirks, repeating my words back to me from yesterday. My face heats. *Those eyes...* I swallow as I look at him, not saying a word.

"I think you broke her," Silver says at my side.

"Wyatt," I squeak. I snap my mouth shut, my eyes going wide at my behavior. *Get your shit together, Dakota.* "What are you doing here?" I know what he's doing here, but I still ask anyway.

"Proving that I'm not trash and spending my last hours in Boston with you. And Sterling, of course." He winks and then sits down on the mat with a huge grin on his face.

"You didn't want to spend it with the guys?"

"They're busy." He doesn't miss a beat.

I feel eyes on us. The women have all stopped talking to observe the incredibly handsome man who has crashed the class.

"Thanks for joining us, Wyatt," the teacher says, her cheeks reddening a bit.

"Happy to be here," he says back.

"All right, everyone. The baby goats are here. I'm going to teach this class like normal, but be aware that the goats will do whatever they wish. Please don't hurt yourself or the little babies." Everyone releases sounds of awe as the goats run toward us. I try to focus, trying to keep my eyes trained forward, but I feel my eyes wanting to steal glances in Wyatt's direction.

GOAL *Suck*

We're instructed to run through a yoga flow, but I'm overly aware of his presence next to me. In downward dog, I sneak a glance at his legs, and in warrior two, I check out his ass and back. He's taken his shirt off, and I nearly drool.

He turns his head and sees me staring, a small smirk appearing on his face. He winks at me and then moves into the next pose. I look down at the ground, examining the pieces of dirt on my mat. I can feel his eyes on me, but I keep my eyes trained there. I feel hot under his gaze, my body craving his attention.

My eyes find him again, and when our eyes meet, his rake over me. I shiver under the intensity of his gaze.

Silver snorts at my back as we move into downward dog again.

"You're enjoying this," I say quietly.

She looks over at me, and even as we're upside down, I can see the amusement on her face. She shrugs, sorta, and then moves into warrior. She made me wear my cute matching set of workout clothes today. At least I can thank her for that.

Wyatt seems to move through the poses effortlessly. I must look like a fool beside him. Even the goats seem to like him. It irritates me that even getting along with goats is easy for him.

As the class wraps up, Wyatt stands, grabbing his shirt and wiping it across his face. I stare for a little too long because he smirks at me before bending down to roll up his mat. He walks away, and I turn to Silver, ready to give her a piece of my mind.

"Why?" I ask.

She raises her eyebrows at me.

"Operation Win Dakota Over." She squats to the ground and rolls her mat. "He wants to put in the effort to win you over, Koda. How could I say no to that?"

"I made a fool of myself. There's no way his offer will still stand."

I mull over how stupid I must have looked. Insecurity riddles my brain, and I *hate* the feeling of it. This isn't me, this is the result of the damage that was done to me.

"Oh, Koda. You did not see the way he was looking at you." My heart skips. *Calm. I'm calm.*

"You're Wyatt Lane," a girl at the front says. Her voice travels, and it makes my stomach drop. "You did *so* good. I didn't know hockey players could do that with their bodies." She waves her arms to indicate his body, and I clench my jaw. A sour taste travels up my throat as I watch the woman lay her hand on Wyatt's arm. He smiles, albeit a little uncomfortably.

"Thanks." He runs a hand through his hair.

"Do you come out to Boston often?" She juts out her hip and swings her hair over her shoulder. I don't hear the rest of their conversation. A couple of other women walk up to him and join in. I feel heat rise to my ears and face the longer I watch.

"Go," Silver urges.

"And say what? He's not mine."

"He wants to be."

I breathe deeply. He looks up from the crowd, and our eyes meet. He smiles at me like I hold the world in my hands. It's the kind of smile that feels like it's only for me.

"Can we get a photo with you?" The women crowded around him all pose.

I feel myself shrinking into my shell. He's *famous*. There's gotta be women throwing themselves at him constantly. I'm just the girl he met at the hockey game. What makes me any more special than the women in front of him now? Why would he want me?

He watches me, and like he can see my thoughts unfolding, he pulls away from the group, a collective "aww" rising as he moves away.

"How are you ladies feeling about lunch? There's a Greek restaurant around the corner."

I stand there watching him, my brain trying to figure him out.

"Great! I'm going to take our mats to the front. Lead the way." Sterling leaves us, and Wyatt steps closer to me.

"I'm here for you. None of those girls matter. I need you to know that."

"But why? Why me, Wyatt?" I fold my arms over my chest.

"I told you in Boston that I liked that you didn't know who I was." He shoves his hands into the pockets of his basketball shorts. "For the first time in a long time, someone treated me like a human being. You talked shit and you made me feel normal. You don't have to trust me right away, but I want, at the very least, a chance to change your mind." He brings a hand to my hair, brushing away a piece that had flown into my face.

"You came to Boston for me?"

"I did." He takes my hand in his. "I meant it. I'd like to take you out."

I think about it. I can't ghost him now, that would just be rude. And he did do goat yoga with us. What do I lose if I give him the chance to prove he's not like Tanner? *Come on, Dakota, be spontaneous for once.*

"You are awfully persistent," I say, and he smiles, dropping my hand before he shoves his hands into his pockets. "I'm coming to Raleigh for a convention in November. How about we go out then?"

"Sounds like a date."

CHAPTER 5
Wyatt

"How did it go?" Damian says as he takes the machine next to me. He loads up the weights, secures them into place, then sits on the bench.

"She finally agreed to let me take her out," I say, releasing a short breath. I put the press back to normal and sit up.

"How would this work during the season?"

"I'm in Boston often enough because of the guys. I'm sure we could make it work."

"Are you ever going to tell me anything about this girl? You haven't even said her name."

"That's because I don't like to share."

He puffs a breath, stopping his reps and wiping sweat from his brow.

GOAL Suck

"I may be a shameless flirt, but I'm no thief." He sits up, throwing his leg over the bench and leaning forward to look at me. "I can see that nearly feral look in your eye. If she looks at you with anything like that, I can confidently say that she wouldn't be mine to take." He pulls a towel from his bag. "Plus, I don't have nearly the same drive as you. I'm not in it for the long haul, currently."

I roll my eyes, pointing a finger at him. "You'll tire of the bunnies."

"Maybe so, but not now." He winks and stands.

I shake my head, pulling my phone from my pocket. I'd planned on shoving my headphones into my ears and finishing my work out, but when I open my phone, I'm greeted by a photo of Dakota sniffing the bouquet of flowers I had delivered for her.

> **Dakota:** Thank you for the flowers. Your note was very sweet.

I type my response, then place my headphones into my ears.

> **Me:** I meant every word. You are my sunshine on a rainy day.

Maybe I'm going soft, but what can I say? I'm a simp. Okay, that's not true. I'm a simp for Dakota.

Rushing away from her in Boston had left me feeling uneasy. I'd just barely gotten her to agree to a date with me and then I was running to catch a plane back to Raleigh.

I couldn't just leave without saying anything, so I'd stopped at a flower shop on the way to the airport. The words that I'd written on that paper were the absolute truth.

Hockey is my life, but I can easily see Dakota slipping in and rearranging my focus. Part of that is scary. I've worked my whole life to be here, and for one beautiful girl to slip in and threaten that…it's truly terrifying.

I don't have the time to mess around. I can't waste it on women who only want me for my money or my fame. That is exactly why I am so insistent on going for what I want.

It could be a fluke, but I don't have a doubt in my mind about what I want. And right now, I want Dakota.

"Pass the ball," Hudson says, the guys already standing in a circle. We're in Texas today for an away game. The guys are all swapping yawns as we kick the ball back and forth before our morning skate. It's not necessary, but it is a good way for us to get our heads on right and work off some of the game-day nerves.

"What are y'all doing for Halloween this weekend?" Liam passes the ball to Damian. He kicks it between his feet, then passes it across the circle.

"No clue," I say. The ball comes to me and I juggle it, kicking it behind me back to Hudson.

"Ladies, we're playing in Florida on Halloween," Hudson says.

"Yeah, but people throw Halloween parties weeks before. Surely, there will be some party I can crash." Liam drops to the ground, tying his shoe. Hudson looks like he's got a retort on the tip of his tongue, but Coach walks out to grab us for the morning skate. I start walking with the rest of the team when Coach calls my name.

"Wyatt," Coach says. "Can I talk to you for a minute?"

"Yes, Coach." I walk to his side, my arms gripping my bag.

"No morning skate for you. I'm benching you today. I got a call from Ryan Hart over at Boston. Apparently, something's happening with Roman and they need help with Lily."

GOAL Suck

My heart pounds, my stomach sinking at his words. I try to keep the panic from showing on my face. "Do you know what's happening?"

Coach shakes his head. "Nothing more than Lily has been crying for you, and I can't refuse that girl."

"What about Jaiden?"

Coach shrugs, shaking his head.

"No clue. Probably with Roman. I need you back for Saturday, but you're good for the next couple days. I've let the team manager know already."

"Okay. Thanks, Coach."

He lays a hand on my shoulder and squeezes. "Go," he says.

I nod my head, running back to my car.

When I strap myself in, I take a moment to breathe. I don't know what I'm doing. I've never dealt with any emergency with Lily. The three of us raised her together when Sarah got pregnant in college. After she was born, Sarah went AWOL and both Jaiden and I stepped in to help Roman in any way we could.

I call Jaiden, the line ringing a few times before he answers.

"Wyatt. Thank God." He's out of breath like he'd been running.

"What's happening?"

"Roman took a solid hit during the game and hurt his shoulder, maybe a broken wrist." I curse under my breath. "It was Boretski. That dude's a monster."

"Where's Lily?"

"Coach Hart called the school, but they won't release her unless it's to a guardian. I can't leave Roman, and you're the emergency contact."

"So she's just stuck there?" I feel the anger rising in my veins.

"Her teacher is going to take her home with her until someone can get her." He pauses. "I think he's going to be out for a while."

"Fucking hell," I say, smacking my hand on the steering wheel. "Okay, I'm on my way."

I end the call with Jaiden, then scroll through my phone, not hesitating to hit the call button next to Dakota's name.

It rings twice, then the sound of ruffling and talking fills my car speaker.

"Hey," she says.

"Dakota. Hey," I say. My voice is panicked, and I know she can hear it.

"What's wrong?"

"Sorry to call you. I didn't know who else to call," I say. I put my car into drive and rush back to the hotel.

"Wyatt, what is it? You don't need to apologize."

"I'm on my way to Boston from Texas. Roman got hurt and Jaiden is with him, but there's no one to watch over his daughter."

"Okay," she says. "What do you need?"

Those four words. I take a breath, feeling the panic calming.

"Can you pick me up from the airport? I can borrow one of the guys' cars once I'm there, but I need a way to get to Lily quickly." I rev the engine as I pull into the parking lot of the hotel. I leave everything in my car while I run through the hotel to my room.

"Yes." Dakota says into my ear. "Send me your flight number and I'll be there."

"I'm sorry to bother you with this," I say, unsure why she was the first person I thought of.

"Wyatt, please. We may have just met, but I'd like to say you'd do the same for me if I needed it." She's right. I would. I'd probably fly across the country for her. Is that crazy?

"Thank you."

"Of course. Be safe, please."

GOAL *Suck*

My nerves are wound so tightly that my muscles ache by the end of the flight. Lily probably has no clue what's going on.

I've never thought about being a father. The closest I've gotten to it was when Lily was born, and we got news that her mother had abandoned her. She's never been alone like this before, and I know that she's extremely attached to her dad.

I remember feeling alone and afraid. When I got news that my parents had passed, I had no one until my grandparents stepped in to care for me. I never want that little girl to experience that same feeling. Maybe that is why I can't stop this feeling of urgency and dread.

I step foot into the all too familiar airport. I'm greeted immediately by the humid fall air. The uncomfortable heat of the second summer mixed with my nerves leaves me feeling sweaty and on edge.

It's not until I see Dakota's worried face that I calm instantaneously. Picking up my pace, I walk down the stairs. I'm struck once again by how beautiful she is. She's wearing jeans that hug every curve of her body and a loose band t-shirt. Her hair is tossed into a messy bun at the top of her head. I want to run my hands over every inch of her, but that would be inappropriate at a time like this.

"Wyatt," she says, her voice shaky. "Are you okay?" I want to hold her, to soothe that shake from her voice.

"I will be," I say. "I'm more worried about Lily."

"How old is she?" Dakota walks beside me as we make our way through the airport.

"She's five." I run a hand through my hair, my heartbeat calming already.

"Do you mind if I ask what happened?" She leads me toward a Jeep, stopping to open the trunk. I toss my carry-on in the back and walk around to the passenger side.

"Nice car," I say. She smiles as she slides into the driver's seat.

"Thanks." She looks at me, waiting patiently.

I sigh. "There's a skater on a rival team that's had it out for Roman for a while now. I don't know the full story because he's always been very tight-lipped about it, but I suspect it has to do with a woman." I shake my head. "Anyway. I guess he got a few good hits in, enough for Roman to break his arm and dislocate his shoulder."

Dakota gasps, a hand coming to her mouth.

"Is he going to be okay? What does that mean for the season?"

"He'll probably be out, depending on recovery. We'll find out soon."

A sad look passes her face. She reaches across the car, her hand resting on mine.

I watch her for a moment. She looks at me so intently. "Thank you for doing this."

"Of course," she says. "Where to?"

"Roman's. I'll take his car so that she'll be more comfortable."

"All right. Lead the way."

We drive in companionable silence, the only sound from the GPS guiding her to his home. When we pull into the driveway, she stops to look at me.

"I'm glad you called, Wyatt."

"Me too," I say. "Thank you again."

"Of course. If you need anything, don't hesitate." She grins at me, her eyes slightly guarded.

"I will." I hadn't planned on this being the next time I see her; these are not favorable circumstances. I also hadn't planned on this feeling so much like a test. This alone proves my theories on Dakota. No puck bunny would have done anything remotely as kind for me.

I shake my head, clearing Dakota from my mind so that my thoughts can't be plagued by the things I want to do to her and the ways I want to make her mine. I can't have that while I'm caring for Lily. *Think of Coach skating naked. That'll certainly kill the mood.*

CHAPTER 6
Dakota

My stomach has been upset since I picked up Wyatt from the airport. He was so different from the other times I've seen him. That confident, cocky man was gone and replaced by uncertainty and worry.

I don't *know* Wyatt, but I know enough for that small fact to make me worry for him. I've been sitting at home alone for several hours, wondering if I should have offered to do more.

Should I call him and offer to bring over dinner or to sit with him? I've been told that I have a very calming energy.

I throw my head back onto the pillow, groaning up at the ceiling. Honestly, what do I lose if I show up and offer dinner? I could just send him a text.

No.

GOAL SUCK

Yes.

No.

Don't be a weenie.

Fine. I'll do it.

Shaking my head, I pull a sweatshirt from a hanger and toss it over my head. My keys jangle in my hands as I pull them from the table and rush out the door, slipping into my shoes on the way out.

My car is warm by the time I finally decide to pull out of my spot and onto the main road. I remember exactly how to get to Roman's place, so I follow the road until I pull up to the curb in front of his home. *Is this crazy? It's a little crazy. Please don't think I'm a stalker.*

I close the door to my car more quietly than I needed to. Taking a deep breath, I knock on the door, my heart nearly beating out of my chest.

It's silent for a few moments until I hear voices on the other side of the door. I panic, almost ready to turn and walk away. Closing my eyes, I turn on my heels, losing my confidence. That's when I hear the door open.

"Dakota?"

I cringe, squeezing my eyes shut and then replacing my grimace with a calm smile.

"Yeah, hi!" I say. Wyatt stands in the doorway, the screen still shut. He's dressed in gray sweatpants, and I nearly go weak in the knees. His hair is disheveled, and I suddenly feel unwelcome.

"Who's that?" a female voice calls from the distance. I freeze. Wyatt looks behind him, then back at me. I shake my head and walk backward.

"Um, nevermind," I say, turning and walking back down the driveway.

"Dakota! Wait!" The door slams, and I hear footsteps running after me.

Picking up my pace, I rush to my car, barely opening the door before Wyatt steps up behind me, closing the car door.

My back's to him, but I can feel the way he's captured me against my car.

"Dakota," he breathes. I don't look at him for several moments, but then I turn, leaning my back against the car. He braces a hand against the door, keeping it closed. His face is so close to mine. I hold my breath, willing myself to meet his gaze.

"What?" I say, my voice low. I'm trying *really* hard not to sound angry, but I don't know how well that translates.

"Whatever you're thinking, I can promise you, you're wrong." He leans into me, his dark hair falling in front of his face.

My eyebrows shoot up. "Really?" I shake my head. "It doesn't really matter. We barely know each other. It's not like we're dating or anything."

"Dakota," he says, an eyebrow raised. He's said my name several times this evening, and a part of me that isn't upset wants to hear him say it again. "That's the nanny."

"And?" He could've been spending time with the nanny alone. It's none of my business.

"And I only have eyes for one woman as of a couple weeks ago. I thought I made that clear."

I open and close my mouth a few times, trying to gather words to say.

"We haven't even gone on a date yet," I say.

"No, but that doesn't mean I'm going to fuck around until then. Do you think so little of me?"

"I'm sorry." I look down at my feet, shoving my hands into my pockets. "I've been hurt before and I was too quick to judge."

GOAL *Suck*

"Don't apologize. I promised to prove you wrong, and this is a part of that." He moves his free hand to my face, pushing a piece of hair out of my face. "Now tell me why you're here."

"I was going to offer to take you to dinner. Or to bring you dinner."

"I'd love to," he says, a smirk blooming on his face. "Let me get dressed." He brushes his lips against my temple. "I'm glad you're here." He turns away from me, leaving me slouched against my car door. I grip onto it for dear life as I feel myself wanting to sink into asphalt.

"I'm glad I'm here too," I say to the sky.

The front door slams a few minutes later. I'm still leaning against my door, trying to catch my breath when Wyatt walks around to my Jeep.

"You okay?"

"Yeah. Yes." I breathe, standing up straight and unlocking my car. He climbs in the passenger seat, looking over at me as I start the car.

"Where were you thinking?"

"Um, there's this old-school burger place down the street. The staff brings your food out to you on roller skates, and we can eat in the car. Does that sound okay?" I look at him as I turn the key in the ignition. He nods.

"I'll never say no to burgers."

"How's Lily?" I ask as I pull away from the curb.

"She's sleeping. She was really upset when I picked her up, but once Char got there, she calmed down. It was a group effort."

"And how is Roman?"

"He's being discharged soon. The team physician needs to clear him before he can be released back home."

"That's good. What happens after this? Can he still play this season?"

"Yes and no. It depends. He'll probably be assigned therapy and will go through a clearance process eventually. If his wrist is truly broken, he won't be able to play again until that's healed."

"How are you feeling?"

He looks at me as I pull the car into a spot next to a speaker. "Honestly, I don't know. Roman and Jaiden are some of my only long term-friends, and I'm always worried about them. They're my family."

"I can understand that. Silver is my best friend, but she's also like a sister, so if anything happened to her, I wouldn't know what to do with myself."

Wyatt watches me, his eyes assessing.

"What?" I ask.

"Just watching for any glitches in the system."

I laugh, my eyes watering. "What do you mean?" I wheeze.

"You're perfect, and I'm making sure you're real and not some robot or something."

"I assure you that I'm very real." He nods, smiling.

"Good. Ready to order?"

I nod, my heart pounding in my chest. I'm extremely glad that I didn't stay home tonight.

CHAPTER 7
Wyatt

"You're a cheater, Wyatt Lane," Dakota squeals, jumping up and down.

After eating, I *really* hadn't wanted the night to end, and I'd like to believe Dakota hadn't either. She'd suggested a walk downtown, so as we walked and talked, we'd stopped outside of this arcade.

I'm absolutely demolishing Dakota at the basketball game she chose. Under normal circumstances, I may have toned it down a bit, but my cock grew at that competitive gleam in her eyes. She understands my competitive nature, and *that* is one of the sexiest things I've ever seen.

"I'm not a cheater," I say, grabbing another ball and tossing it into the hoop. She groans as she misses again, the time counting down.

"I suck at this," she says, grabbing another ball and tossing it. It hits the rim and bounces off in the opposite direction. I laugh, taking a ball into my hand and handing it to her.

"May I?" I ask, stepping behind her. Her breath falters, and I grin into her hair.

"Yes," she says, her voice breathy. I push my body against hers, moving her arms up and into a shooting position. Her eyes flutter as I move my cheek to rest against hers.

"Keep your dominant hand here." I press into the ball, and she moves her hand there. "And your non-dominant hand rests on the side as a guide. All the force comes from here." I push into her arm. The touch is rather intimate, and she shivers. I feel a sense of satisfaction at her reactions.

"When you're ready to shoot, let your fingers roll off the ball. The trick is to keep your elbow in line to help aim." I mimic my motion for her. Her eyes watch my arm, her tongue slipping between her lips. She looks at me, then back at the backboard. Assuming the position, she raises her arm, letting the ball roll off her fingertips. I watch in anticipation as the ball hits the backboard and the ball falls through the hoop.

Her eyes go wide as she looks at me. She screams, jumping up and down, and I can't help but smile at her.

I'm caught off guard as she throws herself into my arms, squeezing me tightly.

"Thank you, thank you," she says into my chest. I wrap my arms around her, breathing in her shampoo. *I really hope she can't feel my erection pressing against her right now.*

"You're welcome."

She pulls away from me, and her face is pink from the excitement. She's beautiful. Incredibly so, really. She's looking at me like I hold the stars, and I really don't want this moment to end.

Moving my hand to her cheek, I brush the skin with my thumb. She's tense at first, but then she relaxes into my hand. My eyes flick between hers, waiting for approval.

Her eyes darken as she rolls her lip into her mouth. That's all the confirmation I need. I dip my face to meet hers.

Her eyes close as our lips meet. At first, it's soft, like a teasing exploration, but then I feel the way she grows more confident, kissing me back with fervor. My tongue begs for entrance into her, swiping across her lips. She tastes sweet, like candy and chocolate.

I press her against the wall of the arcade machine, not caring who's around to watch us.

I move my hand to her backside, her ass filling the space of my palm. She arches into me, and my eyes nearly rollback into my head. She's perfect. Absolutely perfect.

I break away from her lips, peppering her jaw and neck with kisses.

"Wyatt," she says breathily. She presses her face into my shoulder, her face hiding in my shirt. She presses into me again, and I suck on the flesh between her neck and ear. She gasps into my shoulder. "Wyatt," she says again.

"Mmm?" I say in between kisses.

"People are watching."

"I don't care," I say into her neck. "Let them watch."

"One of them has a camera," she says, her voice growing wary. I freeze. *Shit.* We haven't talked about this part of my life yet. I stand to my full height, moving my arms to shield her. With my back to anyone near us, I guide us through the back door and back onto the main street. I slip her hand into mine, sneaking a glance at her. She's watching me, and I smile at the curious look on her face.

We slip into the crowd of people walking, my nerves calming the farther from the arcade we walk.

"I'm sorry. I often forget that I'm more recognizable here." I pull her aside, letting people pass by.

"It's okay. I just"—she plays with her thumb, looking down then back at me—"I didn't know if you wanted to be photographed with me or how any of this works." She looks at me, then her eyes slip back to her feet. I slide my finger under her chin, lifting her head to me.

"That's why you were worried?"

She nods, and I sigh. "At the risk of sounding very arrogant, you did me a favor, but Dakota, I need you to know that I would be honored to be photographed with you. You are the most incredible woman I have ever met. I'm more concerned about the impact that it will have on you."

"What do you mean?"

I purse my lips, mulling over my next words carefully.

"The media can be brutal. They'll spin things any which way until a formal statement is made. Again, not to sound cocky, but the media likes me because of my eligibility."

"Your eligibility? You mean the fact that you've been labeled one of the most eligible bachelors in the NHL?"

I internally scold myself for even bringing it up. "Uh, yeah."

"So you're worried the women are going to attack me if they find out who you're making out with in random arcades?"

I nod.

"You don't need to protect me, Wyatt. I'm familiar with the way these things work. There's a reason that I hated hockey players."

I can't help but notice the way that she speaks in past tense. *Hated.* She hated hockey players. I think that's a point for me.

I open my mouth to speak when Dakota's phone rings. She looks at me apologetically as she pulls the phone from her pocket and raises

GOAL *Suck*

it to her ear.

"Sterling. What's up?" She walks away from me, giving herself some distance, but not enough that I can't hear what she's saying. It sounds like something's happened because the tone of her voice has changed, her words more urgent and flustered. She shoves her hand into her pocket, a frown replacing the smile that was there a moment ago.

She paces the street, talking into the phone. She goes on like that for a few more moments until she sighs, walking back to my side.

"Is everything okay?" I ask.

"The pipes exploded in my apartment building. I guess it flooded the first couple floors."

"So what does that mean?"

"I'll probably have to stay in a hotel tonight. Lani lives in the same building and she's going to her boyfriend's tonight. Sterling's in Seattle for a shoot, so I'm alone."

"You can always come back to the house with me," I suggest. "I doubt Roman would mind."

"Oh, no. I can't impose like that."

"Seriously. His place is huge. I can ask him. They should be home now." I pull out my phone, sending a text to Jaiden. I look up from my phone to see Dakota biting her lip as she watches me. She looks hesitant, and I only want to put her mind at ease.

My phone pings, and I look down at his reply.

"Do you need to grab anything from your place?"

"Wyatt, I can't stay with Roman."

"You can. This is what we do, Dakota. Any time one of us comes to town for a game, we're all crashing at each other's places. If I don't bring you home, I don't doubt that Jaiden will show up at your hotel room to collect you anyway." I smirk at her, and she rolls her eyes.

67

"Fine," she grumbles. "I don't think I have access to my place right now. I have extra clothes at work. Can we stop there?"

"Let's."

The lights are off when we walk through the front door of Roman's home. I flick on the hallway light, leading Dakota through the space. She follows closely behind me.

Dakota creeps down the hallway, trying her hardest not to make any noise. I snort, looking at her. She frowns at me, her eyes narrowing.

"What?" she hisses. I just shake my head. She reminds me of a teenager sneaking back into their home after a night out on the town. It's quite entertaining to see her on edge.

"The bathroom is down there, and the bedroom on the right is yours. I'll be across the hall with Jaiden if you need anything."

"Thank you," she says, her voice barely a whisper. She hesitates, chewing on her lip as she looks up at me. Like some sort of resolve snaps in her mind, she raises up on her toes and smacks a quick kiss on my lips, then disappears into the bathroom.

I groan, adjusting my erection before I walk into the room I'm sharing with Jaiden.

He's sitting up in bed, the little lamp on the side lit. His glasses are perched low on his nose, a book pressed into his face.

"You're home late," he says, a smirk on his face. Kicking my shoes off, I raise a brow at him. I'm barely able to keep the satisfied look from crossing my face.

"I'm bunking with you tonight. Hope you don't mind."

"I'll never mind sharing a bed with your sexy ass," he says, patting the bed beside him. I snort, stripping down to my boxers.

"How's Roman?"

"He's pissed. We both are." Jaiden closes the book, setting it on his chest. His hair is extra unruly tonight. The brown curls are windblown and messy. Quite frankly, he looks like he's been through hell.

"I hope that jackass was penalized."

"They're still rolling through the footage because Coach Hart made a stink about the call. It was bullshit."

"Boretski is the worst," I say. Jaiden nods his head in agreement.

"Oh, by the way, you have just a lil something"—he points to my face—"right there." He flicks my nipple and then turns away, laughing under his breath.

"I fucking hate you," I say.

"You love me. Always have, always will."

I roll my eyes, but I know he's right. Jaiden's family and always will be.

CHAPTER 8
Dakota

I snuck out early to go for my morning run. Everyone was asleep still when I ran out the front door. After several miles, I jog up the driveway to Roman's house.

With both of my headphones in, I walk through the front door and down the hall into my room. I suspect everyone is *still* asleep because there's not a sound to be heard when I pull my earbud out.

The silence leaves me alone with my thoughts, and right now, my mind is fully focused on the way that Wyatt's lips felt on mine. I want to feel it over and over again. Maybe on other places of my body too.

I scold myself, slipping my earbud back in as I walk across the hall into the bathroom.

The lights are still off, so I assume it's safe to enter. I push the door open without any struggle. Flicking the lights on, I toss my clothes onto the sink and then look up to see a naked Jaiden standing in the middle of the room. I freeze, smacking my hand over my eyes and shrieking.

"Jaiden," I shriek, backing out of the bathroom with my hand still covering my eyes. My back meets a wall of solid flesh, the impact of it almost sending me flying forward again. A hand comes to my waist to stabilize me, and I suck in a sharp breath.

"I'm sorry," I say, turning around with my hand covering my eyes. I use my other hand to feel around for a wall, but instead I end up feeling up someone's warm, bare chest. "Ah, I'm sorry," I repeat. A deep chuckle fills my ears, and I recognize it as Wyatt. I peek through my fingers to see him smirking at me.

"Oh my God," I groan. "I'm so sorry." I feel my face heat, the tips of my ears burning.

"You've said that," Wyatt says, his eyes dancing with amusement. I let my eyes roam over him, but only for a moment. When I make it to his waistband, I close my eyes, breathing deeply.

This is not happening.

"I was going to shower, but Jaiden is naked in there and it was dark and...okay, bye," I say, scooting past him and slipping back into the guest room. I close the door, pressing my back against it and sliding down to the floor.

It is wholly unfair that he looks like *that*. I'm well aware that athletes need to maintain a certain physique, but holy hell. I want to run my tongue up his abs just for funzies.

I smack my hand into my face, clenching my jaw. *That sounds ridiculous. You're ridiculous.*

I hide on the floor for several more minutes until I don't hear any noise coming from the hallway. When I peek out the door, the coast is clear.

I run to the bathroom and shut the door behind me, making sure that it is, in fact, empty this time.

I shower and dress quickly. When I leave the admittedly luscious bathroom, I hear the guys talking in the kitchen.

"You cannot say that to a room of kindergartners," Wyatt says.

"Why not?" Jaiden's voice is firm, but there's a hint of humor in it. I walk down the hall, standing there awkwardly. They all look at me, then go back to talking. *Okay, then. We're ignoring what happened earlier.*

"Dakota, please take my side on this." Wyatt's leaning against the counter, a mug in his hands. I walk to his side, standing between him and Roman. Jaiden's seated at the bar-like seating on the opposite side of the counter.

"On what?" I ask. Wyatt slips a mug into my hands, and I smile at him.

"Jaiden thinks that this is an appropriate joke to tell Lily's class for show-n-tell." He pauses, making sure that I'm paying attention. I nod, and he starts again. "What has two butts and kills people?"

"What?" I ask, meeting Romans' eyes. He looks thoroughly amused. He shakes his head, taking a sip from his mug. I look back at Wyatt and his eyes are almost bored.

"An assassin," he says, his tone bland. I bend over laughing, nearly spilling the contents of my cup on the floor. Wyatt slips it from my hand as I wheeze. It's not even that funny. It's more his delivery that has me nearly on the floor with laughter.

"See," Jaiden says, his arms extended toward me. I stand up, catching my breath.

"I'm sorry, Jaiden," I say between fits of laughter. "He's right. You can't say that to a group of kindergartners."

"What?" he says, throwing his hands up. "Why not?"

GOAL Suck

"I really don't think their teacher would appreciate you essentially teaching them curse words. Imagine what kind of calls they would get from the parents when they go home and tell the joke to their parents."

"Told you," Wyatt says.

"Roman," Jaiden pleads. He shakes his head, sipping his coffee as he leans against the counter. His legs are crossed in front of him, his arm and shoulder wrapped tightly in some sort of sports bandage.

"Traitors," Jaiden says, sliding from his chair and stomping to the couch. "Now I need a new joke," he calls over his shoulder.

"How are you feeling?" I ask Roman.

"Sore," he says. "But I'm okay."

"I'm glad. Sorry for crashing your humble abode."

"There's been a lot of sorrys thrown around this morning," he says. He smiles at me, but it looks like he's trying not to laugh. I sigh.

"I don't want to talk about it," I say. The guys exchange amused glances, then look back at me.

"What are you doing today?" Wyatt asks.

"I have to go to the apartments to talk to management and then run to work for a client. My shop is usually closed on Tuesdays, but I made an exception." He nods his head several times.

"What kind of piece is it?"

"It's an anime sleeve. We've been working on it for a couple of weeks now."

"Which anime?" Jaiden asks from the couch. I look over my shoulder at him.

"JJK," I say, smiling. "Do you know it?"

"Do I know it?" Jaiden scoffs. "Of course, I do." He mimes eating his finger, and I look back at Wyatt, my eyebrows drawn together. They're fighting laughter.

"Are you flying back to Texas?"

Wyatt nods. "Since everything is handled here, I'll be back on the ice for the game tonight."

"What time is it?"

"Seven thirty." He walks toward the couch and sits down. I'm suddenly realizing that it's incredibly easy to talk to Wyatt like this. He makes me feel at ease. *Safe.* "Are you going to watch?" He winks at me, and I blush.

"Maybe," I say, drawing out the word. "I don't have a TV to watch it on currently."

"You're more than welcome to come here," Roman says. "Stay as long as you need to." He looks so sincere. I couldn't possibly over impose, but I appreciate the gesture.

"You should watch. I heard there's one of the NHL's sexiest players on the ice today." Wyatt's eyes watch me, waiting for a reaction. I snort.

"That's arrogant," I tease.

"Oh, I was talking about Damian. That ginger beard gets all the ladies."

I really laugh this time.

"I'll have to look him up. Maybe he's single."

Wyatt releases a sound from his throat that sounds almost primal, a growl of sorts. It probably shouldn't make my stomach flutter or send a tingling sensation to my core. Jaiden looks amused, shaking his head. I swear I hear him mumble something, but I'm not listening. I'm watching Wyatt, his face now serious.

"Dakota," he says, his voice deep and dark. "I'm a selfish man, and I very much don't like the idea of you with another man—*especially* Damian." My heart flutters in my chest. I clear my throat, his proclamation doing all sorts of things to my body. I cross my legs under the counter, pressing my thighs together. I hope that wasn't too conspicuous. The mere idea of him staking a claim on me...*This is the shit from my books.*

"Good thing we're going on a date then, right?" I say it to ease the mood because damn, it's getting hot in here.

"Right," he says. "Don't you forget it."

CHAPTER 9
Wyatt

WYATT ALEXANDER LANE SEEN GETTING COZY WITH SHORT BLONDE

That is the best headline they could come up with? *Short blonde.* If I were Dakota, I would be offended. Hell, I'm offended on her behalf.

They didn't mention how beautiful she is, or how the curves of her body could make a man fall to his knees. No, they settled on *short blonde.*

"Wyatt," Coach yells from his office. I clench my jaw, tossing my

GOAL Suck

jersey over my shoulder and stalking to his half-opened door.

"Yes, Coach?" He doesn't look up at me, just gestures to the seat in front of him. I look at it, my mouth going dry before I sit in the seat, my knees knocking his desk as I sit down fully.

He tosses the gossip magazine on the desk, the headline I was just reading on the top page.

"I hope you were actually helping Roman's family while you were in Boston," he says, his eyes trained on his computer screen. I've never wanted him to look at me more, if only so I can see the emotions in his eyes. Am I going to be fucked for this? I squint my eyes at the magazine, then look up at him.

"I was. Scout's honor."

"Who is she?" Coach looks at me over the top of his glasses.

"Someone I met in Boston several weeks ago."

"Is it serious?"

"I'd like it to be," I say.

"As long as she doesn't affect your game play, I won't complain. Got it?"

"Yes, sir." I say, releasing a sigh of relief. I start to stand, but he raises his hand.

"Boston's inquiring about you. Nothing's set in motion yet, but I wanted to give you a heads-up."

"They're rebuilding?"

He nods. "They need defensive relief. I guess they've been asking about you for a while now. The GM just stopped by."

"Okay," I say. I don't know whether to be concerned or elated. Boston would be a big move. The team has several wins under their belt already, and it could be a great career move, but I've also built a life here in Raleigh.

"Go home and rest. Be back here at five for press."

"Yes, Coach." He waves me off, and I leave his office feeling uncertain. Players often have little to no say on whether or not they get traded. It can be difficult to adjust and swallow if they are. I can only wait it out. *Let the madness begin.*

The familiar ping of a point plays on my phone, bringing a smile to my face. I'm dressed in my suit, my shirt still open and my tie draped around my neck. I should be getting ready, but instead, I'm seated on the bed glancing down at my phone.

Holding it in my hands, I send off the text to Dakota, feeling a sense of accomplishment. We've been playing this word game back and forth for the last couple hours. Any time my phone pings, I know it's more often than not a reply back indicating that it's my turn.

> **Dakota: I loathe you right now.**
> **Me: Don't be a sore loser.**
> **Dakota: I'm extremely competitive, Wyatt Lane. Now get dressed so I can watch you play tonight.**

I smirk, finding joy in the fact that she knows I'm wasting time playing this stupid game instead of getting dressed. I press the video call button, propping the phone up on a pillow as I stand and adjust my tie in the mirror.

The ringing stops, Dakota's face filling up my screen.

"What?" she asks, and I laugh. She narrows her eyes. "You look nice."

"I didn't call you to fish for compliments, but thanks for feeding my ego." I wink at her. I can practically feel the eye roll through the

GOAL Suck

screen.

"Oh, shush. Why did you call, then?"

"I just wanted to see your face before I leave for the rink."

She blushes. "Oh, how you flatter me, Wyatt Lane."

I grab the phone, holding it in my lap while I slip on my socks and dress shoes. My suit of choice today is a green slim fit with a skinny black tie. After seeing the way Dakota ogled my arms this morning, I couldn't help but choose something that hugs my body.

"Did you see the article?" I ask. She purses her lips, sighing.

"I'd like to make it known that I am completely average for a woman. You are just giant-sized." I chuckle, taking in the way her eyes twinkle as she talks. "At least the bunnies and hockey detectives haven't found my name yet. They've only got"—she throws up air quotes—"short blonde, to go off of."

"Well, when I finally claim you, we'll have to change that. It'll read, *sexy blonde tattoo artist, the best of her time.*"

"When," she says, her voice noncommittal.

"When," I say. "In case I haven't made that clear already."

She ignores my statement, huffing a breath. "Wyatt Lane, you're going to be late and I refuse to be the reason."

"Fine," I grumble. She licks her lips, and I groan, rubbing my forehead. "Please don't do that. I won't be able to stop thinking about your lips now."

She laughs.

"Bye, Wyatt. Don't suck." She hangs up the call, leaving me alone with my uncomfortable stiffy and memories of the way she tasted in my mouth.

CHAPTER 10
Dakota

I hate packing. If I could just hop on the plane and be there without all of the prep work, I would, but alas, I need my gear and clothing to wear in different climates.

This time it's different, though. Our whole building flooded, so for the foreseeable future, I'll be living out of a suitcase.

Standing in the middle of my room, I rub the back of my neck as I look around at all my belongings. The only thing I really need is clothing. We have the cafe at work, and all of my important things are at work. I hate to say it, but almost everything else is replaceable.

Releasing a heavy sigh, I toss things into my suitcase haphazardly until Sterling walks into my room, dropping something onto my bed with a thud.

"Your sketchbooks," she says, sitting down on the edge of the bed.

GOAL *Suck*

"You're going to need those. Oh, and do you have your flash sheets?"

"Shit." I rummage through my drawer, finally pulling out the laminated pieces I printed for the conference. Silver takes it from my hands, examining them. I'm traveling to Colorado tomorrow, and shortly after, I'll be in Raleigh for the convention. I still have no idea where I'm going to stay while I'm in Boston. I'm suddenly thankful for the days that I'm traveling.

"What's your theme this time?" She hands me back the sheet.

"Geometric floral. I'm only doing a few custom pieces this weekend."

"I wish I could come to Raleigh with you." She makes a pouty face, then winks at me.

"Speaking of, how are things with Jaiden? What is even happening there?"

"Girl, I don't even know. I'm excited to see the boys this weekend, though." She shrugs her shoulders, scrunching her face. "Is Wyatt coming?" She stands from the bed and walks into my closet. I'd forgotten about Halloween this weekend. Let's add this to the list of things I'm stressed about.

"Not that I know of. Also if you see anything in there that I should pack, pull it out." She doesn't hesitate one bit with that request. The next thing I know, a black lace thing smacks me in the face and I feign dramatics. "Careful where you're throwing things. Je-sus." I grab the black lace item and unfold it. It's a corset top—one of my favorites, honestly.

"Your tits look great in that top. Always better to have it on hand, just in case." She winks, then continues rummaging in my things. She tosses a few other items at me before switching to my drawers.

I look down at my phone. I haven't told Wyatt about Halloween. He's supposed to be in New York that weekend. We've been texting nearly every day, and that fact alone excites me.

It's been two weeks since Roman's accident. I'd promised I'd let Roman know if I needed a place to stay, but I've been avoiding that at all costs. It'll be nearly impossible to avoid this weekend when we're partying with them for the evening.

"Why did you talk me into this?" I groan.

"Into what?" She widens her already large doe eyes, blinking at me innocently.

"Halloween with professional hockey players." I narrow my eyes at her, and she sticks out her tongue.

"You'll be fine. We'll sit at the bar and watch Wyatt play. There's absolutely nothing you need to worry about."

"I'll hold you to that."

There is absolutely something I need to worry about. The moment two incredibly well-known Boston players walked into the bar, the energy shifted.

One moment I'm looking down at my phone, the next some random person is literally trying to sit on me to get closer to Jaiden. I clench my jaw in frustration, tossing my phone into the pocket of my racing suit and zipping up the front to cover my breasts. Originally, I'd been going for the sexy racecar driver, but now I want to be even more invisible than I feel.

I stand from my chair, weaving through the crowd of people. Not caring to let anyone know where I'm going, I walk out the front door and into the chilly October air. The second I'm outside, I walk to the side, pressing my back against the building.

"Crowded?"

I look over at the bouncer seated on a chair beside me. I nod, and he gives me a sympathetic smile.

"Didn't you walk in with the Boston players?"

"I did," I confirm, pulling my phone out again and holding it in my hands.

"I thought they'd keep a better eye on you. There's a lot of creeps out tonight."

I stifle an eye roll. *I can take care of myself.* "It's not their job to look after me."

His eyebrows go up. He watches me, his face resembling something close to respect.

"There you are." Roman steps outside, sliding next to me.

"Here I am."

"Needed air?" He nods at the bouncer, who nods back.

"It was feeling suffocating in there. Your fans are—"

"Overwhelming?" He interrupts, and I give him a small nod.

"Exactly that. Very overwhelming. How do you manage it?" I lean my head back against the wall, my nose burning as I breathe in the cool air.

"I've been doing this for five years now. You kind of get used to it. Hockey draws a certain crowd, and I suppose that crowd is here tonight." He shrugs. I give him a sheepish grin, unable to hide the small amount of fear I feel from creeping onto my face. When I was with Tanner, he hadn't gone pro yet. He was in the draft and making his way through the process, but—I mean this with total offense— Tanner sucks at hockey. He doesn't suck enough to not get drafted, but compared to Jaiden, Roman and Wyatt *fucking* Lane…he's got nothing on them.

"He'd protect you." I almost don't hear his words because I'm lost in my own thoughts.

"I know," I say quietly.

"He's family. I know he cares for you. I can only speak for myself, but I'll protect you too."

"Thanks, Roman, but I don't even know what he wants with me."

"I think he's made that pretty clear, don't you?"

I gulp. *I don't like the idea of you being with another man.*

"Not to put the pressure on you, but you're the one who made a clear statement of hatred for hockey players. He won't make a move unless you're clear that you want that."

"How do you know?" I look at him from the corner of my eyes.

"I've known him for almost a decade now. He's one of the best men I know." He looks like he wants to say more, but doesn't. He slouches against the wall, then raises to his full height, his eyes looking down at me. I feel tiny next to him, but that's been a pattern with most of the men I've been around lately.

"What else?" I urge him to continue. He chuckles, shaking his head.

"Because he's one of the best men I know, I think I owe it to him to insist you stay with me." I begin to protest, but he holds up a hand. "Lani told me you've been sleeping on her boyfriend's couch. You'd have a whole room to yourself at my home, and Jaiden won't be there to bother you."

"I can't impose on you, Roman. You have a daughter and I…" I can't even think of another excuse. He smirks at me, his eyebrows raising in challenge.

"My daughter would love to have another female there, I promise you that." I laugh at the dreamy look on his face.

"Can I ask about her mom? Please tell me if that's over-stepping."

He shakes his head, clearing his throat.

"We got pregnant when I was twenty and Sarah was nineteen.

GOAL Suck

It wasn't planned, but I was ready to make the commitment to be a father. I didn't know that Sarah was having doubts until it was too late.

"I'd been considered for the draft, but I decided to wait to be there for Sarah, but when I made it back to the hospital, she'd checked herself out, leaving Lily there for me to take care of."

I gasp, holding a hand over my mouth. "Roman, I'm so sorry. I have no doubts that you're an incredible father."

"Thank you." He looks down at his watch, blinking a few times. "I've been instructed to get to the TV for the post-game interviews." He smirks, and I blink at him. He nods his head toward the door. I sigh, standing up and following him back into the bar.

We walk back to the bar seating, the crowd cleared for the most part. Sterling is seated in Jaiden's lap when we approach them. She grins at me and I mouth an *Oh my God* at her.

When I look up at the screen, Wyatt is seated on a bench, a microphone in his face.

"How are you feeling after your win tonight?"

"Great," Wyatt says. "It's been a long time coming. We've got our sights set on the cup this year."

"I heard that some other teams are looking at you during the trading period. What are your feelings on that?"

"Obviously, I love this team, but I can't control where I end up. Either way, I want to take that team to the finals."

"You're very determined. No wonder you're an all-star this season. We have a more personal question, if you don't mind?"

"Yep," he says, taking a drink from his water.

"Every woman is wondering, now that you're Raleigh's superstar and an eligible bachelor, what are you looking for in a woman?" The interviewer pushes the microphone back at Wyatt, and he looks right into the camera. My stomach flutters, his icy blue eyes looking right at me.

"I'd say that I'm not much into superficial things, but at the moment, a particular blonde with tattoos has caught my eye. I want someone who challenges me and treats me not like a hockey all-star, but like a regular person, because that's what I am." He smiles at the camera, his dimple on full display. My breathing slows as I watch him. The people in the bar disappear; the only thing that matters right now is the screen.

"Is this the woman you were spotted with?"

"All I will say is, she knows who she is." The crowd around them releases sounds of awe and sadness.

"So you won't tell us who she is?" the interviewer pushes. Wyatt's coach comes into view, his arm firmly on Wyatt's.

"If and when they're ready to comment, they will," he says. "Let's go." Coach taps Wyatt, and he stands. Wyatt winks at the camera once more, his fresh-off-the-ice form disappearing.

"Well, you heard it here, folks. Wyatt may, sooner rather than later, be off the market."

The screen cuts back to the ice, the replay footage from the game flashing across the screen. When I finally peel my eyes away from the screen, everyone is watching me. Well, not everyone, but anyone who matters.

"What?" I ask. Jaiden snorts, shaking his head.

"He essentially just laid claim on you."

"He what?" I blink at them. They don't answer me because the screen flips back to the interviews. The general manager for the Raleigh Riders comes into view. They talk with him about his success this season and his hopes for the team going far this year.

They run through a myriad of standard questions until I hear

GOAL Suck

Wyatt's name again.

"There have been several inquiries about Wyatt. What are your thoughts on that?"

"We're currently in talks with one team in particular. I won't disclose who right now, but I'll certainly be sad to see him go."

"What does that mean?" I ask Roman, pointing at the screen.

"When the trading window opens, it's like a game to them. Players will be traded and swapped to build the best team." He looks down at his glass. "Think of it a little like fantasy football. Great players who are on generally losing teams can be traded onto teams where they'll have better chances of winning and vice versa. Just depends on the deals and offers that come through."

"So he could be traded anywhere?" The guys trade looks, and I watch them do it, growing suspicious.

"Yeah, but I know with my injury, Boston is looking at rebuilding. We've had generally good stats, but a lot of players want a change of scenery."

"Oh," I say. I want to ask more questions, but my phone rings in my hand. I smile when I see the name that pops on the screen. I hold the phone up to my ear, answering the call.

"Did you watch it?" Wyatt says into my ear.

"Mmhm." *Words, Dakota. Form words.* The phone rings in my ear, and I look at the request for a video call. I look at the guys and Silver, excusing myself out the back door. When I accept the call, his freshly washed hair is the first thing I see. He looks at me, his eyes growing dark. That's when I realize what I'm wearing. I clear my throat.

"There's this hot blonde at the coffee shop I go to in Raleigh. I'm hoping she'll go on a date with me." He waggles his eyebrows, and I snort.

"You're an ass." We're silent for a moment. I pull a couple strands of hair out of my ponytail and twirl them in my fingers. "Do you mean it?" I ask.

He moves his arm from the back of his head. "I do." His voice is husky and serious. I clench my thighs together.

We talk for a few minutes longer before I end the call. *I'm so totally screwed.*

CHAPTER 11
Dakota

You can learn a lot about someone in a short amount of time. I've learned a lot about Wyatt in the past week. He's a massive flirt, which I already knew. He's incredibly cocky, and his confidence is through the roof. One of the things I've always hated about hockey players is the cocky behavior. But when Wyatt does it, it doesn't feel like he's trying to break me down while he builds himself up. There's always this edge of teasing there that draws me to him. I'm incredibly jealous of his confidence. He oozes it, and I wish that I could be that way.

My phone buzzes, and I see the newest text from Wyatt.

It's a selfie of him with his tongue out. His wet hair is draped in front of his face as he stands in front of a gym mirror. I really don't hate this view because I can see his ass, and it's spectacular.

Wyatt: Like what you see?
Me: I do like going to the gym, so yeah, I guess.
Wyatt: -_- I feel like I should be offended.
Me: Awe, is Wyatt upset?
Wyatt: If I say yes, will you kiss me to make me feel better?

I snort. *He's smooth.*

I am also a liar—a big fat liar. I *do* like what I see. He's gorgeous. I always tell people that I don't have a type. That, too, is a lie. Wyatt is my type. Everything about him. He's intelligent and creative. He's got one of the best senses of humor and is mouth-wateringly attractive. Seriously, like, hot damn.

Sterling tosses a shirt at me. I'm pulling from my massive suitcase into a smaller one for my trip.

"Why didn't I do this last night before our outing?" I bite my lip, folding things quickly until my suitcase is packed and ready to go.

We're due at the airport in less than an hour, and my heart is beating so quickly. I'd packed for both Raleigh and Colorado so that I wouldn't have to worry about unpacking and repacking while I'm there for a few days. *I'm an idiot.* I think that these things will reduce the stress for me, but I'm almost certain that I am creating more stress for myself.

I roll my suitcase to the door, leaving it there while I pull clothes for the flight from my suitcase and throw them on.

"Because you were stressed about Halloween and didn't want to deal with it." Sterling shoots me a look, and I know exactly what she means.

"Speaking of things I do not want to deal with," I mumble under my breath.

I'd promised Roman that I would think about staying with him. I have thought about it, but I'm still not convinced I won't be imposing. Our apartments won't be ready until late November at the earliest; that's nearly a month of sleeping on a couch, and I don't know if my back can handle that. Sterling got lucky. She's gone so often during the hockey season that she doesn't need to worry about places to stay for long. I envy her.

I look up to see her shoving something into the front pocket of my suitcase.

"Better to be safe than sorry." She closes up my larger suitcase and rolls it behind her. "I'm leaving this in their room for when you come back." She walks away from me, and I watch her. She's acting suspicious, and I let that suspicion get the better of me.

Walking to my suitcase, I open the front pocket and pull out a long strip of condoms.

Silver peeks her head back down the hallway, a wicked grin taking over her face. Her face is gone from view when I make an exasperated noise in her direction.

"Sterling Sage, you take these back right now." I hold the strip of condoms out in front of me and waggle it. "Silver!" I repeat. I hear her holding back laughter from the living room.

"I'll repeat myself," she says, wheezing with laughter. "Better safe than sorry. Maybe you'll ride some hockey dick while you're there."

"Certainly not," I say, my face heating. "It's too soon. We barely even know each other."

"Oh, darling. It's never too soon to sleep with someone." She laughs more when she steps into view and sees my tomato-red face. She struts toward me, taking the condoms and putting them back into my bag. "Keep them. I'd rather you have them than not and regret it later."

"I hate you," I groan, walking back into Lani's room.

I have a short break between clients. Sterling is chatting it up with the shop owner, so to pass time, I pull out my phone.

Overall, Colorado has been pretty uneventful. I've done several custom pieces while we've been here. My favorite part is the collaboration I've been working on with the owner. For their social media, we've been working on this large half-and-half piece. Someone volunteered their arm to have it tattooed on them. I designed one half and Barry designed the other.

We'd spent eight hours working on it yesterday while Sterling recorded pieces of it. Sterling has been running through footage and editing the video today, which amazes me. Sterling, the woman of many talents.

I scroll through my photos and stop on one of the tattoos I just finished. I snicker when I send the photo to Wyatt. His response is almost immediate.

Wyatt: Are those hockey sticks?

Yes. Yes they are. Hockey sticks and flowers on a tattoo. Sterling laughed so hard when she learned of that request.

I ignore his question, an idea coming to my head.

Me: Did you know that hockey romance is a genre of book?

I put my phone down on the table while I take a sip from my water bottle. Sterling is relentless when reminding me to stay hydrated and drink my water. I'd rather not get in trouble, so I make sure she sees me when I drink. My phone buzzes with his response.

> Wyatt: I did not. Have you read any?

> Me: Now why would I ever admit something like that to you?

The bell to the front door rings, and my eyes wander up. It's not for me, so I look back down at my phone, the smile barely staying hidden. Three consecutive buzzes light up my phone.

> Wyatt: I just want to know if I'm cooler than the fictional men in your books.
> Wyatt: We can role play if you want. You can pretend you don't know how to skate and I'll come rescue you. Knight in shining armor, am I right?
> Wyatt: Am I making dating a hockey player sound appealing yet?

I roll my eyes, but I can't help but smile.

> Me: You are relentless. Will you ever give up?

I don't want him to give up.

> Wyatt: Never.

I smile, putting down my phone when Sterling walks to my side.

"How's Wyatt doing?" She smirks at me, and I poke her side. She squeaks.

"Fine," I say. "Perfectly fine." She snorts when she sits down next to me. We talk about the rest of the day and our plans for the evening. By the time my day ends, I'm exhausted. We've got one more day here until we head back to Boston. I'm ready to get out of Colorado. There's so much sun. I want my dreary weather again so I have an excuse to look like a vampire.

I'm lying in bed when my phone rings on the bedside table. It's a video call from Wyatt. My stomach flutters a bit, slightly with panic and slightly with anticipation. My finger hovers over the button before I decide to bite the bullet and answer the call.

I lay the phone down while I throw my hair into a bun at the top of my head and brush my eyebrows down to make sure they don't look crazy.

I lift the phone up to my face and see Wyatt lying in bed, shirtless, with one muscled arm supporting his head against the headboard. It's unfair how attractive he is.

"What's your favorite color?" he asks.

"You called me to ask me what my favorite color is?" I spin to my side, propping myself up on my elbow. He smirks at me.

"Well, I did want to hear your voice, but I thought saying something like that would scare you off."

"And you think the things about role playing a hockey romance wouldn't?" I raise an eyebrow at him.

"We're already doing that, so no." He winks at me, and I blush. "So what is it?"

"Uh, green," I say. "Like emerald, olive, and forest green. What's yours?"

"Blue." His screen pauses, and I hear him typing on his phone.

"I wanted to ask how you're feeling about the possibility of being traded."

"I'm feeling okay. Normally, a player wouldn't get a heads-up about this sort of thing, so I can't complain."

"If you had a choice, where would you want to go?" I lay back into the mound of pillows. Sterling is still out for the night. The team plays until late tonight, so it'll probably be hours before she comes back.

"Boston," he says.

"Why Boston?"

"I could name a few reasons." His eyes lock on mine, and I feel tingly.

"Oh?" I tease.

"Oh?" he mocks, smiling at me. "My number one reason is currently the beautiful woman looking back at me."

I blush, looking down at the blankets on the hotel room bed. "You do that a lot."

"Do what?" He moves his arm from behind his head, his neck cracking when he moves it from side to side. I crinkle my nose at him.

"Call me beautiful." My voice is quiet, almost like I don't want him to know that those simple words affect me so much.

"It's only the truth." He pauses, watching me.

"I think I like you, Wyatt Alexander."

"I think I like you too." He looks at me, a yawn overtaking his face. This is so much harder than I'd thought it would be. Staying away from Wyatt is growing increasingly difficult. By the time I make it to Raleigh, I'll have no restraint left, and by the way he looks at me, it's almost as if he's counting on it. I talk with him until I feel the weight in my eyelids and my body relaxes into sleep.

Long fingers tangle in my hair, another hand wrapping around my throat lightly. A mouth comes to my neck, the hot breath tickling my skin. The feel of stubble rubs against me as his face moves, peppering kissing along the way. It's so much. I can feel him everywhere. My senses are overloading at the feel of him.

I arch into the hard body, a gasp escaping my mouth as the hand leaves my neck and travels down my naked body. A weight presses into me, and I don't mind being captured under the Adonis of my dreams. His hand continues roaming, leaving a trail of goosebumps along the way. His fingers slide up my sex, and I moan at the pure bliss I feel. My heart pounds, my breathing ragged as he rubs small circles over my clit.

"You're so fucking beautiful," he says. I blink a couple times as the face pulls away from my throat. His features come into focus, and I realize that it's Wyatt.

He smirks as his finger sinks into me, and I whimper. I buck, urging him deeper. He obliges, adding a second and then a third finger. He moves them inside me, the rhythm perfect and torturing. His thumb pays special attention to my clit.

Every thought and every worry escape me as his fingers pump into me. I reach for him, my hands roaming across the lean muscles of his body. My fingernails dig into his back as my body tenses around his fingers. It's right there, close enough for me to taste. I'm panting as his rhythm increases.

"That's it. You're perfect, baby. Come for me." His voice caresses my ears, sending shivers through my whole body. His lips capture mine, his teeth biting softly. I tense, my body begging to fall over the edge.

I sit up in bed with a gasp, my hand coming to my mouth to quiet the noise. My breath is ragged, my core pulsing with need. I look over to my left to see Sterling's bed still empty. I lay back, my arm resting across my eyes. *Holy fuck.*

When I look at the clock, it shows only ten in the evening. I must have passed out early into the evening. My phone call with Wyatt is still going. The soft sounds of his breathing come from the phone. I swallow, pressing my thighs together.

Breathing deeply, the ache between my thighs doesn't ease.

I want—no I *need* to—finish off the job, but I don't want to give myself the satisfaction. I should be embarrassed. Shouldn't I?

I haven't had sex in so long, and now I'm dreaming of Wyatt's fingers buried inside of me. It was the hottest thing I've ever experienced. Sex with my other partners was never like that, never focused on my needs and my pleasure.

Before I know it, my fingers are sliding down my body. Pushing my panties aside, I slide my finger through the slick wetness there. My breathing increases, my head falling back as I draw little circles over my clit.

Clenching my eyes shut, I picture Wyatt's hands, his calloused fingers brushing over my body, and my pace increases.

I slide a finger inside me, then another, working myself until I feel my body tighten.

That's it. You're perfect, baby. Come for me.

"Wyatt," I breathe, my voice quiet.

Like a wave, my orgasm crashes over me. I whimper, my core pulsing around my fingers. Gasping into my hand, I lay there for a moment, catching my breath.

My face grows hot when I notice that the sounds of breathing have quieted on the other side of the phone. My heart beats, the pounding almost audible in my ears. *I forgot to mute the phone.*

I scramble, grabbing the phone to check if Wyatt is awake. When I move the phone, I hear one simple word in a groggy, husky voice. It makes my insides churn.

"Perfect."

I end the call so quickly, tossing the phone across the bed. *Oh my God.*

How am I going to look him in the face when I see him next week? *Fuck.*

CHAPTER 12
Wyatt

I walk out of practice, my duffle slung over my shoulder and my hockey stick in my other hand. It's six a.m. and we've got the rest of the day for downtime before our game tomorrow afternoon. Damian pats my back as he passes me. He walks onto the bus, and I follow after him.

Coach stops me on my way into the bus. When I glance at his face, I already know what he's going to say. He nods his head, a sad smile on his face.

"This is it?" I ask.

He nods.

"This is it," he confirms.

I lick my lips, looking at the jersey poking out of my bag.

"How long?"

"Maybe six, seven more games. The deal is meant to close at the end of the month."

"Okay," I say.

"They're asking for Damian too."

My eyes widen. I look down the rows of the bus. Damian is watching us. I can't quite decipher the expression on his face.

"Okay."

"Okay."

The ride back to the hotel is quick. Many of the guys are going down to the rec center to play pool or soccer to pass time. I don't know what I plan on doing yet, so I head back to my room.

I sit down on the bed, my duffle at my feet. When I lay back, I pull my phone from my pocket and scroll through my notifications. I don't have any texts from Dakota, and for some reason, that brings a frown to my face.

She's been short when she does respond to me, which isn't often. I'm growing more concerned that she'll decide not to come to Raleigh this weekend. I'll do anything to convince her. I haven't even gotten her yet, so I'm not ready to lose her.

Had I known she was going to react this way, I would have kept my trap shut. But *holy hell*, Dakota is a gift straight from God.

Waking to her labored breathing and whimpers had set me on cloud nine, destination: space. It wasn't until she came with my name on her lips that I felt my cock swell almost painfully.

Perfect. She's perfect.

When she ended the call, my hand found my cock, stroking it until I was panting and cum coated my abs.

I want to hear those whimpers again. I want to be there to see her face. Next time, it won't be her fingers, but mine. I groan into my hands, rubbing my fingers across my face.

I'm scrolling when my phone pings with a notification. I hit it without thinking, the text thread with Jaiden coming up immediately. There's a group of photos that I open and shuffle through.

A growl rips from my mouth as I continue scrolling. The first photo is of Sterling and Dakota spinning on the ice with Roman. The next is a selfie with the four of them. Dakota and Sterling are hugging tightly, their faces squished together. The last couple of photos are of Dakota and some of the Yellow Jacket players talking.

I'm still staring at the screen when Jaiden's texts again.

Better get your ass here before we steal your girl.

He sends a wink emoji with it. I'm on my feet before I can stop myself. I grab my backpack and throw some clothes into it.

I pick up the hotel phone and dial the front desk.

"Hello, Mr. Lane. What can I do for you?"

"Can you get me a rental car, ASAP?"

"Yes Mr. Lane. I'll have them pull one up to the front for you."

"Thank you," I say before hanging up the phone.

I rush down to the lobby, where I find Damian and some other teammates talking.

"Damian," I say, "tell Coach I'll be back in the morning."

"He's gonna kill you if you aren't," he says, shaking his head. I wave my hand back at him and rush out the door to where a black Mercedes Benz waits for me. The concierge hands me the keys, and suddenly, I'm making the drive from New York to Boston.

Two hours and forty minutes later, I pull my car up to the rink. It's almost nine in the morning, so they should still be here. When I drive through the parking lot, I see Dakota's Jeep and park next to it. I leave my bag in the car, grabbing only my gear as I walk through the double doors of the rink.

"Mr. Lane." The security guard nods politely as I pass through the metal detectors toward the locker room. I sit on the bench and lace up my skates.

How the hell do I make an entrance? She's not mine. I can't just roll in there growling. Will she even want to see me? I decide to take a moment to watch before I skate out onto the ice.

The chilled air of the rink hits me immediately. I breathe deeply, feeling at peace. As I walk further through the tunnel, I see them, my blood pulsing.

Sterling is skating backwards, the players skating toward her. I see Dakota skating at her side with a camera in her hands. Jaiden squats low to the ice, his face getting close to the camera Dakota is holding. He rises as she does and his arms come to her shoulders, spinning her around. The laugh that comes out of her is like music to my ears. A twinge of jealousy rushes through me.

Seeing her on the ice is incredible. Something about it is the most attractive thing I've ever seen. The rink—it doesn't matter which rink—is my home. Seeing her in my element and thriving…*damn*. It's fucking sexy. As if this girl could get any better, she does a couple crossovers, looping around Jaiden and making him spin.

Roman pulls off his helmet, his brown skin glowing under the lights. He runs a hand through his cropped hair before he rushes forward and shaves to a stop. He spots me by the doors and skates in my direction. His hand is in a brace, but overall he looks good.

"Intruder," he says, his voice teasing. The others on the ice turn, but I'm only watching Dakota. I can see her eyes light up, then her cheeks redden. She turns away from me, leaning in to speak to Sterling before she skates forward and does a cute little shave. It's quite pathetic, honestly, but I admire the effort. I slip off my guards and place them along the rim of the glass.

I skate onto the ice, meeting Dakota and Sterling. I tower over her naturally, but with my skates on, I must look like a giant next to her. She won't meet my eyes for a moment, her fingers twirling in front of her. My lips pull into a smirk. Sterling nudges her arm, and she finally looks up at me.

"What are you doing here?" she says a little breathlessly. I pull her into my arms, and she tenses. When she relaxes, my heart calms. We'll be talking later, but for now, I'll make her feel comfortable.

"My fault," Jaiden says. He skates over, the rest of the team following behind him. "I sent him the selfies we took along with some threats."

Sterling doubles over laughing. She wheezes when she stands, bumping fists with Jaiden. "Genius," she says. "While you're here, Mr. Hockey Man, show us what you've got. I want to get some good shots." She pushes me further onto the ice, but all I want to do is stay near Dakota.

Sterling instructs Roman, Jaiden, and me to skate toward the camera. The click of the shutter goes off multiple times. We mess around, tossing the puck back and forth.

I feel Dakota watching me, so I sneak a peek at her. She looks beautiful. Her hair is braided and tossed over her shoulder. Her matching beanie and gloves are adorable. She's standing against the wall, her cheeks red as she watches us intently. I'd like to believe she's watching only me. I run my tongue across my lower lip, and she gasps, her face turning down to the ice. I chuckle to myself. Okay, maybe I lied. I'm enjoying the blush that creeps across her skin.

Jaiden passes the puck to Roman. When it comes back to me, I hit it up onto my stick and bounce it into the air.

"Here we go," Roman says, shaking his head. I chuckle and hit the puck into the air a couple times and catch it on the end of my stick.

"Show off," Jaiden yells. I hear Roman tell Sterling that I've always been a showoff. In college, I lived on the ice. We spent so much time there that I had time to create tricks. The ladies sure loved it.

I spin around and stop when I'm facing Dakota. She watches me with another blush rising to her cheeks when I shoot her a wink. I drop the puck and shoot it across the rink, knocking the cone off the top of the goal crossbar.

I hear curses throughout the rink.

"Shit," Jaiden says, drawing out the *i* sound. "Tell me why you're a defenseman."

I smirk, skating toward him.

"You're making us all look bad, man," one of the other players says as he skates past me.

No. I'm just showing off for my girl.

Sterling gasps as we walk through the doors of Roman's home. As hockey player, many of us like to rent apartments, condos, or even homes if they've got a family to account for, but oftentimes, no place is permanent. Trades happen frequently, and then we're uprooted and moved across the country or even cross borders into another country. With Lily, Roman wanted to give her something that felt stable. I don't blame him for that.

"Your home is beautiful," Sterling says from my side. She spins in place, looking at the expanse of the home. It's a two-story home with a modern country interior. I think his mother had a large hand in that. Roman has exactly zero sense for interior design. He tried to decorate our apartment in college, and it ended up looking like the day after a wild party. Or maybe even a haunted house.

I know we won't be seeing Lily tonight. Part of me wishes that

Dakota could meet her, but in time, that will happen. Lily's grandma had kidnapped her for the night, no doubt to spoil the living hell out of her. Rightfully so. She deserves it. That girl has me wrapped around her finger. Lord help any man she brings home. She'll need to deal with three hockey players before he can be welcomed into the family.

"Make yourselves at home," Roman says, slipping off his jacket and slipping it into the coat closet. "We can throw on a movie or a show. The living room is right through there." He points down the hall. "Jaiden, Wyatt or Dakota can show you."

I walk down the hallway and into the open living room and kitchen area. Sterling follows Jaiden and plops into the seat next to him on the couch. I take the love seat.

Something comical happens when Dakota walks next to Sterling and tries to take the seat next to her. Sterling stretches her legs out, taking up the seat and raising a challenging eyebrow at Dakota. I stifle a laugh, but it ends up coming out in a pathetic sounding snort.

Dakota stands there awkwardly for a moment. She holds her thumbs in her hands, then, surprisingly, walks until she's standing in front of me.

"Hey," she says, and it brings a smile to my face.

"Hey."

"Mind if I sit here?"

"Not at all." She slides into the seat next to me, and I lean my arm across the back. Roman walks into the room, grabs the remote, and flicks on the TV.

"What are we watching, friends?"

"Oh, that new superhero movie just came out on streaming." Jaiden smacks his legs in excitement. "We should watch that."

"Down," I say. Both Sterling and Dakota hum their agreements. Roman navigates to the movie and starts it while he throws some popcorn into the microwave.

    Dakota is tense beside me. She's watching Sterling and Jaiden closely. They're cracking jokes, and I see Jaiden run a hand down her leg casually. Finally, Dakota relaxes and leans back into the cushions. Her leg brushes mine, and she looks over, her eyelashes fluttering and her cheeks turning pink.

    "Sorry," she says.

    "It's fine." I smile at her, hoping it looks reassuring. In actuality, my cock is reacting to her nearness. She smells amazing, and her near proximity to me is doing me in. I've been rocking a semi since the moment I saw her on the ice and it's only getting worse. I cough, grabbing a pillow and placing it over my lap. She looks at me sideways, and I shrug.

    The night continues like that. As the movie plays, she relaxes more and I become increasingly aware of her presence. I brush my hand against her leg, her hand resting on it lightly. I hear her breathing stop, and I smile into my other hand.

    I lean into her, my mouth nearly meeting her ear. She breathes deeply, her hands fiddling in her lap again.

    "Enjoying the movie?" I whisper it so only she can hear.

    "Yeah," she says. Her voice is breathy when she speaks. There goes that blush again.

    "There's been a lot of that tonight," I say.

    "A lot of what?" She keeps her eyes trained on the screen.

    "That gorgeous blush to your cheeks. If I were wiser, I'd think you like my attention." She stills, then wiggles in the seat, adjusting herself.

    "Uh, yeah. Um." She stumbles over her words, and I smirk.

    "We haven't talked much since…"

    She shoots me a look, her eyes wide and her jaw clenched. I stifle a snort, relaxing back into the cushion. Moving my arm across the back, I drape it around her and pull her into me. She protests at first, then she gives in, leaning into my chest.

I brush my hand over her arm, and she shivers.

"Cold?" I ask into her hair. When she doesn't answer, I pull the blanket from the back of the loveseat and drape it across us.

She relaxes, her weight pressing into me. I let her relax more, waiting for the right moment.

Slowly, I slide my hand down her arm, slipping it around her waist. She gasps quietly, her head turning to look at me.

"Dakota," I whisper into her hair.

"Hmm?"

"I'm going to talk and you're going to listen. Keep your eyes on the screen, beautiful."

I feel her heartbeat increase, and a beat of excitement rushes through me.

"I don't want you to feel embarrassed about what happened." I nip at her ear, and she leans her head back into me. "Are you going to tell me what happened?"

"A dream," she says. Her voice is so low that I almost missed it. Sterling giggles at something Jaiden says, and we both look over at them. Roman's on the opposite side of Sterling, and they're all laughing about something.

"What kind of dream?" I like where this is going. I slip my hand into her shirt. "Is this okay?" She nods, and I feel her shiver against me. She's silent for a while until she finally whispers back.

"Um, the naughty kind." I reward her candor with another feather-light touch. My fingers slip into her bra. She whimpers as I twist her nipple between my fingers. Oh, how I want to suck them into my mouth. Her breathing grows more labored. I'm hardly paying attention to the movie on the screen—Dakota is the real show.

"Shh," I command. Did Dakota Easton have a sex dream? I'm so fucking hard at the thought of her dreaming about me. "I need you to promise me something."

"Hmm?" She crosses her legs, and I'd give anything to be able to ease the ache that's gathering there.

My lips brush her ear. I don't know if she's ready to see this side of me. Everything in me hopes she doesn't run away now. I kiss the side of her head before I speak. "The next time you come with my name on your lips, I want my cock buried so deep inside you that we both see stars." She freezes, her lashes fluttering. I smile a satisfied smile when she wiggles against me.

"Promise," I say into her hair.

"I promise," she says. I remove my hand from her breast, resting it against her hand. She turns her face to me, her eyes watching me. I slip my hand under her chin, raising her lips, and I bring mine down to meet hers. I kiss her lightly, a promise for later.

When I pull away, her eyes are still closed like she's waiting for more. *Oh, how I wish I could give her everything.*

She looks back at the screen, her hand against mine, our fingers brushing. It's like a game we're playing. I feel like a teenager in a movie theater trying to sneak little touches of affection. I want to touch her and hold her. I want to make her dreams come to life.

My phone rings in my pocket, and I curse it. I don't want to leave her side, but I'll see her soon. It's that fact alone that allows me to rise from the couch and walk away from her as we say our goodbyes.

Pulling the car up to the front of the hotel, I hand the concierge the key and sprint back to my room. I make it back in time for our evening meeting. Damian called me while I was in Boston warning me to haul ass back to Albany.

I don't normally struggle with FOMO, but when it comes to Dakota, I've felt this possessive edge. There are no labels and there have been no conversations. I want her for myself. I won't have it any other way at this point.

I can tell she's still questioning me. I haven't told her outright that I'd like to date her, nor have I told her that my body reacts every time I think about her.

My mind wanders as I walk through the building. I can't get that image of her out of my head, her body leaning against the wall, her bottom lip pulled between her teeth. I want to touch her, I want to feel the smoothness of her skin. And, quite frankly, I'd fucking love for her to sit on my face and suffocate me to death between those juicy thighs.

I shake my head, adjusting myself discreetly as I walk through the doors of the gym. Taking the seat next to Damian, I bump his fist and settle in.

The meeting is short. We discuss our plans for game day tomorrow. By now, we all know the routine. I know where I'm supposed to be and what I'm doing before each game. The rookies are still getting into the groove.

With two games left in the regular season, our shot at the finals grows closer. We're currently top in our division and second in the Eastern Conference. The odds are looking good, but anything can happen in the blink of an eye.

As I walk out of the locker room, Damian stops me.

"Where did you run off to?"

"Boston for a photoshoot," I say plainly.

"For the tatted blonde you were raving about the other night?" He raises an eyebrow, and I look at him sideways.

"I didn't know you paid attention to those things."

"It's hard not to when it's plastered all over the place, Mr. Most-Eligible Bachelor."

"Awe, are you sad? You and the ginger beard aren't getting enough attention?" He laughs, landing a punch on my arm.

"Dick." He coughs. "I'm getting plenty of attention, thanks for asking. There's only a few of us left to get tied down. Just want to know if I'm going to lose you to the other side."

I sigh, the full force of my frustration sounding in that sigh. I've known her for a few weeks now and she occupies most of my brain space outside of hockey. Am I sick?

"Maybe," I say, running a hand through my beard. "So, Boston?"

"Boston," he says.

"How do you feel?" I tap my hand against my knee.

"I think this could be a good thing, but I started with this team, so it's bittersweet." I nod my head at his answer. I understand that feeling fully.

"I'll certainly miss some people."

"Yeah, that little asshole Liam is growing on me." He looks at me sideways with a serious look on his face and then we both chuckle.

After the meeting, I meander my way back to my room. It's time to set my plan into motion. In a matter of days, Dakota will be in Raleigh with me.

Pulling out my phone, I shoot Sterling a text. She responds quickly. Without a second thought, I browse through her suggestions and settle on two. I send the gifts to the address she provided me with, signing off the purchase with a note.

Sterling is my partner in crime. Dakota is mine. It's time that I make that the truth.

CHAPTER 13
Dakota

On my way out of Lani and Dane's small apartment, I stop by the front desk to pick up my mail. I received a call this morning that there was a package delivered for me.

I'm suspicious for a couple reasons, but the main two are that I haven't provided this address to anyone and that Silver has been glancing at me all morning with this glimmer of mischief on her face.

"Hi!" I say, my voice higher than it needed to be. I clear my throat and try again. "I'm Dakota, and I was told that there was a package for me?" The receptionist nods her head, grabbing a package from behind the counter and handing it to me. She then slides a piece of paper toward me, asking me to sign in confirmation that I received it. *Strange.*

Taking the package in my hands, I walk back out of the office, grabbing the handle of my suitcase more firmly.

Silver waits for me by the curb, her cherry red Shelby GT500 parked and ready for me to load my suitcase into it. I've always loved her taste in cars. We're opposites in that way. I've always loved trucks and more rugged off-roading types of cars. Silver, on the other hand, loves the sports cars that knock you back against the seat when you gun it.

"Get in, loser," she yells from the driver's seat. I roll my eyes, lifting the trunk and slipping my suitcase into it.

We pull up to the curb of the airport a few moments later. This is where we part ways. Sterling is off on her next adventure, and I'm headed to Raleigh for the convention. She slips out of the car and walks around to the back where we meet. She pulls me into her arms and kisses my cheek.

"Open that on the plane," she says, pointing to the package in my hands with a wink. She slips back into her car and waves as she pulls away.

After I make it through security, I find a seat near the window of the airstrip. I stare out the window for a few minutes, but curiosity gets the best of me.

I pull the tie loose and unwrap the package. It's a book with a note on the top. I hold the note between my fingers, flipping it over so I can read the carefully written words.

Dakota,
Heard this book was one of your favorites.
I found a bound copy for your collection.
See you soon,
xx
Wyatt

My heart flutters in my chest as I pick up the book and look it over. I can't help the gasp that leaves my mouth as I inspect it. It's a bound copy of one of my favorite fanfictions to ever exist. I've been dying for a physical copy for ages.

My eyes sting as I stare at it. My fingers brush the pages, the feel of it like magic between them. Bringing it to my face, I sniff. It smells like magic.

"Holy shit," I mumble. My heart continues to flutter. Who is this man and why is he surprisingly perfect? I'll never admit that to him, but goodness.

I still as a revelation hits me. I *like* him. I've said it before, but I mean it in my heart this time.

In my lull between clients and at the end of a busy travel day, it's become second nature to talk to him. Are we friends? What is happening between us? Would he do something like this for a friend?

I play back our last interaction. There's definitely sexual tension there. I'm so attracted to him that I let him touch me *like that* while his friends were in the same room. Am I suddenly an exhibitionist? *No...yes?*

I should be embarrassed. I should be asking Silver to pick me up and telling her that I'm canceling this whole trip.

Before he showed up at the rink the other day, I'd been thinking of canceling. I couldn't fathom looking him in the eye after what I did. But I don't want to run away from this.

Wyatt makes me feel something. He makes me feel special and important.

I was so afraid to see him, but when I did... *oh God.* I could hardly breathe. Not to mention, every time he breathed, I pictured his hands on my neck and his mouth on mine. That wink—oh God, that wink. I clench my thighs together thinking about the way he winked at me before knocking that cone off the opposite end of the rink. I feel myself winding up so tight over the feel of his hands on my breasts and the way his breath felt against my ear as he bossed me around.

I'm so anal about every detail in my life, and it was like he just knew that I needed someone to command me, to tease me like he did.

These are highly inappropriate thoughts for an airport. I shake my head, trying to clear Wyatt from my mind. It works, but not for long.

Another feeling rushes through me. What if he doesn't like me? What if he just wants a casual fling or a friends-with-benefits situation?

I'm not that girl. If he wants some casual hookup, I know that I'll have to walk away, and that is the part that pains me.

I should honestly get an award for the amount of overthinking I'm doing right now.

We board the plane, and I decide to shut my thoughts down and rest as I travel across states to see the man who could potentially hurt me. *Fuck—I'm doing this again, aren't I?*

I step off the plane onto the jet bridge, feeling a bout of anxiety creep through my body. This is nothing new for me. I've been here before, been a part of this convention, and I'm familiar with this process. What I'm not familiar with is the fluttering in my stomach. I wasn't prepared for the way my body is practically on fire with anticipation.

After grabbing my suitcase, I slip my jacket around my shoulders, pulling my arms through slowly. The cool air hits my face as I walk through the tunnel toward the car rental station. I feel a shiver rush through my body, so I shove my hands in my pockets after ringing the bell for the front desk.

"Can I help you?" A male voice says from behind me. I recognize that voice. My heart pounds as I whip around. I almost fall over when I see who's standing there.

Wyatt's leaning in the doorway, his eyes trained on me. He's dressed for the cooler weather, and I can't help but stare, drinking him in. Just like always, he's stunning.

I hadn't known what this moment would be like, but with my racing heart and blank mind, I hadn't expected this. Just like last time.

The corner of his mouth raises, his hand leaving his pocket as he stands straight in the doorway.

"Surprise," he says, his eyes smiling. He licks his lips, and I nearly fall to the floor.

"How?" I manage to say. Maybe it's the fact that there's no one with us that makes this moment different. I'm unsure of what to do next.

I think he sees the battle in my eyes. He takes a step toward me, pulling me into his arms. I stuff my face into his sweatshirt, quietly breathing in his woodsy mint smell. I suddenly feel awkward and unsure of myself.

"Sterling sent me your itinerary. I flew back early from Detroit so that I could pick you up." He says it into my hair because we're still holding each other, and I'm starting to feel weird again. He releases his arms, allowing me to step out of his embrace.

My face meets his chest, and I almost feel bad that he'd have to bend to kiss me or to rest his chin on my head. "I know we weren't meant to meet until tomorrow, but I wanted to be here."

"I thought you were playing tonight?" It isn't quite a question, but I say it like one anyway.

"We had interviews this morning after our game last night. No game play until Monday."

"Oh, congratulations, by the way. One step closer to the finals, I hear." He looks at me a bit stunned. "What?"

"I didn't know you were keeping up with hockey. You're a hater." He smirks at me, his eyes teasing.

"Yeah, yeah. I can't judge all hockey players, okay?" I bend down, ruffling through my carry-on until I pull out the bound book. I try to keep the excitement at bay, but I feel it slipping. "Thank you for this. I've wanted a bound copy for years."

He smiles at me, the hint of a dimple appearing on his cheek. I hold back the sigh I want to release.

"You're welcome. I'm glad you finally have a copy." He turns, opening the door and letting me out. "I've cleared my schedule this weekend, so I'm all yours."

I follow behind him.

"You do know I'm here for work, right? And what about my car?"

"You'll take mine. I've got extra." He says it like it's no big deal. I nearly stumble over my feet.

"I can't take your car, Wyatt. You barely know me. How do you know I won't crash your car? Better yet, how can you trust I won't steal it?"

"I'll take my chances." He watches me. His dark hair is ruffled today, the little curls of his hair more prominent now. My stomach flutters again.

He releases a breath, then takes my suitcase from me, our fingers brushing slightly. I feel my cheeks redden. What are we even doing? Do I want to sleep with him or date him? Or both? My brain hurts. "So you have two options." He rolls my suitcase behind him, walking toward a lifted black Bronco. "I can take you to your hotel, or you can come back to my place and we can eat dinner together?"

"And then I can go to my hotel?" I fold my arms over my chest as I walk.

"Or you can stay in my guest room?" He turns his head back to look at me, an eyebrow raised.

"Or you can take me back to my hotel."

"How about we have dinner, and if you're comfortable, you can stay. If you're not, I'll take you to your hotel." He clicks a button on his keys, the car roaring to life. The trunk swings open, and he puts my suitcase in the back. He walks around to the passenger side and opens my door. "My lady." His hand reaches for mine, Mr. Darcy style, to help me into the car. He closes the door behind me, then jogs to the driver's side.

"What would you like to eat?" He pulls the seatbelt across his lap and I stare at his hands. He's wearing rings on his middle and pointer fingers. It's one of the sexiest things I've ever seen, and I can't explain why. I cough lightly to cover up the fact I'm drooling over his hands.

"I love Mexican food. I'll never say no to tacos and margaritas."

"Tacos it is."

We stop at a taco truck on a corner street. Wyatt lets me stay in the car while he orders for us. I don't mind that so much because I have the opportunity to watch him. I want to touch him, to run my fingers over the expanse of his body, just to feel him. My stomach flutters. *That damn dream.*

When he pulls his door open, I see his breath as he passes me the to-go boxes. "Hold on tight," he says, sending the car into reverse and pulling onto the main road. The further we drive, the more my brain overthinks. Is this weird to be going to his house? I don't even know him. I wonder where he lives and if it's some sort of bachelor pad.

My thoughts stop when a song I love comes on the radio. I don't even think before I reach across my seat to turn the volume up. When

I sit back in my seat, I see a small, amused smile on Wyatt's face.

"I love this song," I say, closing my eyes and nodding my head to the beat.

"Good taste," he says. He pulls off the main road into a parking garage. After driving up a few levels, he parks near a set of double doors. He lets himself out before walking around to grab my suitcase from the trunk and open my door.

"Do you have anything else you need to do tonight?" He takes my arm as I step out of the truck.

"No. The team is setting up my station for me, so I just show up with my gear." He nods his head as he pulls the doors open. We walk through a beautiful lobby space. A black desk rests against the back wall, the woman behind it waving to us as we walk through the lobby toward a set of elevators.

"Evening, Mr. Lane," she says.

"Evening, Jenna." He continues walking, and I follow after him. My eyes scan my surroundings, trying to take in all I can. I look down as I walk, making sure to step on the black tiles instead of the cream ones. It's childish, but a fun habit I have when walking on multicolored floors. The hallway narrows, the cream stone walls closing in as the elevators come into full view. Wyatt hits a button, and a second later, the doors open for us. He guides me inside. When I turn around from the incredible view, Wyatt has pressed the button for the twentieth floor.

"If you enjoy that view, you'll love the view from the condo." His eyes gleam as he looks down at me.

We've been mostly quiet since he picked me up, and I'm oddly comfortable. When I'm tattooing, it's easy to talk to people. Usually, my clients start conversations and because of the type of clientele I attract, we often end up nerding out about books we've read. In the outside world, I want to babble to fill the silence. It's a nervous habit, but with Wyatt, I don't feel the need to do that. I feel comfortable enough to just listen and observe.

The elevator slows to a stop. Wyatt enters a key into the wall, the doors opening to reveal a simple living space.

"Welcome to my condo." He rolls my suitcase to a stop near the bar in the kitchen.

Grabbing the food from my hand, he sets it down on the counter, then offers to take my jacket. I let him pull it off my shoulders as I slip my arms out. When he places the jacket on the back of one of the stools, I take a spin, looking at his space.

It's surprisingly empty, but I guess since players can be traded and swap teams often, it would make sense not to make one place feel permanent. The living room is essentially one large open space. Glass windows surround the whole area, giving us an incredible view of the city. I step toward the windows, taking in the expanse of the view. The sunset is on full display now, the purples and blues more prominent.

"It's beautiful, isn't it?" Wyatt walks up beside me, standing at my side as we both look out at the city coming to life in the evening.

"Mmm," I say, smiling. "This is the closest I've felt to home in a long time." I see Wyatt look at me. I turn my face to look at him. "My father worked in a big high-rise building and my favorite part of my day was going to visit him in the evenings when he couldn't be home for dinner. My mom would pack food for us and we'd bring dinner to him." I shove my hands into my pockets. "He had a view like this from his building."

"That's a good memory to have. Raleigh is a beautiful place to be. It's why I left Boston. I fell in love with this place."

"Makes sense." I don't bring up the fact that he could be coming back to Boston. I wonder what's happening on that front.

"Would you like to eat?" Wyatt leaves my side to walk into the kitchen. He pulls out plates from the cupboards and places them in front of the chairs on the table. I nod, pulling out a chair at the table and lowering myself into the seat. I cross my legs before reaching for one of the styrofoam containers.

"They're all the same, so take as many as you want." Wyatt takes the other container out and places the tacos on his plate. He walks back to the fridge and pulls out two beers, popping the caps off and then setting one in front of me.

"Lime?"

I nod my head, taking one from the plate and squeezing it into the bottle.

I take a couple tacos from the container and put them on my plate. Folding one up, I take a bite, nearly moaning around the bite. I sigh, taking another bite, and my eyes practically roll back into my head.

"Good, right?" Wyatt smirks, shoving the whole taco into his mouth. I laugh, almost choking, so I take a sip of my beer.

"So good," I say.

We finish dinner quickly, talking lightly between bites. I lean back in my chair, a hand resting on my belly.

"So, why hockey?" The moisture on the outside of my beer bottle drips down my hand, so I take a napkin and wipe off the bottle and my hand.

"My grandpa was a hockey player," he says. "My parents passed away when I was little, so I was raised by my grandparents." He takes a sip of his beer, then continues, "There was this story they told when I was little that always made me wrinkle my nose in disgust. They were so in love all the time. When I was a kid, I thought it was gross, but now I appreciate it more.

"I guess in grade school, my grandfather had overheard my

grandma talking about how she had this dream to date a hockey player. 'Some kink of hers,' or something as my papa said." He laughs. "Anyway, he started taking lessons and made the high school team, then went on to play in college. He didn't go pro or anything, but he was a simp for my grandma, and I admire him for it. It took her a while to notice, but they eventually started dating and got married their junior year of college." He looks off into the distance, probably lost in a memory.

"That's adorable, actually. Are they still alive?" I grip my beer tighter, emotion clogging my throat. I miss my own grandparents dearly.

"No," he says. "They got to see me go pro, and shortly after, Gran passed. Not long after that, my papa passed as well. They were always together, so I saw it coming."

"I'm sorry," I say. I want to reach over and grab his hand. Instead, I look up, searching his eyes.

He clears his throat, wiping at his mouth. "Anyway. Tell me about you. Why are you a hater?" He winks, smiling a smile that tells me he's teasing. It's my turn to clear my throat. *Someone who was supposed to love me, hurt me. That's why.*

"It's complicated." I stare intently at the lip of my beer. Maybe these confessions will scare him away and I won't need to worry about the distance or about the fact that he's a hockey player.

"We've got time," he says. "Only if you're comfortable, though." His blue eyes watch me. There's something different about the way he watches me. I've been in relationships before, but none of those men have watched me like Wyatt does. He watches me like he wants to memorize and to know. He pays attention in a way that makes me feel like he cares.

In the beginning of my relationship with Tanner, he gave me just enough attention to make it seem like he cared. Then one day, that just stopped. Everything I'd say was less important to the point where I'd stopped sharing.

I stare back at Wyatt, trying to see any ill intent in his expression.

"My ex is a hockey player," I say, sighing. "And I feel like it sounds immature to hate hockey and all hockey players, but there was a lot that happened between us, and it was easier to make a blanket statement to protect myself."

"It's not immature," he says. "If someone hurt me, it'd be an easy decision to do something similar to protect myself too."

"Thank you," I say, looking at him through my lashes. I mean it too. I didn't feel like there was any judgment coming from him, and that makes me feel safe.

CHAPTER 14
Wyatt

H er ex *is* a hockey player. Not *was*. Is. I don't even know what he did, but it must have been something serious if she's created an opinion against all players. I wonder if he's gone pro. Is he a man that I've shared the ice with?

Dakota rubs her wrist absentmindedly. I watch her as she thinks. She's in some sort of internal battle with herself, probably wondering how much to share with me. I don't blame her for being hesitant. For her to trust me at all says a lot to me. She looks down at her arm, rubbing circles over that tattoo that wraps around her wrist.

"Can I ask you something?" She looks at me intently.

"Of course."

"What are your intentions here, Wyatt? I don't want to stay in your guest room or be vulnerable with someone who has no intention of sticking around. I want to make it clear that I'm not the kind of girl to have a casual relationship."

The question throws me for a second. Her blunt statement makes me like her more. I respect that. She bites her lip as she waits. I hold her gaze as I speak, my voice dropping an octave or two.

"Dakota, I wouldn't have invited you to stay at my place had my intentions been casual." I reach across the table, capturing her hand in mine. "I intend to win you over, however long that may take. I intend to date you, to make you mine. And I intend to destroy everything that man ever did to make you dislike my sport and the people in it. Does that answer your question?" I run my tongue across my lower lip before pulling my hand back and taking a sip of my beer. She watches me the whole time, and I stifle a smile.

"Uh." She coughs, blinking a few times. "Yeah. Uhm. Actually, it does. Thanks."

I smile. "Great. Glad that's settled." I lean back in my chair, stretching my arm above my head. "What would you like to do now? I'm sure you're tired after your flight." Her eyes track my movements, her lips pursing. I glance down at my watch. It's only six-thirty.

She looks at me for several moments, then a smile fills her face.

"Do you trust me?" She looks at me expectantly. There's an almost giddy sort of energy behind that statement, and it's adorable.

"Of course," I say, removing my hand from the back of my head and leaning forward to look at her. I hold her gaze and she looks back at me with fervor.

"I propose a competition since I lost so badly last time."

"Okay. I like where this is going. What are the stakes?"

"If I win, tomorrow you have to let me tattoo you at the convention. And if I lose, I'll let you tattoo me." She gives me an almost-wicked grin, and it does all sorts of things to my cock.

"You sure you want me to ruin your perfectly tattooed body?" I wink, and she laughs.

"What makes you believe you'll ruin it? And don't you think you're jumping the gun a little? You don't even know what we're doing yet."

"I'm just trying to start off oozing confidence. If you win, it won't be much of a punishment to let you tattoo me, considering you have more talent in your pinky finger than I do in my whole body." She snorts at me.

"Says the professional hockey player. Have you seen yourself play? You're incredible, Wyatt." My body heats at the way my name sounds coming out of her mouth. It reminds me of her breathy moans, and suddenly my erection is pressed against the zipper of my jeans.

"Don't say things like that to me before we're meant to compete." I groan. She raises an eyebrow at me.

"You don't want me to feed your ego?" She pauses, biting her lip on a smile. "Wyatt…"

An almost feral instinct in me wants to lift my dining table and toss it across the room to be closer to her. That little minx is trying to throw me off my game.

"Oh, you're good," I say, arranging my face into neutral calm.

"I really thought that was going to work." She chuckles into her hands, her green eyes bright and beautiful. "Do you have any card games?"

I nod. I head down the hall and into the back room where I've begun packing boxes. I'm keeping this room a secret from her…for now. I pull out my box of games and carry it back to the table for her to rummage through. She pulls out *Phase 10* and shuffles the cards so that we can go through the game together.

"My brother and I used to play this game together for hours. I don't want to brag, but I'm pretty good."

"Oh ho! Here we go," I say, fanning out my cards. "Prove it." I raise an eyebrow at her, and she raises her chin in mock indignation.

"You're on, Wyatt Alexander."

"I like it when you call me that."

"Wyatt Alexander?"

I nod.

"My grandma was the only one who called me that. To everyone else, Lane is an important part of my identity. To the people I care about, I'm just Wyatt Alexander, a kid from a small town."

"I like Wyatt Alexander," she says. "I like the guy behind the hockey helmet."

We look at each other for a few moments. I wonder if she realizes how important those words are to me.

She draws a card, moving things around and then dropping her phase to the table. I glare at her, the competitive monster in me roaring to win.

After about an hour, we're tied, neck-and-neck. I'm sweating, not because I have anything to lose, but because this has gotten intense. It's almost dangerous, but she hasn't run away scared yet.

We're on the last phase, and the game could end at any moment. I look away for one second, and suddenly, she's slapping cards down onto the table, a shit-eating grin spread across her face.

"Told you." She tosses her hands in the air. "I've lost against you *twice,* and I couldn't let it happen again."

"Damn," I say, flipping my cards over and showing her my completed phase. She cackles, her eyes watering.

"I'm a winner," she cheers. She does a little happy dance in her seat, and I want to hold her in my arms. She's adorable.

"Okay, okay. Rub it in, why don't you?"

"What should I tattoo on you next?"

"You can do anything you want. I trust you." She eyes me, her cheeks flushing.

"You don't even realize how much I love those words, Wyatt Alexander. Every tattoo artist *dreams* about someone saying that to them."

"Well, it's the truth." She looks at me for a moment, then her hand comes to her mouth as she covers a yawn. I look over at the clock on the stove.

"It's getting late. Let me show you to your room." I stand from the table, grabbing her suitcase and carrying it with me down the hall. I twist the handle for the guest bedroom and push the door open. "There's extra blankets in the closet, and the bathroom is the first door on the left." I set her suitcase down in the room and step back into the hall.

"Thank you, Wyatt." She turns away, then pauses. "Actually, one more thing. I wanted to know if you wanted to come with me tomorrow. You don't have to stay the whole time, but I thought it would be fun. Obviously, you'll be there for my victory tattoo, but usually Sterling comes to these things with me, and I won't really have anyone there I know."

"Sure," I say. "What time do we need to leave?"

"Eight."

"Sounds good. Goodnight, Dakota."

"Goodnight, Wyatt Alexander." She smiles, watching me as she closes the door. I take a breath, my heart beating hard. *Mine.*

I toss and turn in bed for hours. By the time I finally give up on sleep, it's almost two in the morning.

GOAL Suck

I hadn't realized it would be so difficult to sleep with a beautiful woman across the hall. I desperately wish she would creep across the hall into my room. I've fallen asleep with her on the phone, but now that she's here, I want her to actually be *here*, in my bed and in my arms.

I still when I hear the careful creek of the floor as Dakota creeps down the hall. I smile to myself. I must not be alone in my inability to sleep. Not willing to let this moment pass, I toss the blankets aside, not caring to throw on a shirt or pants before I walk down the hall after her.

She's standing at the sink, her back to me when I say her name, my voice lower than normal. She squeaks, turning around so fast and dropping the glass she was holding.

"Sorry." I chuckle. "I didn't mean to scare you." My bare feet pad across the tile floor to the cabinet. Pulling out a broom and a dustpan, I kneel to the floor, picking up the broken pieces of glass. I look up at her and realize that she's holding her breath. She's wearing an oversized tee. It stops around the middle of her thighs, and I nearly choke on my own tongue taking in how beautiful she looks. I can see her nipples poking through the shirt.

"Why have you stopped breathing?" I ask from the floor. She sighs, adjusting her stance as I sweep around her legs.

"You're not wearing pants," she says a little breathily. I look down at myself, seeing only my boxers.

"You're not wearing pants either," I say, standing to my full height. I take a step toward her, and she gasps. I smirk, resting my free hand on her waist and moving her aside so I can dump the broken glass. When I'm finished, I set the broom aside, not caring to step back from her.

"Wyatt," she breathes. Her eyes are blown, and I feel my forearm flex when I tighten my grip on her waist. She looks up at me and licks her lips, and that's when I feel my control snap.

I press into her, bringing my lips to hers. Bringing my other hand to her, I slide it up her side, bunching the shirt in my fist.

My cock stirs in my boxers when she pulls my lip into her mouth and bites. She gasps into my mouth when I press my erection into her waist. She must feel it. There's only a thin barrier between us.

Our tongues battle, her hand coming to my hair and fisting it. Her other hand roams across my back, her nails skimming across my skin. The feel of it leaves goosebumps all over me.

My mind goes hazy with arousal. I growl into her mouth, sliding my hands under her shirt and gripping her waist to lift her onto the counter. I use my thigh to support her further, pressing it between her legs and adjusting her weight.

I ache to have my hands all over, to line myself up with her and to hear her scream my name as we fuck right here on this counter. I hold her face between my hands, kissing her like my life depends on it.

"Dakota," I groan between kisses, "tell me about the dream." I could beg. I could get on my hands and knees and beg her. I need her to stop me before I go any farther. I need to hear those words from her mouth first, to know that she wants me too.

"Dream?" Dakota mumbles, her head falling back as I suck at her neck.

"The naughty one, Dakota." I say her name like it's a prayer. This is getting dangerous. She bucks into me, and suddenly I'm aware of the wetness against my thigh. She freezes, her hands no longer roaming across my back or pulling at my hair like it's keeping her grounded.

She scrambles, her eyes wide. "Oh my God." She scoots back on the counter, moving away from me. "Oh my God," she repeats. "I'm—"

"Don't you dare say you're sorry," I growl. "Don't you dare."

"Wyatt…"

"No. You have nothing to be sorry for. That"—I point to her—"is completely natural, and, quite frankly, hot as hell." She doesn't respond for a long while until she nods, albeit reluctantly.

"Dakota, I need to know…" I almost grimace at the way my voice sounds. *Desperate.*

"What?"

"Who was in this dream?"

She blushes, her hands folding in her lap and pressing down into the t-shirt.

"Wasn't that obvious?" I shake my head, and she sighs. *I need to hear you say it.*

"Me," she says.

"And?"

"You," she whispers.

I swallow, feeling relief wash over me.

"That's all I needed to know," I say. I extend my hand to her, and she takes it. She jumps off the counter, her grip tight on my hand. This beautiful woman stands there staring up at me, and I want nothing more than to claim her.

I make myself turn away. *Tomorrow.* "Goodnight, Dakota."

"Wyatt, wait." Her voice is pleading. I look over my shoulder at her. She adjusts her weight, her lip pulled into her mouth like she's battling with herself.

I promised myself that I would win her over, but I also know that I need her to be sure that this is what she wants too. Until then, I'll wait.

She slumps slightly, her eyes downcast. "Goodnight," she says.

My heart sinks. I don't know what I was hoping for, but it certainly wasn't that.

"Goodnight, beautiful."

CHAPTER 15
Wyatt

The conference is packed with people from all over the country. I've been by Dakota's side for over an hour now, and I've witnessed her speaking to people from every state and some from other countries. I'd known she was popular, but this is a level I wasn't expecting. I have no experience with this, but compared to some of the other tables, Dakota's has been packed from the moment the doors opened.

I enjoy watching her in her element. I'd gathered that Dakota is more of an introvert. At first, she'd been quite shy with the people coming and going. As time has gone on, she's grown more comfortable with everyone coming to talk to her.

When she's working, she looks so at peace. I watch the way her hands trace the lines and the way she bites her lip while she concentrates. It makes me think about how she bit her lip last night in the kitchen. I wanted to kiss her goodnight, to take her to bed with me and to wake up with her by my side. But that didn't happen.

Dakota's working on a custom piece for a woman from Guatemala. She'd seen her work on Instagram and booked when she saw that Dakota was coming to this conference. They'd been talking through DMs on the kind of piece she wanted, and they'd settled on a custom piece for her arm. It's a geometric piece, a stack of books within it. The top book is laying open, a castle coming out of it along with a bunch of other creatures and plants. I'm not much of a reader, but I imagine it's symbolizing your favorite book coming to life.

I'd taken a chance to look over her flash sheet. I couldn't count on two hands the number of women who have come by to get the "smut slut" tattoo—whatever that means.

"Do you design your own tattoos?" I'm watching her arm as she tattoos. She's got a patchwork type sleeve on her right arm. There's a myriad of different tattoos on her skin. I'll have to ask about them later. She dips the needle back into the ink and then moves back to the woman's arm.

"Some of them." She draws the straight outer line of the diamond, then continues, "Lani's done most of my recent tattoos. I'd hoped that over time she'd want to become an artist in my shop, but that hasn't happened yet."

"She's not an artist?"

"No. She's got an amazing eye and mad skill, but she only tattoos for fun. One day, I'll convince her to get licensed." She starts shading pieces of the tattoo, wiping away extra ink. After a few more minutes, she wipes at the tattoo, revealing the final product. This is my favorite part.

Every time she shows them the final product, I can see the pride in her eyes. She lights up like a Christmas tree in the most subtle ways.

It's in the way her eyes gleam or the way that she sits up taller, her chin raised a little higher. She should be proud. It makes a difference when an artist can create a small community as well as provide work that they're not only proud of, but that people love.

The woman stands, her eyes looking at her arm in the mirror. "It's beautiful, Dakota. Everything I'd imagined and more. Thank you!" She throws her arms around Dakota, pulling her into a hug. "I'm so excited to finally be able to meet you. This has been a dream of mine." Dakota smiles as she pulls out the aftercare supplies.

"I've gotten as far as I have because of people like you who have supported me, so thank *you*. I'm glad you like it." Dakota taps the chair, and the woman sits back down. "Okay, so, leave this on for at least forty-eight hours and then you can wash it gently. I'm giving you an extra piece to put on if anything happens. If you have any questions, don't hesitate to reach out, love." She smiles wide, giving the woman one last hug before she leaves the booth. I'm still watching her as she cleans her station.

She taps the seat, giving me a wide smile. "Your turn."

I groan, pretending to be upset, but in actuality, I'm excited to see what else she creates.

"I'm thinking of Medusa for this one." She sets up a row of black inks and assembles her tattoo gun.

"Whatever you want," I say. I lay down on the table with my arm up. I nearly fall asleep as she draws on my arm. It's only until the sound of the gun stops and the vague feeling of being watched overcomes me that I open my eyes. She stares down at my arm, admiring her own work.

"Want to see it?" She wipes away the excess ink and slides her chair away from the table. I sit up slowly and look into the full-length mirror.

GOAL *Suck*

"Holy fuck! This is incredible." I twist my arm around to get a full look. Medusa's snakes wrap into the other tattoos, melding the three tattoos together. Half of her is a beautiful woman, her hair long and wrapping down my arm, the other half of her is cracked almost like stone.

I'm sitting in the chair, admiring her work, when I feel someone approach.

"And that's a wrap." The voice comes from our right. A lengthy man approaches the table. He's eyeing Dakota's ass as she's bent over wiping down her area. "Great job today, Dakota. It was nice having you here again this year." I watch him, my eyes narrowing. He looks at me for a moment, then looks away.

"Thanks for having me, Jude. It's a pleasure." She stands up straight.

"Of course. You're always a hit." He shoves his hands into his pockets. "Anyway, I wanted to know if I could take you out to dinner?" I almost laugh, but I keep my face neutral.

"I've actually got plans already, but thank you for asking." He takes a step closer to her, and I clench my fists.

"Oh, come on. I owe you at least that. Let me take you out." He's completely ignoring my presence.

She stills, her eyes flicking to me. "Sorry. I can't." That's all the cue I need to know that she's uncomfortable. I slap my hands down on my thighs as I rise to a stand. I take a step toward him, extending my hand. I tower over him, so he looks up at me.

"Hi. I don't think we've met. I'm Wyatt." He shakes my hand lamely, clearing his throat.

"Uh, hi. Jude." He looks back at Dakota. "Is he with you?"

She nods her head, her lips pursing.

"How do you know Dakota?" he asks me.

"He's my plus one today." Dakota takes a step toward me. He frowns slightly, his eyes squinting.

"Wait, I know you." He waggles his finger in my direction and I purse my lips. "You're Wyatt Lane, the hockey player. Yo, dude. Big fan."

"Thanks, bro."

"Anyway, I better be off. Have fun, Dakota. Hope to see you around here again." He practically speed-walks away from the booth. Dakota huffs a breath, her features softening. She turns to me, her hands tucked into her jean pockets.

"Thank you. He's relentless. *Every year.*" I nod, watching her as she finishes packing up her things.

"I'd like to take you out and show you the city." I put my hand on her back as we walk through the emptying building.

"Okay, yeah. Let's do it."

"I didn't think you were a science kind of guy."

"Judging me again, are you?" I smile at her as we walk through the natural science museum. She stops in front of the T-rex skeleton, a little sound of exasperation leaving her mouth. I hide a smile.

"Ugh, yes, I am. I'm sorry."

"We'll need to fix that, then." I smirk at her.

"How do you suppose we do that?"

"How about I tell you five things about myself and you can do the same? We are getting to know each other, after all."

"At this point, I'm sure all five things will shock me." She wraps her arm through mine as we walk.

"We'll see." I think over what to share with her. "Okay, I got it. One, I was a biology major in college. Two, as a kid, I wanted to be a paleontologist." We keep walking, but she's not looking at the exhibits. She's watching me, her arm looped through mine, and I couldn't be happier.

"So you like bones?" She smirks at me. I snort.

"I *liked* bones. I didn't get very far."

She laughs, her hair falling into her face as she leans forward. "Okay, continue."

"Three, my birthday is on April seventh. Four, I hate, absolutely loathe, tomatoes."

Dakota snorts, her steps slowing as we continue.

"Last one, I love children and hope to have my own one day."

Dakota's eyes smile. She holds my gaze, then looks away.

"My turn, I guess. Since you shared your birthday, I guess I'll share mine. I just turned twenty-three on September tenth. I have an older brother named Dallas. And yes, my parents have a thing for city names." She looks down at her feet. "I grew up in Canada, but my mom is originally from California, so I like to consider myself half-American. My mom moved her life to Canada to be with my dad. How many is that?"

"Three. You've got two more." Her grip on my arm tightens as a kid runs past us, his father following close behind.

"I'm a wizard. I got my letter to wizard school when I was eleven."

I toss my head back on a laugh, and she smiles at me.

"One more," I say.

She stops walking, unhooking her arm from me. I immediately feel a small sense of loss. She slips her arm out of her jacket and rolls up her sleeve. She points to the ink on her arms.

"I became a tattoo artist because someone in my life told me I couldn't do it. They repeatedly told me that I wouldn't make it and that

I wasn't talented enough. They said and did other things that hurt me too, but I look back and thank them for those nasty words. Without them, I wouldn't be where I am today." She points to a specific tattoo on her arm. It's a sword, wrapped in vines and flowers. "There's a book character I love. She's a warrior and fought against all odds. This tattoo is a nod to her and a reminder to myself that I fought to be here and that I deserve it." She clears her throat. "Not every tattoo has some deep meaning like that, but a lot of them do. I'm kind of intense sometimes."

"I like that. I'm sorry that happened, but I'm glad you didn't let it stop you."

"Me too." She slips her arm back into her sleeve, then fiddles with her fingers a bit. I take her hand in mine, lacing our fingers together. She looks up at me and her face relaxes as she takes a breath.

We finish walking through the entirety of the museum. We came at a good time; not many people were left, and many of the exhibits were empty for us to wander. After the museum, we made our way to a restaurant to eat before we landed back at my condo.

"I'm kind of surprised we weren't bombarded by your fans," she says, taking a seat on the couch next to me.

"Oh, that was intentional. Roman told me about Halloween, and I wasn't ready to share you quite yet."

"Oh, so I'm yours to share?" She winks at me, her legs moving closer to me. I don't answer. Instead, I watch her. I need her to say it, to willingly become tethered to me.

"So…I go home tomorrow." Dakota smoothly rests her leg across my lap. The longer she's here, the more comfortable she gets. She's got this hard outer shell that needs to be cracked in order to get to the deeper portions of her. I think she's built up walls of protection, and I'm learning the ways to earn her trust. She's grown more comfortable, finding ways to subtly touch me. This is progress, and I can't complain.

"You do," I say, my hand drawing small circles over the top of her foot. A movie plays in the background, but I haven't been paying much attention.

"I'd like to see you again. I'd like to keep seeing you, actually." My hand stills on her foot.

"I'd like that too."

"I don't know how this is supposed to work, Wyatt. I've never done a long-distance relationship before."

I raise my eyebrow at her, the corner of my mouth lifting.

"What?" she asks.

"A long-distance relationship."

Her face drops. "I thought that's what you wanted."

"I do. I just like hearing you say it." I could shout for joy, but instead I resume my small circles on her ankles.

"What? That I want to be in a relationship with you?" She smiles, her cheeks reddening. Her pale skin paired with that beautiful blush is one of my favorite things.

"Is that what you want, Dakota?"

"Well, what would it look like if we were doing what *you* wanted?" she counters, avoiding my question. I want to feel upset, but I see what she's doing. She's making a challenge out of this. Her eyes darken a little.

"Tell me about that smut slut tattoo," I say. I hold her leg, my hand roaming her ankle and calf now.

"Some people watch their porn," she says. "I read it."

Well, damn.

My hand goes further up her leg, rubbing as I go.

"I like to read smut. My brother calls them porn books, but I really just love romance and the community that I've found with these books." I continue rubbing, her voice growing breathier. "I think that there's a certain amount of shame that comes with being a woman and talking about sex. Society has made it normal to shame women and to make us feel bad for wanting sex, for asking for what we want, or for dressing a certain way. I talk about my sex books because I'm tired of being shamed for sex." I move my hand a little higher, watching her with a blank expression. She tosses her head back onto the cushion, her face growing red. When she looks up at me again, she breathes deeply. "Smut slut is basically a gang of people who read smut like me. Like a code word for a secret club." She bites her lip. "Wyatt, what would it look like if we were doing what you wanted?"

"Dakota, I said I was going to win you over, and that's what I intend to do. But I won't do anything unless you make it explicitly clear that you want it too. I'd like you to ask and to not be afraid to ask." My heart pounds as I speak. She watches me, her eyes darkening. I see the moment she makes a decision, and my cock twitches in my jeans the moment she moves toward me and sits across my lap, her arms on my shoulders.

CHAPTER 16
Dakota

I don't do this. I don't make the moves, and I certainly don't mount a man I'm not dating, but here I am, sitting across Wyatt's lap with my arms wrapped around his shoulders.

That's the funny thing about this situation. We're not dating *officially*, but over the last month, my mind has been fully entranced by Wyatt. I've realized it before, but this man has me in the palm of his hand, and now it's my turn to act.

There's something so empowering about taking control. Wyatt's put the ball in my court. He's explicitly told me to make it clear what I want, and right now, I want to taste him. I want to pepper kisses along his neck and to breathe in that woodsy smell that makes me want to bathe in him. For once in my life, I feel like one of those girls in my books. I feel like a sexy woman and someone worthy of attention.

I draw my lower lip into my mouth as I bring my hand to the back of his head. My fingers slide through his hair, the softness of it brushing my fingers. My thumb brushes behind his ear, and his eyes flutter shut. I feel his breath quicken and then his hands grip my waist.

I lean in slowly, watching him as I get closer. His usually light eyes are now dark, inky blues. As I lean in closer, I feel a magnetic pull toward him. I close my eyes before our lips meet.

It's gentle at first, the touch light and testing, and then it grows more urgent. His hand comes to the back of my head, the other lowering to my thigh.

Every time he kisses me, it's like a religious experience. His mouth teases me, sending shivers throughout my whole body. He doesn't need to speak for me to understand the passion behind those kisses.

I'm not certain that this type of kiss is reserved only for me, but for now, I can pretend like it is.

I part my lips, and I feel him draw my lip into his mouth and bite. *Just like that damn dream.* I smile, releasing a small breath before pulling back. I want him to remember this, to remember me. This fluttering in my stomach and this battle in my head is new and dangerous. I don't want this to end.

No one has made me feel like this before. I'm attracted to Wyatt, but there's more. I want to *know* him and to be important to him. I *want* him to want me, and I want him to win me over. I wasn't rooting for him at first, but I want to trust him fully and to let him in. I don't know how long that will take, but I want to try.

He breaks our kiss, his lips pressing against the skin between my neck and ear. He nips lightly at the lobe, rolling it between his teeth. I moan, rolling my hips in his lap.

I feel his erection growing between my legs, and my mind wanders to last night. When I felt him last night, my mind short-circuited.

GOAL *Suck*

Even now as I'm mounted on top of him, I have no questions about the sheer length of him. It's intimidating and yet so damn fitting. *Of course*, Wyatt Lane would have something like that hiding in his pants. I want to hold it, to touch it.

Wow. Slow down, Dakota. He groans against my neck, his lips brushing against my skin. I feel hot, my body on fire at his every touch.

He raises his hand over his head and I instinctively flinch. I regret it the moment it happens.

Wyatt's lips leave my neck, his eyes wide open. He's breathing heavily, his eyes trained on me. His jaw clenches, and I shrink into myself. He looks angry. I hope he's not angry with me.

"Who hit you?" His voice is deep, almost like a growl. I close my eyes, liquid burning behind them. This is so embarrassing, but the relief I feel is instantaneous. "Look at me," he says. His voice is more gentle now. "Was it him? Your ex?" I don't trust my voice and I certainly don't trust myself to look him in the eye, so I nod.

He doesn't breathe, or at least I don't feel him breathe for a while. I lean in, resting my head against his chest. When I finally pull away, he's still watching me.

My eyes are wet. He takes a hand and gently wipes under my eyes. "Let me make one thing *very* clear. I need you to know that if we enter into this relationship, I will never hurt you. I will never touch you in a way that causes harm, and I won't raise a hand to you. I certainly will not tolerate anyone else hurting you, either. So I promise you, if I'm to become your boyfriend—which yes, Dakota, I very much want to be your boyfriend and to put a label on this because I don't think I can go another day where I'm worried that someone else will take you away from me. *If* I'm to become that to you and I *ever* meet this ex of yours, I'll make it very clear that he's a disgusting excuse for a man.

And if he comes near you, I'll end him." His hand brushes against my face, pushing my hair out of my eyes. I lean my cheek into his hand, my face fitting into the expanse of it.

"Thank you." I don't know why I say it, but I do. Maybe it's because at this moment, I feel so safe. I want to feel protected, and those words from his mouth make me feel safe. I kiss his nose, then rest my head into his chest. He wraps his arms around me, holding me close to him.

I don't know how long we stay like that. I decide to break the silence. I turn my head that's now resting in his lap and look up at him. He looks down at me.

"I want that," I say. He watches me. "I want to date you, to call you my boyfriend, and to let the world know that the short blonde has laid claim to Wyatt Alexander."

He raises his brows. "Are you sure? I won't be quiet about this. Once it gets out, there's a chance for the media to pay attention to you." *I won't be quiet about this.*

"So if someone asks you during an interview, you'll tell them that you're seeing someone?"

"Most definitely. I plan on letting the world know that you're mine." He runs a hand through my hair, and I shiver. There's something almost animalistic about Wyatt Alexander. He's territorial and growly, and for some reason, I find it incredibly attractive.

"Good. Then we're on the same page." I smile at him, wiping the remaining tears from my eyes. His face softens, and he looks at me like I hold his heart in his hands. *Shit.*

He presses his lips against mine in a tender sort of way. When he pulls away, he smiles.

"Okay," he says.

"Okay."

Wyatt drives me to the airport in the morning, and the sour feeling of sadness works its way into my throat. Beginnings are supposed to be fun and exciting.

I've never done this before. Long distance is new to me, and the feeling of doubt creeps its way into my mind and tugs. I'm not expecting this to be easy. We're still learning each other, and my *stupid* flinch had to ruin our moment.

"So I decided that I'm going to be staying with Roman until I can move back into my apartment." I twiddle my fingers, not looking up at him yet.

"I think he'll love that. Lily will too."

"Yeah. I hope so. I'm meeting Lily tomorrow, so we'll see."

"She'll love you. I told her that she needs to approve of you before we can date." He holds up his finger to his mouth like it's a secret.

"Oh, did you now?" I laugh, my eyes smiling at him.

"I did. I guess we'll see if she approves."

"I guess we will."

"Dakota, I've been meaning to ask you…" He smirks at me. "Will you come to the game on Friday? Watch me cream Jaiden and Roman?"

"You're playing Boston?" An excited smile crosses my face.

"Indeed, and I want you to be there."

"Then I will," I say. "Are you staying for Thanksgiving?" I can't help but wonder if he'll be there with us. Roman invited us to his home since we aren't going home until Christmas.

"I am. They're my family, so my holidays are usually spent in Boston." I can't help the smile that springs free on my face. Then as quickly as it appears, it's gone as Wyatt pulls the car into the airport parking lot.

Wyatt steps out of the car, my suitcase in his hand as well as his own. The team is flying to Tennessee for their game tomorrow. I look down at my feet, my toes wiggling in my boots. When I release a breath, I can see it in the chilly morning air.

We walk in silence into the airport. I know it won't be long until I see him next, but I'm already aching to finish what we started.

We check in, stopping when we can't continue together any further. He pulls me into his arms, placing a kiss into my hair.

"I'll see you soon, *girlfriend*."

I laugh, shaking my head at him.

"I'll see you soon, *boyfriend*."

"One day at a time," he reminds me.

"One day at a time," I confirm. "I'll see you soon. Call me when you land." I rise up on my toes, kissing him again before taking my bag from his hand and turning away.

"Thank you. For being so patient with me and for not wanting casual."

"For you, always." He kisses the top of my head again before walking back to his gate. I watch him walk away from me before I turn and walk in the opposite direction.

I have barely a moment before I'm boarding the plane and on my flight home. It's only then that I realize how tired I am. When I'm home, I'm generally a homebody and comfortable with the to and from work routine. Spontaneity is not a strength of mine, but it seems as if Wyatt is always making moves on the go. Me…well, at the end of the day, I get to watch movies or cuddle up with a good book. I'm comfortable and used to my routine and my plan. This is new territory, and I'm admittedly scared.

GOAL *Suck*

Pulling out my Kindle from my purse, I scroll through, picking my next read. I don't make it very far because the next thing I remember is waking up to the sound of the landing announcement. My neck is stiff and sore, but after rolling it out, I gather my things and hunker down until landing.

As I ride the escalator down to the airport entrance, I see Sterling holding a hand-drawn sign. It reads "World's Biggest Raleigh Riders Fan." I roll my eyes, a laugh escaping my lips when she jumps up and down after spotting me.

"Hey, babes," she says. "How was your *ride?*"

"I expect you're going to be making sex jokes for the foreseeable future."

"You would be correct." She waggles her eyebrows at me, then turns to walk out the door. "So tell me everything. Don't leave a single thing out."

I spend the whole drive recapping my weekend with Wyatt. When we get to Dane's place, Lani is there with Thai food, and suddenly I'm starting over to fill her in. The girls gasp when appropriate and fangirl over every detail.

"He actually *said* that to you? That'd he'd end Tanner if he came near you?" Lani shovels a bite of Panang curry and rice into her mouth.

"He *did*! I almost want to tell him his name just to see what would happen." *I won't. But I want to.* Sterling snorts, her eyes amused.

"I think I like him. Tanner deserves to be punched straight in the dick." She sips her drink. "Multiple times. Over and over again."

Lani raises her drink. "Hear, hear." We all laugh, clinking drinks and eating. I take a look around the table at Lani and Sterling, and I can't help but smile. I *love* my friends, aggressively, and I'm beyond thankful that they're here to share this moment with me.

"You've got that mushy look on your face, Koda." Sterling's cheeks rise, her eyebrow wiggling.

"Just thinking about how thankful I am for both of you." I stare down into my drink. "Do you think it's too soon, too *fast*, to put a label on it?"

"Koda. Have you *seen* that man? I'd lick him, pee on him, anything I could to lay claim on him as early as possible to make all the puck bunnies back the fuck off." Sterling watches me.

I've never thought about the puck bunnies before. I'd known enough about hockey before Tanner, but I'd still asked questions, eager for his attention and approval.

I'm a damn liar, acting like I hate hockey. I *love* hockey. I love that I can slowly accept that part of myself again and that I don't need to fake it.

"In all seriousness, relationships range in levels of commitment. As time goes on, you'll get to know each other more. That *is* the whole point of dating. I don't think it's too soon. If you're both on the same page, I think it's perfect timing. Take it at your own pace, love."

"Thank you," I say.

I lay on the living room couch, my phone resting on the cushion beside my head. Wyatt's voice fills my ears as he speaks.

"I'm glad you made it home safely." There are sounds of shuffling in the background. It's later in Tennessee than here, so he should be asleep right now. When he finally settles down, I hear the groan he releases, probably from soreness.

"Me too," I say.

"So you're meeting Lily tomorrow?"

"Thursday, I think. We moved it because they were going out of town, and I didn't feel comfortable staying at his place alone." I sigh. "I think I'm more nervous to meet her than I am for...well, anything at this current time." His answering chuckle sends shivers through me. I smile into my pillow.

"Don't be. She's perfect, and like I said earlier, I'm sure she'll love you."

"Tell me about her," I say. He's quiet for a moment, the only indication that he's still there is the breathing on the other end of the call.

"She's a special girl," he says finally. "I think I fell in love with her the first moment I saw her." I can hear the smile in his voice. Hearing the note of softness in his voice makes my insides feel squishy. "I've always wanted kids, but this was different. Sarah had just left and he was...broken. But looking at her just changed you. There was this little innocent creature lying in a crib, and all three of us couldn't fathom how anyone could abandon her."

"Roman told me some of the story, but I didn't know that it broke him."

"Oh, it did. He wouldn't ever admit it, but he was broken for a while. He'd given up his dream for them, and suddenly she's gone. Not to mention that he had to watch his two best friends go through the draft. It was a hard time, but look where he is now."

"Does Lily travel with him?" I pull my pillow into my arms and hold tight.

"She did, but now that she's in school, not so much. It's hard to separate the two of them. As much as Lily is dependent on him, he is on her as well."

"I have no doubt that she's a part of his support system. She sounds like a great girl."

"She is, and there is absolutely nothing about you that someone couldn't like, so don't be worried."

"Okay. Fine," I concede. "Oh, the girls wanted me to ask if they can accompany me to the game on Friday."

"The girls or you?" He laughs, and I scowl.

"Hey, Silver is the hockey fan, not me," I tease.

"Fine, fine," he says. "Text me their full names, and I'll add them to the list."

I smile to myself, my eyes nearly closing with how wide my smile is.

"Okay," I say, and I can hear the yawn he releases. "Go to bed, Wyatt. I'll talk to you tomorrow."

"Mmm. Okay. Good night, *girlfriend*."

I laugh, my cheeks hurting from my smile.

"Goodnight, *boyfriend*." I press the button and place my phone on the nightstand.

Swinging my legs off the couch, I sneak down the hall into the kitchen. Sterling turns around at the sound of my footsteps. "I thought I heard you in here," I say. "Can't sleep?" I lean against the kitchen island.

"No. I'm kind of anxious for tomorrow." She pulls out the mint chip ice cream and scoops a bit into her bowl. I reach for the tub and scoop myself some. We both take a spoonful and moan over the minty chocolaty goodness. "God, this is why you're my best friend. You just *get* it." She rolls her eyes, taking another bite. I laugh, then lick the chocolate off of the spoon.

"So tell me, why are you anxious about tomorrow?" I walk to the couch, sinking into the cushions a moment later. I pull my leg into my chest, my bowl of ice cream resting gently on top of my knee. Sterling sits across from me.

"I've been feeling really creatively stifled lately. I don't know if

I'm just not being fulfilled anymore or if it's something simple like a creative drought. I love what I do, but Koda..." She squeezes the decorative pillow close to her chest. "Working in the shop with you and taking care of the shop with Lani and Julia...that's the most fun I've had in a long time—outside of traveling with you, of course. God, I love hockey so much, but I don't know what's wrong with me." She lays her head back onto the cushion and stares up at the ceiling.

"Have you thought about the fact that you got into this to prove to someone that you could? You're just like me, Silver. Now that you have, what challenges are you going up against now? Where's the next fight?" I bite my lip and look at her closely. "Silver, this career was partially a game for you. I know you love hockey and you love photography, but are you really doing what you want to be doing? As for working in the shop, I want to make it clear that you are just as much a part of that business as I am, so you are more than welcome to bother my staff anytime you need." I wink at her. Her nose wrinkles as she laughs. She shakes her head.

"You're right. I'm going to stick to the commitments I've made, but I think that I need a break." She shovels another bite of ice cream into her mouth. She wipes at the corner of her mouth, then raises her eyebrow at me. "Are you sure you don't mind having me in the shop?"

"Sterling, I would literally die without you there at least once a week. So yes, please, come work in my shop whenever you want. Just, you know, let me know so I can put you on the schedule." I laugh, and she tosses a pillow at me.

"Oh, speaking of, Wyatt's getting us tickets to see him play on Friday. They're playing Boston, and I thought you and Lani would want to come with?" I say it more like a question than a statement. Her eyes go wide and she springs to her feet, jumping up and down on the couch. I laugh, walking back into the kitchen to place my bowl in the sink.

"Yes!" She squeals. "Does this mean you're finally done pretending you hate hockey?"

I turn around, my back leaning into the sink. I roll my eyes in the most dramatic way possible.

"I suppose so," I say.

"Great. So now we need to load you up with gear and jerseys…" She keeps talking, but I'm not listening. The lizard brain is creeping in, the fears of seeing Tanner again gripping at the corners of my mind.

"Dakota." Sterling stands and her voice brings me back to the present. "What was that?" she asks. My eyes drop to the floor. I breathe deeply, my eyes squeezing shut.

"Silver, I'm so scared. I don't know how to trust people. I don't know Wyatt enough to trust he won't do what Tanner did. I think I'm broken, and I'm so fucking frustrated because I desperately just want to get laid and date and to not have this voice in the back of my head telling me that everyone is going to hurt me." I slide down to the floor, and Sterling comes to sit next to me. She takes my hand in hers and squeezes. "What if I see him again? I've avoided games like the plague, and starting a relationship with Wyatt opens that door again."

"Let me ask you this: considering how Wyatt reacted, do you trust that he would protect you if you ran into him together?"

I mull her question over in my head. Wyatt's face had been one of pure rage. He's known me for a little over a month and was already reacting in such a strong way.

My life has been nothing but a perfectly calculated plan; I've got a routine and a plan for everything. I've even had a routine and a plan for what my love life could look like. My mother would slap me for my closed-off thoughts about it being too soon to know whether someone is important to you. My parents knew after a month. And I knew after a couple weeks that Sterling was going to be my best friend. So is it too much for my head and my heart to be in agreement that maybe, just maybe, it's not too early to trust that Wyatt will protect me?

"I think I do. The way he reacted to it felt so genuine, and I didn't even tell him the whole story. He just *knew* something was wrong." I turn my head to look at Sterling, and her grip on my hand tightens.

"I know that you know that I would go to jail for you. If I *ever* see that man's face again, I can promise you that I won't hesitate to act. I just want you to have someone else in your life that will fight for you in that way. I don't know Wyatt well, but I know a lot about him. I wouldn't have even entertained the idea of the two of you together had I questioned him."

"I fucking love you," I say.

"I fucking love you too," she replies.

CHAPTER 17
Dakota

Walking through the front doors of Roman's home feels different this time. It's my third time here, and I can feel myself shaking from nerves. It feels ridiculous, though, because she's a five-year-old girl. *A five-year-old girl who needs to approve of you.*

I stifle my sigh as I follow Roman down the hallway into the kitchen. The smell of pasta wafts into my nose and sends my stomach rumbling.

"Smells delicious," I say to Roman's back.

"Spaghetti is Lily's favorite." He looks back at me before he addresses the curly-haired girl sitting at the table with her back to us. "Lily, I'd like you to meet Dakota. Dakota, this is Lily."

Her little hand stops writing, her pencil immediately forgotten when she turns around and looks at me. I'm immediately struck by

GOAL *Suck*

how similar to Roman she looks. Her light brown skin and curly brown hair are a perfect replica of Roman's, if not a few shades lighter.

She looks at me with beautiful amber eyes, which, once again, are just like her father's.

"Daddy, is that her?" she asks Roman.

He smiles, nodding. "You're Uncle Wyatt's girlfriend?"

She slides from her chair and walks toward me. I kneel on the floor in front of her so that we can be eye level.

"I am. Is that okay?"

"Depends," she says with a mischievous smile. "Do you like fairy princesses and superheroes?" I laugh, clapping my hands in front of me.

"I do. Is that a determining factor?"

"Uncle Wyatt doesn't really like them. I think he just pretends so that I'm happy." The statement makes my heart twist.

"Maybe, but I'm pretty sure he has a pair of fairy wings at his house." Her eyes go wide with glee. It's one of the cutest things I've ever seen. I'm understanding why Wyatt loves her so much.

"He does?" she asks, jumping up and down.

"He does," I confirm. I look up past Lily and see Roman smiling. He nods his head toward the kitchen, and I look back at Lily, grabbing her hand. "I need to talk to your dad for a moment, but I heard that you like to do hair. Would you maybe want to play with mine later? I have a lot of it." I swish my ponytail behind me, and she gasps.

"Yes!" she squeals. Standing, I walk to Roman in the kitchen.

"I think you're the perfect addition to this friend group," he says, his voice low. "Thank you." He swipes at his face, pulling the pot from the stove and dumping the water out in the sink.

"So does that mean I can stay?" I tease.

"Of course. Stay as long as you need." He tosses the pasta in with the sauce, giving it a few stirs before he calls Lily over to the table.

The table is already set when we sit down. "Lily, would you like to say grace?" He scoops some pasta onto a plate and sets it in front of her.

She smiles, folding her hands in front of her and bouncing lightly in her chair.

"Grace," she says loudly, giggling.

I snort, covering my mouth when I see the reprimand on Roman's face. She sighs loudly and closes her eyes.

"Thank you for this food and for the hands that prepared it. Thank you for Dakota and for Daddy and for Uncle Wyatt and Uncle Jai and for my teacher. Amen." She looks up at both of us, and Roman shakes his head, chuckling.

"Dig in," he says.

We finish dinner quickly. I try to offer to help clean up, but Roman shoos me off when Lily asks to braid my hair. She nearly sprints up the stairs to her room, and when she returns, she's holding a small bin with hair ties, brushes, and cute accessories.

After several minutes, I'm seated on the floor, Lily on the couch while she brushes the length of my hair and places several braids and hair pins throughout.

Roman's at the table, looking through a stack of paper, when the alarm for the front door chimes. The door closes, the alarm beeping again. Heavy footsteps sound down the hall, but I'm not paying much attention because Lily is telling me all about her friends at school. Her tale has gotten exciting, and I can't help but *ooh* and *ahh* when she shares the exciting bits.

I look over at the TV, my eyes locked there until I catch sight of a dark-haired figure in the corner of my eye.

The hands still in my hair as Lily leaps from the couch and runs across the room.

"Uncle Wyatt," she screams. I see him drop his bag, lifting her in his arms and standing to swing her around. She giggles, and I smile wide, my insides mush once again. He kisses her cheek, and she squeals in delight.

"You're getting so big," he says. "I won't be able to do that much longer." He sets her down, and she pouts.

"No, I'm never growing up." She places her hands on her hips and shakes her head at him in a sassy manner. I snort, looking at Roman.

"I don't know where she gets that from," he says.

I stand, just now remembering that my hair probably looks crazy. Wyatt winks at me, and I blush as I make my way to him.

"Do you like Koda's hair, Uncle Wyatt? I braided it."

"It looks perfect, little one. Good job." When I reach them, he twists his finger, and I make an exaggerated spin so he can get a good look. He pulls me into his arms and places a gentle kiss on my lips. "Perfect," he says into my ear, and I shiver. *That damn word.*

Lily makes a *blech* noise and runs to her dad. Wyatt laughs, kissing my head before releasing me.

"Why *blech*, Lily?" He raises an eyebrow. "One day when you get a boyfriend, I won't *blech* at you."

"Daddy says I'm not allowed to date until I'm thirty." We all laugh, and Roman shakes his head.

"Lord help the man," Wyatt says.

"You're here early—and in a rival member's home, no less." Roman smirks at him. We all sit down, Wyatt taking the seat next to me. He leaves little space between us, and part of me feels guilty and part of me feels incredibly safe.

"Lily, who do you want to win? Uncle Wyatt or your dad?"

Lily splays out on the couch, her stuffed pig now firmly grasped in her arms. She looks between the two of them.

"Depends on what I'm getting for Christmas," she says finally. I laugh loudly, clasping a hand over my mouth.

"I think I like you a lot," I say to Lily. *A woman after my own heart.*

"Can we keep her?" Lily whisper-screams. We all laugh again.

"I certainly plan on keeping you," Wyatt breaths into my ear. His hand grips my side, and I try to keep a straight face when my insides are going wild. It's been barely four days since I saw him last, and my body feels on fire with his nearness.

"Good," I say.

CHAPTER 18
Wyatt

I skip morning skate with the permission of Coach. I've got a very important meeting that I can't miss.

Pulling up to the building, I switch my car into park and climb out, my legs carrying me inside and up two flights of stairs. I opt for the stairs instead of the elevator because it helps me get the nervous energy out since I'm not able to skate with my team.

The realtor waits at the door for me. She greets me warmly and opens the door, allowing me to walk around and get a feel of the place.

I already knew before this visit that I wanted this place to be mine.

Walking through the small space, I click the tip of my pen in my hands several times. The click of the realtor's heels sound around me as she does a walk through, a phone held close to her face. She says a series of words in French, then waits as she listens for a reply.

I breathe, walking to the window and looking down over the city.

"It'll look different at night," she says, tucking her phone away. Her accent is more mellow than it was when she was speaking her native tongue.

I met Amelie in college. She came here from France for an education and ended up dropping out to do realty. She's damn good at it too. Every place I've owned or rented since I started has been found by her.

"I know," I say. "Everything okay?"

"Yes. The owner was a little hesitant about the rush, but they've finally agreed." She extends her hand toward me, and I take it. "Congratulations, Mr. Lane. It's been a pleasure working with you." She smiles at me, releasing my hand.

"Thank you," I say.

"You can come pick up the key on Monday."

She leaves me alone for a moment to take in the view. *Welcome back to Boston.*

"Honey, I'm home," Jaiden calls from the front door. Roman and Jaiden barrel down the hall, kicking off their shoes and coming to sit on the couch.

It's game day, which means that we all went to morning skate and now we're back home for a few hours.

I grab the sandwiches I'd been making and hand one to each of them. Jaiden shoves the sandwich in his mouth and groans around a bite.

"Pastrami and swiss," he says, his mouth still full.

"I don't even remember why this became our game-day sandwich."

GOAL Suck

I sit on the couch, bringing the sandwich to my mouth and taking a large bite.

"I think it was an accident," Roman says. "They only had pastrami left at the cafeteria deli, so that's what we got." We all nod our heads, the memory coming back.

We finish our sandwiches quickly, each of us leaning farther into the couch. Jaiden's hands are behind his head, his feet kicked up on the small table. He looks at me and breaks the silence.

"How did it go? Did you get it?"

"I did," I say. "I pick up the keys on Monday." Something like excitement twists in my gut.

"Does she know?"

"No." I shake my head. "I'd planned on telling her in Raleigh, but I don't know why the words wouldn't come to me."

"They're making the announcement tonight."

"After the game," I confirm. "I've got a set of interviews lined up already."

"I hope for your sake that this secret is a good one."

"Me too, man. Me too."

The team videographer is crouched on the ground as she films each of us walking off the bus. Everyone is dressed to the nines in their suits and ties. Game-day dress code requires that we dress professionally for many reasons, but I know that it makes for good content on social media.

Katya rises slowly, moving around as we walk. I know she'll turn this into a slow-mo shot later. It's her favorite.

She zooms in close as one of the players tugs their jacket or winks at the camera. Damian is a fan favorite. His golden-brown hair and bright red beard are sexy as hell, and I'm not even afraid to admit it.

There's screaming and the flashes of cameras all around us as we walk through the arena doors. I adjust my tie and wink at Katya as I walk through the door. Damian shoots finger guns, then runs a hand through his hair. He fist bumps me as we walk through the second set of doors.

"Big day," he says. I nod my agreement. *Big day, indeed.*

I breathe deeply, running a hand over my scruffy beard. I've been growing it out, much like the other members of my team. We all have our superstitions and game day routines. I've got my lucky underwear on to help me through the day.

Coach walks into the locker room. We go through strategy and video footage of the Boston players. I pay extra attention, finding that I want to learn about my future teammates.

"This is a bittersweet game for us." Coach tugs on his tie. "The official announcement is being made tonight, but this is our last game with Damian and Wyatt."

The guys sulk, patting us on the back and offering congratulations. I feel Hudson's eyes on me. He nods at me, and I nod back, a bit of sadness caught in my throat.

Coach continues, spouting off a spiel about how he's proud of us, and no matter what, he's proud to be the coach of this team.

Coach is one of the best men I have had the privilege of knowing. I think that many of us wanted to take this team all the way for him more than ourselves. Coach deserves this the most. That man is the most committed to the game I've seen in a long time, and it's admirable.

He leaves us to dress, the volume in the locker room increasing. We dress, each in our own way. Damian slips his lucky bead onto his

GOAL Suck

lace and knots it so it won't come loose. He pats me on the shoulder before standing.

The moment I skate out onto the ice, my head is in the zone. My mind shuts out everything—well, almost everything. I take a loop around the ice, stopping in front of the glass by the penalty box. I see her immediately. She's seated with Sterling and Lani. Hudson's wife, Rachel, is on the opposite side of Dakota. She taps her arm when she spots me.

Dakota's eyes meet mine, and I'm nearly knocked off my feet. She smiles wide, waving from the other side of the glass. Suddenly, I'm wishing for the barrier between us to disappear. Urgently. She's dressed in our colors, blue and black. I pray to God that she's got my number on her back. She looks beautiful.

The crowd cheers, and I don't need to look up to see the camera watching me. I balance the puck on the end of my stick and then flick it in the air. I toss my stick and catch it, then catch the puck on the end of the stick. Shooting her a wink, I skate back to the team. Her pink cheeks make it all worth it. I can't wait to kiss that beautiful mouth later. My cock twitches in my gear, and I have to push the thought aside.

I'll get questions about that later, but I'll worry about it later.

The moment the puck hits the ice, I look over at Damian. He nods at me, and everything else disappears but my team and the ice.

CHAPTER 19
Dakota

"So why aren't you up in the wives' box?" Sterling shoves some popcorn into her mouth.

"The women up there are a bunch of bitches, if I do say so myself. Not all of them, but a lot of them."

"I heard it's like a sorority and a competition between all the wives," Sterling says. I'm just listening as they talk. Lani is watching me, and I smile at her. There's still a bit of unease, but I'm excited to finally be here.

"Oh girl, it is. I'm technically the top of the food chain because my husband is the captain, but I don't like to follow their petty rules. It's a competition on who looks the best and who's brought the most expensive designer purse. I don't subscribe to that." Rachel nudges my arm. "So stick with me and I think you'll survive." I laugh, a half smile

GOAL *Suck*

taking over my face.

I suddenly feel slightly self-conscious. Wyatt mentioned the press and that it was possible that we could be photographed together tonight. I'm wearing ripped black jeans and a long-sleeve shirt with a Rider's jersey over. The thing is massive and covers my butt. I made sure to do my hair and makeup extra special today, but the knowledge that the women are wearing designer clothing and carrying fancy purses sends anxiety rolling through my stomach.

"Is it like that on every team?" I ask curiously.

"Naw," she says. "Hudson's been traded plenty of times, and there's always some of it, but overall, the wives are pretty great. I don't know what it is about the damn Raleigh team, though."

"That's comforting, I guess. Not like I'm thinking that far ahead or anything. We just started dating."

"Lady, have you *seen* the way that man looks at you? He wanted to eat you through the glass. Plus, I have *never* seen Wyatt show off like that for any woman." Her southern accent comes out as she talks, and I adore it.

Sterling leans in and whispers in my ear, "I've known her for less than twenty minutes, and I already want to keep her." I laugh, my body shaking. *I also want to keep her.*

"So, Lani, what do you do?" Rachel turns to look across us to Lani.

"Currently, I'm a manager and receptionist for Dakota's tattoo and bookshop, but I'd like to eventually get into tattooing."

"I would die for you to start tattooing," I say, and Lani grins.

"So I've heard—several thousand times."

"I must never let you forget your talent."

Rachel watches us, then smiles. "I'm suddenly hoping for Hudson to be traded to Boston so I can spend all my time with you three." She chuckles.

"Oh, trust me. You'll be seeing a *lot* of us. I can promise you that." Sterling's eyebrows waggle, and we all crouch over with laughter.

The hours go by quickly as we sit and watch the game. There is no doubt in my mind that they're going to win today. Wyatt is an absolute beast on the ice. It's one thing seeing him in videos, but in real life, he's a force to be reckoned with.

I almost feel bad rooting for Wyatt over Roman and Jaiden, but each time Raleigh scores, my heart races and I forget about my worries. I'm team Wyatt all the way.

Wyatt's jersey is number twenty-seven. I watch him fly across the ice like it's the easiest thing in the world. Damian is number eight, and the way the two of them work together makes my heart soar with excitement. The score remains close the whole game, and I feel my palms sweating as I watch each move of the puck.

They almost move as one at certain points. By the time the final period has come around, I'm practically shaking in my seat. My eyes are glued to the game, my fists clenched at my sides. Wyatt skates at full force, spinning in a circle to avoid a burly player heading straight for him. The center skater passes the puck, and Damian catches it, passing it back when the center moves back into position.

My palms are sweaty as I watch the seconds tick. With six seconds left to spare, we score. I jump up, screaming with joy. Sterling hugs me as we bounce up and down. The guys all swarm on the ice in a big sweaty pile. The cheers are deafening, but I hardly mind. My eyes are locked on Wyatt as he turns around and holds his stick above his head, eyes in my direction. I don't know what overtakes me, but I bring my hand to my mouth and blow him a kiss.

The excitement dies down, and I hear the announcer calling for attention. The team is all by the wall, chittering when the voice gets

GOAL Suck

louder, an interviewer popping onto the large screen.

"Darla, we have some bittersweet news for Raleigh Fans."

"We do, Frank. Today, Raleigh is saying their goodbyes to Wyatt Lane and Damian LeDuke. They will be joining the Yellow Jackets this season," Darla says.

"What a great way to close out their seven-year stint with the Riders, though, don't you think?"

"Definitely. One last win to finish off their journey. Well, from all of Boston, we welcome you to The Hub. Stingers up, everyone!" Everyone raises their pinkies and buzz as Wyatt and Damian skate across the ice, waving as the cameras capture their faces.

I stare in shock when Wyatt disappears from the ice, no doubt to shower before he's swarmed for interviews.

Sterling taps my arm when she sees my face.

"Are you okay?"

I nod my head. "Yeah. I just don't know why he didn't tell me."

"Maybe it was a surprise?"

I shrug my shoulders. "Maybe."

Don't get me wrong, having Wyatt in Boston sounds amazing, but a part of me feels…irritated. It feels weird to find out with the rest of the world. I swallow down my annoyance and stand, following after Rachel.

CHAPTER 20
Wyatt

The adrenaline high that I feel after a win is unlike any feeling. It's euphoric. The world practically moves around me as I float through this feeling.

We're all showered and back in game-day attire. We've been through rounds of interviews, and I ache to hold my girl in my arms.

As I walk out of the interview area, someone stops me.

"Wyatt," they call out. I stop, turning to find the source of the voice. A young woman who I recognize waves from across the room, and I nod.

She strides toward me, stopping when she gets close enough to talk.

"Hi," she says, extending her hand. "Nice to see you again." It's the same woman who interviewed me the night I declared that I may be seeing myself off the market.

"Nice to see you as well," I say, shaking her hand. "What can I do for you?"

"Would you be willing to answer a few questions? I saw the exchange before the game, and I wanted to offer to create a formal statement from the two of you." She shoots her eyes across the room. When I follow her gaze, I see Dakota standing with Lani and Sterling.

"I'd like to ask her first if you don't mind."

She nods a few times. "I'll just be over here when you're ready."

Word of my change in relationship status hasn't gotten out yet, but tonight...tonight, I intend to change that. This would be the perfect opportunity. I want the world to know that Dakota is mine.

A tang of something else burns at the back of my throat. It's that sour feeling I've had since I learned of the abuse Dakota endured. A part of me wants to goad him, whoever the hell he may be. Maybe seeing his former girl in the papers will bring him out of the woodwork, then I can put a face and a name to this piece of shit.

The crowd parts, cameras clicking as Roman and Jaiden enter the press area. Lily is clutching tightly to Roman's side. In the distance, I see Dakota standing by the door. Her arms are folded across her chest, and the thought that she's feeling slightly uncomfortable makes me want to rush to her side and protect her.

Lily breaks away from her dad and runs toward me, her little legs carrying her quickly. I tug my pant leg up before I drop a knee to the ground to catch her in my arms. Lily crashes into my chest, her little head nuzzling into my neck.

Her wild curls are piled high on her head with a bright blue scrunchie. I'm surprised Roman let her wear one of our colors. I smirk at him over her head, and he rolls his eyes. I look past them, right at Dakota. She's watching us, of course. She shifts on her feet, her arms coiled tighter around herself.

"Uncle Wyatt!" Lily screams. I wince a bit, then hug her tightly to me. "Daddy says that you're staying in Boston. Does that mean I get to see you all the time now?"

"Yes, it does." I boop her on the nose. "Is that okay with you?"

She nods, and my heart swells.

I look over to see Liam stop in front of Dakota. The muscles in my jaw flex. Liam places an arm on the wall and faces Dakota, saying something to her that makes her blush. I clench my jaw so tightly a tooth could crack. Out of all the men on my team, it had to be Liam. Fucking Liam.

"Lily girl," I say, lifting her into my arms and walking past a group of people. Roman protests slightly, but when he turns and sees Liam by Dakota, he stalks close behind me. "I have something I need to take care of. Go to your dad, okay?" She giggles when I pinch her side gently, then I lower her to the floor. Now seems like a good time to stake my claim.

"Liam is an idiot," Jaiden says under his breath. Liam is still talking to Dakota. She's not listening, though; her eyes keep flicking to me, and Liam is too stupid to notice. Sterling and Lani reappear, drinks in hand, as I stop in front of Dakota and Liam.

"A bunch of us are going out to celebrate. You should come join us," I hear Liam saying. He looks over at me when he finally notices my presence. "Oh, 'sup, Wyatt?" He says it like a question. He's trying to brush me off. Dakota looks at me, her eyes growing more and more amused. She must see *the look* on my face. Liam, again, is too stupid to notice.

From my side, I hear Lily whisper, "Daddy, what's happening?"

"I'll tell you in a second, baby," he says, snickering.

"'Sup, Liam," I say through gritted teeth.

GOAL Suck

"I was just inviting..." Liam blinks a couple of times.

"Dakota," she says.

"Right. I was just inviting Dakota out with us to celebrate. There's gonna be some other bunnies there."

"Oh shit," Jaiden says. Roman gives him a look, and he stutters. "O-ooh shoot," he corrects. "Don't say bad words, Lily."

Dakota laughs, her eyes smiling so bright that the flecks of gold in her green eyes seem to shimmer.

"I'm not a puck bunny," she says. "And I think you're pissing off my boyfriend by insinuating so." The word "boyfriend" coming from her lips makes me *so* hard. I want to crush my lips against her right here in front of everyone. I just might.

"Wait, the Yellow Jacket is your man? Wrong team, baby. How about you switch sides?"

A growl tears from my mouth. Dakota's mouth twitches.

"Not them, dipshit." I don't even care that I cursed in front of Lily. I reach my arm out to Dakota, and she takes it. She moves into me like she'd been waiting to do that for ages. I feel a sense of peace as I rest my chin against her head and breathe deeply. She smells sweet, like peaches and strawberries.

Liam takes a moment to register, then he pushes off the wall, standing back a few inches. "Oh, sorry, man. I didn't know she was your girl. You are a Yellow Jacket now, though, so I wasn't wrong." I narrow my eyes at him and he mutters something under his breath before turning and walking away.

"Was that necessary?" Dakota laughs into my chest.

"Yes. It was absolutely necessary," I say into her hair. I never want to let her go. I want to hold her like this for the rest of eternity. When we pull apart, Sterling is looking at me. There's an expression on her face that I can't quite decipher. Approval, maybe?

"We need to talk," Dakota says.

"We do," I say. "But first…" I press my lips against hers, and she melts against me.

The sound of a throat clearing breaks us apart. Dakota's cheeks are red as she brushes her fingers against her lips. I smirk, taking her hands in mine.

"Why didn't you tell me?" She eyes me as we walk away from the group.

"I meant to. There are several reasons why, and one of them is that I wanted to surprise you."

"In all honesty, Wyatt, I love surprises, but I also didn't enjoy finding out with the rest of the world. It felt… impersonal, almost?"

I nod my head. "Noted. I'm sorry. I do have another surprise for you, later. And this one is just for us." I kiss her forehead.

"Mmm. I like that."

"Anyway, there's a reporter who asked if we'd like to do an interview. I'll only agree if you feel comfortable." Dakota pulls her lip into her mouth, her eyes looking between mine.

"You're ready for that?"

"Dakota, I've been ready since the moment I laid eyes on you." She smiles, her eyes softening.

"Be brave, Dakota." She mumbles it to herself, but it makes me smile.

"Okay, let's do it." She takes my hand in hers and walks toward the reporter, looking determined to conquer the world.

The interview went more smoothly than I'd anticipated. The reporter seemed to take Dakota's nerves in stride, adapting the questions to make her feel comfortable.

I didn't mean to throw her to the sharks like that, but she took it well.

When I went pro, I went through media training. I realize now that Dakota has no experience on this front.

We were assured that the article would be released on Monday, so we will at least have the weekend to ourselves, which goes perfectly with my plans for us.

We're walking from the cars to the restaurant when I pull her behind a larger car. My lips crash into hers; the kiss is electric, my body zinging with the contact. She whimpers, her mouth opening when my tongue brushes across her lips.

I bring my hand to her head, my fingers tangling in her hair and her beanie nearly falling off her head. She presses into my body, and I feel my cock swell in my pants. I groan, and she smiles into my mouth.

"I missed you too," she says, her eyes still closed as our foreheads press together.

"So fucking much," I say. "Come, before they notice we're missing."

"Too late," Jaiden yells, a trickle of laughter echoing after him. I not-so-subtly adjust myself before stepping back into view.

"I can't fucking wait to be alone with you," I murmur as we walk.

"Soon," she says.

Sterling, Lani, and Jaiden are deep in a heated discussion over this book that apparently all of them have read. Dakota is smiling so wide her eyes are squinting, small tears leaking from the corner of her eyes.

Lily is sitting next to Dakota, drawing on a paper mat. Dakota told her that she's a tattoo artist, and now Lily wants to draw something worth tattooing. She's been at it for at least twenty minutes now. I love her commitment.

Roman raises an eyebrow at me. "A lot's happened since I saw you last, huh?"

"It went well," I say, and Dakota grips my hand under the table. I'd told her about our conversation before our weekend together.

"You look happy," he says. "That's good."

I nod. "I am." Our conversation is cut short when I hear Sterling's voice raise.

"We were robbed, I tell you. Robbed. I will accept nothing else as canon. The only thing that is canonically correct is this relationship, and if you disagree with me, you're *wrong*." She smacks her hands down on the table, and Dakota wheezes with laughter.

"No, you are wrong. She was meant to be with that red-headed weirdo."

"Jaiden Thomas, you are *wrong*. We"—she signals to Lani and Dakota—"are a part of a group chat, and I can provide you with texts upon texts with better fucking stories than the trash we got. Trash, I tell you."

"Trash," Dakota and Lani repeat.

"We got matching cups and everything. You do not want to mess with my girl gang on this," Dakota says to Jaiden. The girls look at each other. "Dragon dick is the best dick." They all nod.

I try my hardest not to laugh at the look Jaiden gives me. It's three against one, and I don't even feel bad for him. I don't even know what they're arguing about, but I'd take Dakota's side on this. I get a feeling it's from one of her smutty books, and I fully support that addiction.

Jaiden looks at me and Roman. We shrug, giving him looks that say just give up. He huffs a breath, his shoulders shrugging. My mouth drops open. Roman's eyes go wide.

"I never thought I'd see the day," I say.

"What?" Sterling asks.

"Jaiden *never* gives up. He quite literally has to win every argument. It's like a game to him," Roman answers her.

"I think you broke him," I say, waving a hand in front of his face.

"I lost," he says, his hands coming to his face. We all bust up laughing. I can't imagine a better way to celebrate our win than this.

CHAPTER 21
Wyatt

I lied. This is a much better way to celebrate our win.

Dakota and I parted ways with the others and made our way back to my hotel room. She's seated on the kitchen counter while I fry bananas in butter and sugar for our bananas foster.

"Taste," I say, raising the spoon to her lips. She takes a bite, licking her lips after I pull the spoon away. Her eyes close, and she moans.

"Oh my gosh. That is so good." She wiggles her legs, and I smile. I walk to the smaller counter and grab our bowls of ice cream, handing them to her. She holds them while I pour over the banana mixture. She wiggles anxiously, her eyes watching me the whole time.

I hand her a spoon. She takes a small bite, and her eyes go wide.

"Where have you been my whole life?" She takes another bite, licking her lips, and I stare at the way her tongue moves across her mouth.

Without thinking, I dip my finger in the ice cream and swipe it across her nose. She freezes, her mouth dropping open.

"Wyatt!" Before I can step away, she grabs my tie and yanks me forward, my bowl of ice cream forgotten on the counter behind me. She scoops some ice cream onto her finger and swipes it across my nose as well. She surprises me with what she does next, and there's not a bone in my body that can be disappointed by it.

With her hand wrapped in my tie, she pulls me closer to her until I step between her legs. She moves her face to my nose and licks the ice cream off my nose. When I can't quite function properly, she smirks and tries to pull away.

"Oh, no, you don't." My hands come to her hair, my mouth capturing hers. The ice cream from her face smears on mine, and I couldn't care less. When my tongue runs across her lips, I taste the sweetness from the ice cream on her.

Pulling away, I step away from her, my finger held high.

"Don't you dare move." I take a step backward, pulling my spoon from the bowl. When I return, I step between her legs again.

"Can I tell you something that is incredibly sexy?" she asks when I press into her.

"What?"

"You, in that damn suit." She wraps her hand in my tie once again. I'd intended to leave a trail of ice cream down her body that I can lap up, but I think I want to see where she's going with this.

She stops pulling when my face is a breath away from hers. I had no idea it would turn me on this much to see her practically demanding what she wants. It's so fucking sexy.

"Also, I lied," she says. "I fucking love hockey. Please invite me to every game possible. I want to see you like that every chance I get."

She pulls my mouth to hers, and I groan into her.

I kiss her gently at first, then more urgently.

Her hands roam over me, eventually slipping under my suit jacket and venturing over my arms. I shiver at her soft caresses.

She pushes my jacket down, and I break our kiss to shove the now-offensive piece of clothing off and toss it to the floor. Her lips come to my neck, and I groan as she nips at the sensitive flesh there.

"Fuck," I say. "You know, we don't have to do this right now. I want to move at a pace you're comfortable with."

"Wyatt," she says, her lips still kissing up and down my neck.

"Hmm?"

"Shut up." She captures my lips again, and my eyes nearly roll back into my head when she bites my lip. Her hands work the buttons on my shirt, and I assist her. She tugs off my shirt, her hands meeting bare flesh.

She leans back, her eyes roaming over my body.

"I'm suddenly feeling insecure," she says. "How the hell do you look like *that*?"

"You haven't even seen the best part yet, love." I wink at her. I tug at the jersey she's wearing, and she slowly pulls it off her body. She's wearing a slim tank top underneath.

In one swift motion, I lift her from the counter and bring her to the couch across the room. It's lower to the ground and more suited to my plans.

I set her down gently, pressing her back into the soft cushions.

I kiss her cheek. My lips brush her shoulder, then her bicep. I kiss my way down until I'm kneeling before her.

"Let me share something with you, Dakota." As I slip my hands under her tank, she shivers. I kiss her belly. Her body is magnificent, and I haven't even seen it all. I just *know*. "There are only two people who can bring me to my knees."

I slip the sleeve off, exposing her shoulder. It slips further, her white lacy bra thing showing. I push off the other sleeve until it falls to her waist. I look up at her, asking for permission before I cup her breasts in my hands. Her head rests against the back of the couch.

"Who are the two people?" She breathes when I push the lace out of the way and pull her nipple into my mouth. *God, I've been waiting for this.* Her voice has gone husky. As if she could get any more beautiful, she whimpers when I flick her nipple with my tongue. Her lower half presses into me.

I palm her breast, massaging. Finally, I pull my mouth away, switching to give the other one attention. "Lily, of course. There will never be a day when I let her believe that she's not a fierce warrior."

"Mmm," she says. Her eyes are closed.

"And now you," I say. She gasps when I nip lightly. "If there is ever a day you're feeling insecure, please tell me so I can tell you how beautiful you are." I suck her nipple back into my mouth, then pull away with a pop. She moans, and it's like music to my ears. "Over and over again."

I trace the tattoo on her sternum with my fingers. It's a serpent twisted around a rose. It suits her. I kiss it, unwilling to resist. She gasps, bucking her body into me before she blushes.

"Sorry, I, uh…I haven't been touched like this in a while." A rumble forms in my throat. The amount of trust it must take to be here in this moment with me makes me light-headed with pride.

"Do not ever apologize to me for your feelings." I fix my eyes on her. Her baby blues are mostly gone, her pupil so blown out that I can't help but smirk. "Thank you for trusting me with this," I say. "I won't hurt you, Dakota. My hands are meant for your pleasure and never to cause harm."

She stills, her cheeks reddening. "Pleasure, huh?"

"Fuck, yes," I say. She swallows, her throat bobbing when she takes my hand and places it on the button of her pants. I smirk. "Ask," I say. "I want to hear you say it."

"I, um, I want pleasure, with your hands," she says. "They're quite big, you know." She licks her lips, and I nearly laugh, but it doesn't feel like the right time.

"You know what they say about big hands," I say as I flick the button loose on her jeans with one hand. She presses into me, her breathing increasing as I undo the zipper on her jeans. With time, I'll teach her that she doesn't need to be shy around me. She can ask for exactly what she wants. I can't wait for the day when she outright asks to ride my fingers.

I pull her jeans down, my hands grazing her hips as I slip them down to her knees. I look up at her through my lashes as I bring my hands to her hips.

"Do you mind?" I ask as I lick my lips. Her eyes go wide, then she nods slowly. I slip her panties down and pull her toward me as I bury my face into her pussy. At the first swipe of my tongue, she bucks her hips, a gasp leaving her lips.

"Oh God," she says. With the flat of my tongue, I swipe across her clit. I look up at her again before removing a hand from her waist and bringing it to her center. She gasps as I tease her entrance with my middle finger.

"Wyatt. Please," she breathes. I'm not one to deny a please, so I slowly slip my finger inside of her.

"You're so fucking tight," I say. She whimpers as I move my finger inside of her. Her legs shake, and I move my shoulder to support her.

I want her mouth, so I rise and twist us so that I can capture her mouth in mine. I pull my fingers out when I bring my lips to hers. She

GOAL Suck

immediately protests, and I chuckle against her lips.

"More," she says.

"Yes, ma'am." I add a second finger, pressing into her slowly. She clenches around me at first, but when she relaxes, I release a groan as I pump my fingers into her. She moves her hips, taking over the pace I'd set. A wicked grin takes over my face when she takes control. I bite her lip, and she gasps.

She rocks against me, and my cock swells in my pants. It's painfully hard, but I don't care. Dakota's breaths have gone ragged as she moves on my hand.

"That's right, baby. Ride my fingers." I bring my mouth to her breasts again, tugging at her nipple lightly. Dakota shatters then. Her pussy clenches around my fingers, her breath coming out in quick gasps. I pump into her as she rides out her orgasm.

"So fucking beautiful," I rasp. She slumps forward into me, and I withdraw my fingers before lifting her and placing her back down into my lap when I'm seated firmly into the couch. She rests with her head against my chest until her eyes open to watch me. I bring my fingers to my mouth, sucking the taste of her off my fingers. She blushes as I do it. *So shy.*

I place a kiss on her forehead. Her eyes flutter shut, then open wide again. I see her hands move before I can stop them. She reaches for my waistband and tugs.

"Dakota," I say, groaning when her fingers make contact with my skin. "Tonight is about you. We don't have to."

"But you just won." She looks at me, her eyes assessing. How she worded that bothers me. It's like I would expect that from her.

"What we just did is the best way I could have celebrated that win. I need you to know this isn't transactional. We can take this slow, but I don't want that to make you feel like I don't want it. I do—oh

God, do I ever. But I will not make you do anything you don't want to do, nor will I expect anything from you."

She looks down. I wish she would look up at me so I can see what's going on in that head of hers.

She finally looks up at me, her eyes squinting at me. "You are a freak of nature, Wyatt Alexander." She fiddles with her hands. "Either I was sorely mistreated, or you're setting the standards impossibly high. Higher than I thought possible."

"Now you're just stroking my ego."

"I mean it though." She lays her hand on my cheek and I lean into the touch.

Taking a moment to feel her warmth, I reach down and slip her pants off her ankles. I hold them in my hands when I slip and arm under her legs and sling her over my shoulders.

"Wyatt," she screeches. "Put me down!" She laughs as we walk down the hall right into the bedroom. "Wyatt," she says again, a little out of breath. "I can't feel my face."

I chuckle and kick the door closed behind me. I often get what I want, and tonight I don't want to leave this room for at least twelve hours.

CHAPTER 22
Dakota

Waking to the feel of Wyatt's lips on my chest is probably one of the best ways I could have ever wished to wake up. It's not even light outside, which brings a smile to my face.

His hands cup my breasts as he makes his way down my body until his hands slip under my bare ass and yank me toward him. I wrap my legs around his back, his face coming to my already sensitive clit.

With one swipe of his tongue, I arch into him, my hips rising off the bed. He growls into my core, and I smile. My body feels hot; every touch has my sensitive body aching for more. I roll my lip into my mouth, but I can't stay silent. I moan, his tongue doing amazing things to me.

"Wyatt," I breathe.

"Shh," he says into my pussy, and I laugh. "I've dreamt about this for weeks and it's finally coming true."

"But Wyatt," I protest, my hands gripping his hair. I moan as he sucks my clit into his mouth, unable to form words for a moment. I feel my body tense under his touch.

"You taste sweet, just like you smell," he says, licking his lips as he looks up at me.

"I want you," I say. "I want you." He continues his tortuous rhythm.

"Let me make you come first, love." He continues sucking, his hands gripping my breasts. When he takes the flat of his tongue and swipes up my pussy, I shatter. It takes no time at all for him to leave me panting and begging.

"Where's my name on your lips when you come?" He looks up at me, and I slow my breathing enough to look up at him.

"I promised, not until I have you inside me."

His eyes are so blown I can barely see the blue anymore. A wicked grin spreads across his face.

"I want you to scream my name," he says. He sits up, his erection leaving a tent in his boxers. I reach for it, but he raises an eyebrow at me. "Wait, beautiful." I glare at him, and he smirks.

He reaches down and pulls his suit pants from the floor where he'd discarded them earlier in the evening. Slipping a foil packet from his wallet, he eyes me, his gaze dark and that perfect smirk in the corner of his mouth. I look over his body, enjoying how perfect he looks. His muscles flex when he brings the packet to his mouth and rips.

My mouth goes dry when he winks at me, pulling his erection from his boxers and giving it a few strokes.

"Holy shit," I breathe. I watch the way he strokes himself. His hands are big, but he barely fits in the palm of his hand. The tip gleams and not just from the precum that seeps out from the slit. I swallow, and he pumps his cock in his hand again.

There's a small piercing through the ridge of his cock. Not like I know much about piercings, but I believe they would call it a king's crown piercing.

"Wyatt Alexander...you look so innocent from the outside."

He smirks.

"Far from it, love." He rolls the condom, on and I almost wish I could experience the feel of him without it. *Another time.* "You sure about this?" He leans over me, his arm now resting on the pillow by my head.

"I've never been more sure of anything in my life."

"Good," he says, lining himself up. He pushes into me slowly. I gasp, feeling myself stretch around his length. He's incredibly thick and long, and my body reacts to him immediately.

"Fuck," he says, groaning. I gasp, clenching around him. He continues pushing, filling me up, until suddenly he's pulling out and pushing back in. I can barely breathe, the feel of him is intense and unlike anything I've felt before. The slight scratch of the metal on his cock drives me wild, and I never want it to stop.

"You're fucking perfect," he grits out, his voice breathy. I grip at his back, digging my fingernails into his skin and urging him deeper. He groans, his movements growing more frantic.

"Faster," I beg. "Wyatt, please."

He doesn't hesitate. He presses into me again, the slap of our bodies and our harsh breaths the only sounds in the room. His mouth finds mine, his teeth biting into my lip. "Bite me," I say, and he smiles into my mouth.

"So bossy," he says. He bites my lip hard, and I moan. That, combined with his movements, I don't last. I feel my body tense around him, my eyes rolling back into my head as he presses into me again, and I break. I don't forget, though. I don't forget to scream his name, to plead and beg as I come around his cock so hard that I see light behind my eyes.

He watches me like his life depends on it. He pumps into me a few more times, then I feel him shatter too, his hard body slumping beside me. He breathes, our bodies still connected. His mouth peppers kisses on my shoulders.

"Dakota, you've ruined me." He pulls himself from me, then places a kiss on my neck. His hands roam across my stomach, and I sigh happily.

"What do you mean?"

"I must keep you forever now. There will never be anyone like you, Dakota Easton." He stands, leaving me in bed. I hear him clean himself up in the bathroom, and I want to follow him, but I find myself lost in thought. Forever is a concept that seems almost scary. I'd been prepared for a forever with Tanner, and he'd destroyed that the moment he first hit me. I'd just used his infidelity as an excuse to finally run.

Wyatt returns to the bed, his naked body a sight for sore eyes. I try to smile up at him, but it doesn't quite reach my eyes.

"Tell me," he says.

"It's been incredibly hard for me to think about forever since my ex. I'd been committed to him despite the things he'd done to me. I was willing to stay. At first, I was scared. Hearing you say that scared me, but it feels so different with you. I know we've only known each other for a month, but"—I rub my thumb between my fingers—"I feel so safe with you. Can I tell you something I haven't told anyone outside of Silver?"

"Always. You can tell me anything."

"I made that blanket statement about hating hockey players because it felt safe, and I won't lie, it was safe. But hockey was my life growing up. I loved it, and I bonded with my family over it, and over the years, I had to suppress that because I was so afraid to see him again. I just couldn't." I feel a tear slipping from my eye. "You gave this back to me, Wyatt. I don't feel like I need to be afraid anymore because for some reason, as long as you're there, I know that I'll be okay." I swallow, watching for his reaction. His eyes wander between mine, his face so soft and so open.

"I meant it when I said that I would protect you, Koda. My grandma didn't call me a warrior for no reason. You are important to me, and I swear to you that I'll do whatever I can to make you comfortable. He can't hurt you again." My breath leaves me. I throw myself into his arms and hold him tightly. *What did I do to deserve Wyatt Lane?*

He holds me tight in his arms, his hands running through my hair until I slip into sleep once more. When I wake again, I'm still wrapped in his arms. I smile into his bare chest, kissing him and snuggling back into him. *I've dreamt of this, and now it's finally coming true.*

"Is it dumb if I tell you I've never toured Boston?" I spin around in a circle as I walk with Wyatt through Quincy Market. He laces our fingers together and pulls me close to him.

It's a dreary day in Boston. The ground is slick with rainwater, and a chilled breeze flies through the marketplace. I'm bundled up, my toque keeping the heat from escaping through my ears.

"Nothing you say will ever be dumb." Wyatt looks down at me, and I melt under his gaze.

"Wyatt Lane," someone yells from a distance. I feel Wyatt shift slightly. He stands taller, his eyes hardening, yet his face remains soft and friendly. "Wyatt," they call again. I don't know where the voice is coming from exactly, but then I see two people walking through the marketplace to approach us. We stop in front of a flower stand, the two gentlemen walking faster, weaving through the crowd.

"Wyatt," the guy pants. "I'm such a big fan. My buddy here and I saw you and wanted to say hi." Several people around us turn in our direction. I feel suddenly uncomfortable under their gazes. When I turn my head, several people are pointing and whispering. I know for a fact it's not because of me, though.

"Hey, man," Wyatt says, taking the guys' extended hands. He pulls me closer to him like he's worried I'll run away or disappear suddenly.

"Can we get a photo? You wouldn't mind taking a photo for us, would you?" He looks at me, his phone extended. I look up at Wyatt before I take the phone.

"Sure," I say. Wyatt's face changes again. That goofy, cocky man makes an appearance. I step away from him, the guys standing at his sides. He throws up a shaka sign, giving the camera his biggest toothy grin.

One of the men pats Wyatt on the back. "Congrats on the win, man. I think you'll take our team to the finals this year."

"True, that," Wyatt says. He smirks at me when I hand the phone back. He slips his hand back into mine, and I feel his breath brush my ear as he chuckles.

I wander down a ways, stopping to look at a stand with an assortment of beautiful crystals and jewelry. Wyatt's browsing a booth behind me somewhere. It's not hard to find him, though; his bright teal hoodie is the first thing I see outside of his height. He looks like a giant in this crowd of people.

I pick up a jade pendant and roll it between my fingers. I'm lost in admiration when my phone rings in my back pocket. I pull it out and bring it to my ear, not even bothering to see who's calling me.

"Hey," I say into the phone. A deep growly voice answers, and I roll my eyes immediately.

"You're in so much trouble, sis."

"Dallas, what the fuck do you want? And why am I in trouble?" He doesn't answer me; instead, I hear the phone beeping. Dallas is requesting to FaceTime me.

"Answer it, dork," he says. I roll my eyes again and hit the green button. His face pops into frame almost immediately.

"What?" I say, giving him my best bored face.

"This." He flips the camera to show his computer screen. "Pops saw it pop up on his Yahoo news thingy. That old man still doesn't understand the internet."

I squint my eyes, bringing the phone closer to my face. It's a picture of Wyatt, I know that off the bat. There's a blond under his arm, his name across her back. It takes everything in me not to smile. Wyatt's kissing the top of her head, and Liam is standing there in the distance, looking embarrassed. It had been taken shortly after Wyatt laid claim when Liam was trying to make moves. You can't really tell it's me, but my family isn't stupid.

The headline reads: *Sorry Ladies, Looks Like This One's Finally Off the Market.* My heart soars, but it's mixed with a bit of panic. I thought we had until Monday to worry about this article.

When I look up, Dallas has switched the camera back to his face.

"You're dating Wyatt fucking Lane, Dakota?" Almost as if Dallas' voice conjured him, Wyatt sidles up to me, a bouquet of flowers in his hands.

"I got you these," he says, kissing the top of my head. A gasp comes from my phone, and I pull my lip into my mouth to stop myself from laughing. "Oh, sorry. I didn't know you were on the phone." Wyatt looks into the screen at my brother. "Hi." He waves, and my brother raises a hand, waving with a shocked look on his face.

"You okay there, Dallas?" I say. He opens his mouth then closes it a couple times.

"Hi," Dallas says. "You're Wyatt Lane."

"I am," he says. We move away from the booths and away from peeping ears. I sit down on a bench, my phone held out in front of me. "You're Dakota's brother, right?"

"The one and only. I'm cooler than her, just in case you were wondering."

"Fuck off," I say. "We both know I'm Mom and Dad's favorite. Don't even play." Someone laughs in the background of the call.

"Why am I not the first to know about this? Do you not love me, Toot?" *That fucking nickname. Of course, he'd pull that one out.* Wyatt looks at me sideways, his eyes swimming with amusement.

"I do love you, *Tookie*. I just love Sterling more." I smirk, and Dallas groans.

"Whatever," he says. "When are you coming home? I hope you know that by the end of the week, everyone here is going to be talking about you." He mumbles something, and I pull the phone closer to my face.

"Say that again," I say. "Louder." Wyatt's hand creeps up my thigh as we sit there. The amusement is rolling off of him in waves. I think that he would absolutely love my family.

"I said"—his voice increases a couple octaves—"traitor."

"Damn right. And I have no regrets. The Thunders can fucking suck my ass. I'm team Wyatt now," I say, poking at my brother's buttons. Wyatt coughs at my side, hiding his laugh.

"You're really going to make your family hate me," he says.

"Oh, don't worry. You play hockey. Mom and Pops will love you for that fact alone." Dallas gives him finger guns. "Speaking of, when are you coming home, toot?"

"Toot," Wyatt says under his breath, and I glare at him.

"I don't know. Does Tanner still live there?" Dallas groans. The name leaves my mouth before I stop it. I purse my lips, avoiding Wyatt's eyes. I feel him tense beside me.

"This? Again? Get over it. He dumped you, it's not a big deal." Dallas rolls his eyes, and my mouth goes dry. I swallow over the lump that's forming in my throat.

"Right," I say. "Not a big deal." I feel Wyatt move closer to me. I know he's going to ask me about it later.

"So does that mean you'll come home?" Dallas looks over his shoulder, someone walking around in the background. Probably his long-term girlfriend. He speaks, then looks back at the camera. "I gotta run. Come home soon, and bring Wyatt with you—if he makes it that long." He chuckles, and I wish I could punch him through the phone.

"Don't be such a keener and maybe I will." I flip him off, then end the call. I release a deep breath and hunch forward a bit, my hands coming to rub my temples.

Wyatt looks forward for a moment, his hand coming to my back.

"Go ahead and ask," I say. "I know you want to."

"So…Tanner. That's his name?"

I nod.

"And your family doesn't know?"

"No," I say into my palms. "They don't."

"Why?" Wyatt pulls me into him. I press my face into his chest and breathe.

"They loved Tanner. They still do. My family sees him often, and I didn't want to ruin that for them." I'd been labeled as dramatic so often that it became a personal mission to change their minds. Being the only girl in the family, I tried my hardest to be a tomboy and to reel in my feelings. My mother came from a family of all men; she has six brothers. She doesn't have the same tolerance, so I'd just taught myself not to feel. I wasn't some drama queen looking for attention.

"Wyatt, I hid everything from them. His bruises were always in places I could cover—until one night he snapped and nearly broke my nose. I had to go home that night and pretend like I'd been rough housing with the dogs and one of them gave me a black eye. I just…I couldn't ruin their perfect image of him, and he was going pro, it could've ruined everything."

Wyatt's jaw clenches, but I know that his anger is not at me. "Dakota, that's not your problem. Those were *his* choices, and it would've been *his* consequences to pay, not yours."

"It's too late to say something now, though. No one would believe me."

"I will," he says. "I believe you."

"If only it were enough," I say, my voice low. He looks at me, his eyes sad. I know he wants to fight me on this, but he doesn't. Instead, he takes my hand and guides me through the market.

CHAPTER 23
Wyatt

After tossing and turning all night, I finally remove myself from Dakota's grasp at five a.m. When I need to blow off steam, I usually take to the ice, but since I'm new to the Yellow Jacket's, I don't feel comfortable skating there alone.

My head's been fucked since Dakota admitted that she didn't think anyone would believe her. I want so badly to punch that fucker right in the face for what he did to her. *I won't, but I desperately want to.* He doesn't deserve to share the ice with some of the best people I know.

After she fell asleep last night, I scrolled through my phone until I found him. It was like I couldn't stop myself. I needed to know who he was and to put a face to the name.

Sitting on the couch, I look down at the floor, a frustrated groan leaving my lips. I run my hands through my hair. *I hate this.* I want to protect her, but I feel powerless in this situation.

I clench my jaw, lacing up my sneakers and tossing on a hoodie. I walk through the hotel suite quietly, but I stop when I hear soft footsteps down the hall.

Dakota yawns, rubbing her eyes. She's wearing an oversized tee and shorts, and my stomach clenches. She shifts her weight when she sees me watching her.

"Where are you going?" She reaches toward me, and I give her a soft smile, pulling her into my arms.

"I was going to go for a run. I couldn't sleep."

"Can I come with you?" She bites her lip, her eyes watching me. It's almost as if she's afraid I'm going to say no. Sometimes I catch her looking at me like she's waiting for the other shoe to drop.

"Of course." Her eyes brighten, her eyebrows raising a tad.

"Really?" I nod, and she scrambles out of my arms back into the room. When she emerges a moment later, she's dressed in leggings, a sweatshirt, and running shoes. She looks beautiful as always.

"Ready?"

She nods her head several times.

We walk down to the lobby. Walking out the front doors, Dakota gives me a mischievous glance from the side. I barely have a moment to register what's happening before she takes off running down the street.

"Last one there is a rotten egg," she calls, and I laugh, running after her.

We make it several miles before she slows. She bends over, panting, in front of a small coffee shop. I stop beside her, my hand on her back as I catch my breath.

"You'd think," I pant, "with longer legs, I'd be able to keep up with you." I pant again, gulping in large breaths of air. She somehow laughs from her crouched position.

"How'd that logic work out for you?" She punches my arm and stands up again.

"Not well," I wheeze. She snorts, nodding her head toward the coffee shop.

"Coffee?"

"Yes, please."

We walk into the shop, and Dakota grabs a table before walking to the counter and ordering for us. When she returns, she sets the coffee in front of me before sitting down.

She faces me across the small table. The weather has chilled enough that I almost regret wearing my basketball shorts for this run. Normally, I run warm, but it's cooler than normal for late November. The coffee quickly remedies that, though.

With the first gulp, the hot liquid warms me from the inside out. I feel my body relax. It's then that I notice that my head feels significantly clearer.

"So tell me, why were you running off this morning?" Dakota holds her coffee in her hands, keeping it close to her face.

"I needed to blow off some steam," I admit. A concerned look crosses her face, and I immediately scramble to remedy it. "I found Tanner on social media last night, and I don't want to let it go." She opens her mouth to speak, but I stop her. Her face twists, and I smile, shaking my head. *So stubborn.* "But I will let it go because you asked. Doesn't mean I'll like it."

Her mouth twists to the side, her eyes downcast. I watch the rise and fall of her chest as she thinks. I can see several protests cross her face, but finally, she huffs a breath and shakes her head.

"Thank you," she says. She sets down her coffee and grabs my free hand. She brings it to her lips, kissing it tenderly. "I'll make you another promise. If and when I'm ever ready, I'll tell you first." My heartbeat increases. It's not exactly what I wanted, but honestly, I think it's better. It's a promise to let me help her through this. That's all I could ask for. This is her trauma to heal from, not mine.

"Deal."

I pull my phone from my pocket and see the text I've been waiting on pop up on my screen.

"I have a surprise for you."

She raises an eyebrow at me. "Oh?"

"Oh," I mock her, and she laughs. I love it when she does that. "Yes, let's go."

We pull up to the condo building, stopping at the front office on our way up. With the key in hand, I lead Dakota up to the fifth floor and stop when we make it to the front door. Her eyes are still closed, and I smirk at the way she keeps trying to peek through her fingers.

"No peeking," I scold her, and she giggles. I make quick work of unlocking the door and shuffling her through before she can peek again.

Standing behind her, I hold her shoulders as I speak into her ear. "Okay, you can look now."

She removes her hands from her face and blinks several times, her head moving around animatedly as she looks around the empty condo.

"Is this yours?"

"Yep. I'm officially a resident of Boston."

She steps out of my grip and walks right to the large windows.

GOAL *Suck*

She peeks out at the view, and a small gasp leaves her mouth.

"You're right next to my shop," she says, holding her hand over her mouth.

"That may have been intentional," I confess.

"Awe, is Wyatt going to come visit me at work all the time now?"

"Actually...I was hoping you'd stay with me. At least until you can move back into your apartment. Or stay. Whatever you want," I mumble the last bit under my breath. For someone extremely confident, I'm suddenly feeling uncertain.

"I don't know. You won't get tired of seeing me?" I nearly roll my eyes at her words. When she smiles at me, I shake my head.

"You think you're funny." I pull her toward me, squeezing her waist. She squeals when I pick her up and set her onto the counter. "If you choose to stay, we'll need to christen every surface, I hope you know." I drop my voice low, bringing my lips to her neck. Nipping at her flesh, she arches, her head thrown back against the cabinet as I lean into her. "Make the neighbors real familiar with us," I breathe. Her chuckle turns into a moan when I slip a hand into her pants.

"Wyatt," she breathes, and I feel my cock grow in my shorts. The way she says my name like that is branded on my mind. It's so *damn* perfect.

"Say it again," I say, sliding her panties aside and circling a finger over her opening. "Say my name again."

"*Wyatt.*" She moans when I slide my finger inside of her. My teeth nip at her neck, then move to her mouth. It's not until we hear the sound of a phone ringing that we freeze. "Ignore it," she says.

"It could be important," I say into her mouth. She groans, nodding her head. I remove my fingers from her and slip them into my mouth. It's still the same sweet taste that drives me wild. She shakes her head at me, pulling the phone from her pants pocket.

A panicked look crosses her face before she answers the call. "Lani, what happened?" I hear a frantic voice on the other side of the call. Dakota nods, taking it all in. "Okay, I'll be right there."

She ends the call and looks at me. "Someone leaked the name of my shop online," she says. "Lani says there's a line down the street, and she's freaking the hell out."

"That damn article," I say. "Okay, let's go."

CHAPTER 24
Dakota

A loud, annoying honk sounds behind me as I pull up in front of my building. What is normally a deserted side of town is packed, the street lined with cars in both directions.

My heart pounds in my chest as I take in the scene. The only reason I'm sane is the hand that's gripping my thigh. I'm reminded of his experience with this sort of thing. He experiences it every time he's on the ice.

"Do you want me to come with you?"

"Can you persuade people to go away?" I say, trying to keep the hysterical laugh from slipping out.

"I can certainly try." He squeezes my leg again and extracts himself from the car, the crowd screaming the moment they see him. He walks around to my side and opens the door for me.

When I step out, he pulls me under his arm, keeping me close to him. It makes me smile that he's working so hard to keep me safe.

We have to practically shove our way to the front door, and the moment I see Lani, her face is full of relief.

"Oh, thank God," she says, walking up to us. "And you brought the big guns. Good."

I shake my head and take in my surroundings. The crowd of people hasn't lessened. The protector in me kicks in, and I feel a rumble in my chest. I certainly can't stand up for myself, but for my friends, I'd do anything.

Grinding my teeth, I look at Wyatt sideways, and he studies me intently. The moment he sees the fire behind my eyes, he grins.

Walking back through the front doors, I whistle loudly.

"Ay!" Everyone stops talking and turns to look at me. "I'm going to need y'all to form two lines."

"Who even are you?" someone yells from down the way.

I grit my teeth again. I see Wyatt move from inside the shop, but I hold my hand up.

"I'm the owner of this shop, and you can either listen to me or move on." The person doesn't respond, so I continue. "Whoever is here for me, please stand to my left, and whoever is here to see Wyatt Lane, stand to my right." I see a couple of my regulars in the crowd and wave them forward. Wyatt holds the door open for them, and they walk up the stairs to the bookshop.

It takes a moment for the crowd to arrange themselves, but when there are finally two lines, I call Wyatt forward.

"Are you okay taking care of these people while I figure out this line?" He nods, kissing my head and stepping over. I smile at him and then turn back to the line in front of me.

"Please come in two at a time. Lani and I will help everyone as quickly as we can. Okay?" I see several nods, and that satisfies me. Lani props the door open, and people shuffle in two at a time.

Several hours later, I'm slumped on the little couch at the back of the tattoo shop. I don't think I've ever talked to so many people in my life. Okay, that's maybe an exaggeration, but so many people were here for *me*, and that confuses me.

When I'd made it to thirty-thousand followers on my Instagram account, I hadn't realized the scope of my business. That had come the moment I'd been able to open a shop of my own.

I've worked hard for this, so much so that even before today, my schedule was booked out months in advance. It's crazy to say that I'm now booking into November of next year.

I don't think there's ever been a moment that I've looked back and thought, wow, I've finally made it, but now as I sit on this couch, I feel overwhelmed. Not the bad kind of overwhelmed, though; I feel thankful that this journey has brought me here.

I feel my face fall as Tanner's voice enters my head. *You're only here now because of Wyatt.*

"Stop that, Dakota." Lani points her finger at me from across the shop. I purse my lips, raising an eyebrow at her. She turns to Wyatt who's walked through the door and is wiping off his shoes on the welcome mat. "Please tell her that her business isn't thriving all because of your fame." She looks back at me, her finger still pointing at me.

I scowl, my eyes pleading. "That wasn't—"

"Yes, it was," she interrupts. "That's exactly what you were thinking, and I won't have it. I've *seen* you build this place from the ground up. I've seen the blood, sweat, and tears that you put into this business, and yes, maybe Wyatt has attracted a new crowd, but you were making it before this. You *deserve* this, Dakota. More than anyone." Her eyes are hard when she speaks to me. I sigh, looking at Wyatt.

"She's right, you know. I have proof of it on my body. You're incredibly talented." He shoves his hands into his pockets and shrugs.

I have half a thought to roll my eyes at both of them. It's hard for me to accept the compliments, but I do it anyway, shoving down that *stupid* voice that tells me not to.

"Thank you." I don't need to say anymore. Those two words convey everything I need to say.

"Great!" Lani claps her hands together. "I think this is cause for celebration." She pauses, raising a finger to her lip. "Plus, I really need a drink."

"You're one sexy bitch," Silver says, walking into the bathroom. We're getting ready at Dane's place with Lani. Wyatt is with the guys at Roman's, and we're meeting later.

I feel like I'm getting ready for prom or something; the three of us crowded into this bathroom, the smell of a curling iron wafting in the air.

I finish my last curl, then slip out of the bathroom to throw on my outfit. It's cold tonight, so unlike the girls, who are wearing dresses, I've chosen to wear my black lace corset top with a pair of faux leather pants and a blazer.

Silver holds a pair of heels on the tips of her fingers as she approaches me. "Even with these heels on, Wyatt will still be a head taller than you." I take the heels from her and slip them on, taking extra care to clasp the strap around my ankle.

"Perks of dating a six-foot-five hockey man," I say, and Silver smirks at me.

"I wouldn't know." She winks, retreating to the bathroom once more. "He's going to want to rip that outfit off you immediately. I'm calling it now," she remarks from the bathroom, and I shake my head.

We slip out the door at exactly five p.m. and make it to the club by five-thirty. It's packed for a Sunday night, but this club is worth it.

"I can't believe you convinced the guys to come here," I say into Silver's ear. It's loud, and I really don't want to yell. She smirks at me.

"I don't even think they know what they're getting themselves into." We slide into a large circular booth at the front of the building near the stage. We've just ordered our drinks when the guys walk in. Silver winks at me when she sees the look on Wyatt's face.

I slide out of my seat to greet him, and his eyes rake over me so slowly I feel almost naked under his gaze. It sends a shiver down my spine. He pulls me into his arms and smacks a kiss on my lips.

"You're fucking gorgeous," he says.

"Thanks," I say, slipping my arms around his neck. He kisses me again, and then releases me as we slide into our seats.

"What is this place?" Jaiden asks when he slides into the seat next to Silver.

"You'll see." Lani, Sterling, and I share a conspiratorial glance.

"I have a bad feeling about this," Jaiden mumbles, and we all laugh.

"I was right to have a bad feeling about this," Jaiden says as the drag queen grips his arm and drags him up to the stage. We all wheeze at his deer-in-the-headlights face.

Crystal Lier places a wig on Jaiden's head and hands him a

microphone.

"It's your turn to sing, pretty boy." She struts to the side, leaving Jaiden on center stage. We all shriek with laughter. My stomach hurts from laughing so much, but oh, is it worth it.

When the music first blasts, Jaiden stands there looking rather uncomfortable, but then something kicks in and he begins strutting across the stage, popping his hips and gesturing animatedly to the lyrics.

He lip-syncs perfectly, the crowd cheering him on at every moment. I look over everyone at the table, enjoying their reactions.

Wyatt is watching intently, a very amused smile on his face. Roman and Lani are laughing, the latter nearly crying, and Sterling is watching Jaiden like he's the only man in the room.

I hadn't seen it before, the way she looks at him. Has she always looked at him like that?

The song comes to a close, and I blink several times, plastering a smile on my face. Wyatt's grip on my leg tightens, and I look over at him. I'm enamored completely with him.

His presence is safe, which is new to me. Even my own family doesn't provide this kind of comfort. For the first time in a very long time, I feel like I can breathe easy.

"What?" he asks.

"I'm just happy," I say.

It's about damn time.

CHAPTER 25
Wyatt

Walking through the black and yellow locker room as a member of this team is a new feeling. I've been here before to tour and to visit the guys, but never have I been welcomed as a member.

Damian's already seated at one of the empty benches. The guys aren't here yet, so I take the seat next to him.

"Weird, huh?" He's leaning forward with his elbows propped on his knees.

"Yup." *Very weird.*

"Wyatt," a burly player says from my right. His hair is tied up in a tight bun, and his beard is full but trimmed. I recognize him, but we haven't talked much before. "Glad to have you on the team, man. Welcome."

"Glad to be here," I say.

Several other players shuffle in, looking our way but not saying much. I'm familiar with several of them, but now that I'm officially a newbie, it feels strange. There's going to be a period of adjustment, but it'll be worth it.

Jaiden and Roman sit opposite me, the former giving me a flirtatious wave with a wink. I chuckle, shaking my head.

Coach Hart walks through the side door. He's one of the most respected coaches in our conference. I feel a sense of pride being able to sit in this room with him. He nods in our direction and stands in the middle of the room with his arms crossed in front of him. He's a large man, which made him an incredible enforcer.

He runs through welcomes, making an official announcement of our arrival. Both Damian and I are issued official jerseys. My number twenty-seven has carried over to this team.

Without sparing another moment, we gear up for practice.

An hour on the ice concludes and we hit the weight room, running through mobility and conditioning training. It's different from what we did in Raleigh, but I have no doubts that I'll pick up on their routine quickly.

Jaiden and Roman make small talk with Damian while I run through drills. When I finally pull my headphones from my ear, I catch the tail end of their conversation.

"You fuckers talking shit about me?" I ask, sitting up from the floor.

"Always," Jaiden says. He sets the weights down and tosses a towel over his shoulder.

"Are the movers coming today?" Romans asks from beside him.

"They are. I'm meeting them after this."

"Need help?" Dawson, the team captain asks, surprising me. "We're a team now, and I've got two hands and lots of free time after this." Several other guys chime in.

"I won't say no to help. Beer and pizza on me?"

"Great."

"It's quite comical seeing a bunch of burly hockey players bonding over a dancing video game." Dakota walks through the door, setting her purse down on the newly assembled kitchen table. She places a kiss on my lips and looks around.

"It's not a dancing video game," Jaiden says from in front of the screen. His arms are flailing wildly as he keeps up with the person on the screen. "It's a serious rite of passage that both Damian and Wyatt have yet to participate in."

Dakota watches him, her lip pulled into her mouth as she holds back a laugh.

"I'm busy," I say, pulling Dakota back into my arms. The guys hoot around me, and she blushes.

"Get a room," Damian says, but he walks over to the table and shoves a slice of pizza into his mouth. He wipes his hand on a napkin before extending it to Dakota. "I'm Damian. I've heard about you, but we've yet to meet. You're gorgeous." He winks, and I growl at him. He laughs, throwing his arms up. "So feral, this one. I'm just stating a fact."

Dakota shakes her head, laughing. "Nice to meet you. You came from Raleigh too, right?"

"I did."

"Good." She smiles at him. "You two together are a dangerous pair. I'd really like to see the Stanley Cup in Boston this year." She beams at me, and I feel my cock twitch.

That's my damn girl.

"Glad to know someone recognizes talent," Damian says, running a hand through his hair.

"We've got lots of talent, asshole." Dawson waves his arms in the air as the woman on the screen dances. When he stops, he looks at Damian with a frown. Damian laughs when they turn back to the screen, doing some sort of twerking movements. He walks toward the group, leaving Dakota and I alone again.

Shaking my head, I pull out a seat for Dakota and then one for myself. She looks around the room, taking in the newly furnished place.

"It looks nice. Cozy."

"It does. I had help."

"Clearly," she says, winking. "I have good news." She waggles her eyebrows, and I snort.

"Oh?"

"Oh?" she mocks like I always do with her.

I deserved that.

"Aida Monroe contacted me. She wants to interview me for an article she's doing. She listing top successful business women in Boston, and I was nominated."

"That's amazing, Dakota!" I say, pulling her hand into mine and giving it a squeeze.

"Thank you." She blushes, her eyelashes fluttering. "It feels surreal. Someone's labeling me as a successful businesswoman. I never thought I'd see the day."

"You deserve it."

"I don't deserve you, Wyatt Lane." She leans toward me.

"You do," I say, pressing my lips to hers. "You absolutely do."

GOAL *Suck*

Dakota left my bed early this morning to do her interview.

I smile up at the ceiling, feeling a sense of rightness. I hadn't realized how much I missed Boston. I've been able to see Lily every day this week for dinner, and that alone makes me happy. But now there's another woman in my life.

I've known for a while now that I could see Dakota fitting into my life. She's so easy to be with.

Hockey is a very time-consuming sport. It's hard to foster relationships when you're already in it. Most people find someone in high school and marry young. Those women follow them, making their own careers along the way.

At that time, I'd been rebellious and nowhere near ready for a long-term relationship. But now…now I'm happy that I waited. I want Dakota, and now that I have her, I refuse to let her go. Call me a sap, I don't care. That woman is incredible and deserves all the love and affection in the world. I just want her to believe it too.

I drive to Roman's home to help with preparations for Thanksgiving tomorrow.

After Thursday, we'll be on the road off and on until Christmas.

This is always a hard time for me, not having my family here anymore, but the guys make it better. And now I have Koda.

The house smells of yams when I walk through the front doors. Rounding the corner to the kitchen, I see Roman wearing an apron decorated with dachshunds wearing tutus. He's pulling something out of the oven when he spots me. Lily is seated at the counter, crayons spread across her workspace. She's humming happily, and that makes me smile.

"Don't even make a comment," Roman says. I shake my head, my lips pursed.

"Wasn't going to."

Lily turns from her seat and looks at me.

"Uncle Wyatt," she says, her eyes swinging back to the paper in front of her. "Can Dakota help me draw something for school?"

"Oh, I see how it is. You don't even like me anymore." I slide my lower lip out, letting it quiver. It's my best sad-puppy-dog look, and it doesn't even phase her.

"She's better at drawing than you." Roman snorts, and I blink several times.

"I gotta admit, I'm wounded."

"I still love you, Uncle Wyatt," Lily says, giggling.

"Okay, good." I blow a raspberry against her cheek, and she squeals.

Loud footsteps plow through the front door. Jaiden walks in with Sterling trailing closely behind. She looks at me, her eyes wide, and I feel my stomach drop.

"What happened?" I say without thinking.

"Show it to him," she says to Jaiden. He grimaces, and then hands me his phone.

I read through the words on the screen quickly. I feel the tension in my body increase the further I get. My fist clenches, my jaw tightening. If it's ever been possible to have steam come from my ears, it would be now. I swallow, the bitter taste in my mouth growing.

When I finish reading, Sterling is looking at me with a panicked expression. I sigh, gritting my teeth. Jaiden starts to speak, but I shake my head.

"I gotta go," I say, not looking back as I slam the door behind me. I vaguely hear Jaiden asking where I'm going, but I'm not listening. My ears are ringing, and I'm seeing red.

CHAPTER 26
Dakota

"We are honored to have you here with us today, Dakota." Aida stands near the camera, the bright lights almost blocking her face. "We're just going to get a few shots of you for the article in a couple different outfits."

"Okay," I say, feeling slightly uncomfortable. The makeup artist brushes at my face, and I sit still so she can add the final touches.

When we're finished, I pose in front of the camera for an hour, changing outfits when instructed. By the end, I'm laughing and feeling more comfortable.

"That is exactly what we want," Aida says. "Now when I interview you, you'll be loosey-goosey." She laughs, snapping a couple more photos.

"That's smart," I say, my body contorted in some sort of lean-back pose. These are the last couple shots, and I want to make them count. I'm wearing a power suit, the blazer open to reveal my sternum tattoo. My hair is up in a high pony, and I feel incredibly sexy.

"Okay, can I have you take a seat over here? Liz is going to touch up your face before we begin rolling again for the video portion." She steps away from the camera, her hands brushing through her hair. I hadn't known this process was going to be so time consuming, but I'm surprised that I'm actually having fun.

Taking a seat in the chair across from Aida, I take extra care to sit up straight and not slouch.

When Aida sits across from me, she instructs several people around her, then finally slips an ear piece into her ear. She nods to the cameraman, and that's when I know we're rolling.

"Thank you for sitting down with us today, Dakota," she says.

"Thank you for having me," I say. Aida smiles at me before speaking again. She crosses her legs in her chair.

"Of course. We're happy to have you. I'm interviewing several women this week for our Boss Babes article, but I have to be honest, I was very excited to meet you."

I laugh, blushing a bit.

"Thank you. I'm honored, really. I was surprised that I was even nominated for this." I hold my hands in my lap to keep from fidgeting.

"Why is that? You're a successful businesswoman and have been for a while now. I think you deserve it." She tilts her head at me.

"It's been a whirlwind," I admit. "Yes, I've worked hard to be where I am today, but it's been weird to think of myself as a *boss babe*. It hasn't really hit me." My foot rocks, knocking against the leg of the chair.

"Well, that's all changed now, hasn't it? I understand that you've experienced a recent influx in your business."

I nod my head.

"I have. At first, I was blaming the change in my relationship status, but I've been assured many times that I've earned this. I'm just now starting to believe it."

"Yes. I agree that the change in your relationship did bring attention, but from what I saw in my research, you were thriving even before that."

"I was. I had a pretty solid following on social media, and, I mean, I run my own business now, which is amazing and a dream all on its own."

"I'm sure the readers and watchers would love to know more about your business. So for people who aren't familiar with what you do, can you tell us a little about your business?"

"Of course. I'm a tattoo artist. I opened my own shop when I was twenty-one and expanded it into a bookstore and coffee shop as well. I'm an avid reader, so my shop specializes in bookish and pop culture tattoos. Almost all of my artists work in that realm, but not everyone."

"When you say bookish and pop culture, can you expand on that a bit?"

I nod several times.

"Many artists will find a style and stick within that. The artist I did my apprenticeship with did fine line and floral tattoos, which are really more delicate than say the traditional style of tattooing. I incorporated what I learned there into what I do now. I design a lot of anime tattoos and fantasy pieces that tie into different fandoms of books. I've been expanding more; like for Wyatt, I've been doing Greek mythology."

"I've seen some of your work in my research, and it's absolutely stunning."

"Thank you," I say.

"Can you share how you got into tattooing?"

"I can. I've always loved to draw. I would spend hours drawing on myself and my friends. It expanded to my friends asking me to paint their calculators in grade school, and then I was drawing fake tattoos on people's bodies during lunch. One day, it just clicked that I wanted to tattoo. I had a few people in my life discourage me, but I kept going, and here I am."

"Here you are," she says. Her face grows more reserved. "In my research, I found that you'd dated a hockey player in the past?"

I freeze, my body feeling stiff.

"I don't feel entirely comfortable discussing that," I say.

"Of course," she says, shaking her head. "I only bring it up because your ex has recently come out and released a statement. He'd said some ugly things, and I wanted to give you a chance to address them."

"I wasn't aware that he'd made a statement," I say, raising an eyebrow at her.

"I think it was just released today. He's been claiming that your success was attributed to him and that he'd supported you fully on your endeavors. There were other things, but I won't go into them. I fully believe that your success is your own." I look around the room, unsure of what to say. Aida waves at the cameraman, and they cut.

"I'm sorry," she says. "I didn't mean to corner you. Would you like to read it?"

No. "Yes."

Someone hands the article over to me, and I run through the words quickly, my face growing paler every second.

GOAL *Suck*

TANNER MORIN CLAIMS EX-GIRLFRIEND IS OUT FOR FAME.

When NHL bad boy Tanner Morin was questioned about his former girlfriend, he claimed that she was 'out for fame.' The successful tattoo artist and business owner has recently entered into a relationship with all-star Wyatt Alexander Lane. The duo were spotted together in Boston after news of his trade was released.
Morin claims that ex always wanted to be a successful tattoo artist. "I supported her through her whole journey," he says. "When my career went south before the draft, she left me in search of someone better. I attribute some of her success to me, though."
We asked him if he was happy for her new relationship, and all he had to say was that he's glad that someone's taking care of his ex-lover.
"Once a puck bunny, always a puck bunny," says Morin.

In a matter of seconds, I experience several emotions: anger, sadness, fury, mortification, and fear.

"I have to go," I say, rising from my seat. I start to walk away when I hear slight protests. "I'm sorry. Thank you so much for having me. I have to take care of something."

When I pull up to Roman's home, I don't see Wyatt's car out front. My heart panics, the blood rushing through my body at an alarming pace.

It's when Sterling opens the door that I know. *They've seen the article.*

"Where is he?" I ask.

"I don't know," Jaiden says. "He stormed out with steam literally coming out of his ears."

"Can I come in?"

Jaiden nods his head toward the hallway, and I follow after him. The moment I walk into the kitchen, I lock eyes with Roman and feel the tears falling.

"Lily, baby. Can you give us a moment?" Lily nods, climbing down from her chair. She stops and hugs my legs before she runs upstairs. I choke down a sob.

"I told you that we would protect you," Roman says. "I think that he just needed to blow off steam."

"It's your story to tell," Silver says from behind me.

"I'll tell you more later, but the gist of it is that I have a shitty ex who's a hockey player and that's why I told Wyatt I hated hockey players. Admittedly, y'all are some of the greatest people I know, so I'm sorely mistaken. But now that shitty ex is saying fucked up shit on the internet about me, and it makes me very, *very* angry." I huff a breath and look between the three of them.

"Are you okay?" Silver grips my hand.

"Not really, but I will be. This is just…*argh*." I toss my hands up and pace. "He always has to make it about him and ruin a good thing."

"Go find him," Roman says. "We'll be here when you get back." I nod sadly and jog out the door and right to my car. I hear footsteps running after me.

"Try the rink," Jaiden says. "He likes to go to the rink." I nod my thanks and pull away from the curb.

GOAL *Suck*

I panic the whole drive there. I'm so angry about this. I can handle the slander against me but to insinuate that I'm dating Wyatt for the fame...I'm not okay with that.

Wyatt isn't just another hockey player to add to my repertoire. I didn't need his fame to help my business. I didn't even *want* to feel this way toward another hockey player but here we are.

When I walk in, the security guard waves me through. My hand stills on the door handle. I peek through the window, my heart calming a bit when I see Wyatt. He's skating across the ice, the puck shuffling as he goes.

I sneak in quietly, tiptoeing toward the ice as I watch him skate. When he makes it to the other side, he spins and runs across the ice to the other side, shaving to a stop. He does that several more times before he slows, his breathing ragged.

I stand in the entryway of the rink, watching him. When he looks up, meeting my eyes, I smile at him sadly.

I see the man I saw the night of Roman's accident again. He looks at me with a note of vulnerability, and it breaks my heart.

He skates to me, not saying a thing, just wrapping his arms around me and breathing me in like his life depends on it. He lifts me up, my feet dangling off the ground until I wrap my legs around his waist. When I feel his breathing slow, I pull away so that I can look at his face.

"Are you okay?" I ask, my voice quiet. His eyes narrow at me, his jaw clenching.

"Fuck, Dakota," he says, pressing his forehead against mine. "I should be asking you that."

"Well I asked first, so tell me, are you okay?"

"Yes," he says. "But Tanner better be thanking God that I'm not on a plane right now. I could kill him for what he said about you."

I feel my stomach drop, then I laugh-sob.

"What's wrong?'

"I thought you were going to be angry with me," I admit. "He insinuated that I'm dating you for your fame, and I know that's the opposite of what you wanted in a partner."

He sets me down, then links his hand with mine. "I'll never believe a word that comes from that man's mouth, if he can even be called that. He's no man." He shakes his head several times. "Fuck. Dakota, you were successful without me. Why would I believe anything he says? You didn't even know who I was when we met."

"True, but the increase in business and the article don't make me look good," I say.

"Stop that," he says. "You've earned this. You." He looks at me, his eyes gleaming with mischief. He grabs my hands and pulls me out onto the ice with my high tops still on my feet. I shriek.

"Wyatt!" I say, trying to keep the laughter from my voice. I slip, and he catches me.

"I'll leave you on the ice until you admit that you've earned this. We'll stay here all night if we have to."

I laugh, slipping again. "Okay, fine. Just get me off the ice."

"Say it," he says.

"Fine, fine. I earned this."

"Good." He picks me up and skates with me in his arms across the ice. I laugh, my face going numb.

"Put me down," I say through laughs.

"Yes, please, put her down," a man says from outside of the rink. My eyes go wide, and I slam my mouth shut.

"Coach Hart," Wyatt says. "I'm sorry. I was just blowing off some steam so I won't beat someone up."

"Save those punches for Tuesday," he says, shaking his head as he walks away. I look at Wyatt, and he laughs.

"I think I like Boston," he says.

CHAPTER 27
Wyatt

"Happy Thanksgiving," Dakota says as we walk through the doors of my condo. It's past midnight, and we're due at Roman's home in less than seven hours.

I'm exhausted, but thoughts of sleep have long gone when I see the look on Dakota's face.

"I have something I'm incredibly thankful for," she says as she prowls toward me. She watches me as she drops to her knees before me, her hands slipping to the waistband of my jeans.

I watch her like a predator watching its prey. She's the most beautiful thing I've ever seen. Her pupils are dilated, her tongue slipping across that perfect mouth of hers.

The sight of her before me, on her knees and aching for me, makes me ravenous.

She flicks the button on my jeans loose, sliding the zipper down slowly. I feel my blood running hot and my heart pounding in anticipation.

"I think it's time to get to know the neighbors," she says as she frees me and takes my cock into her hand, stroking it once…twice.

I groan a guttural sound when she licks the head, paying special attention to the little piece of jewelry.

"Fuck," I hiss when she sucks me into her mouth. I've remained still until now. Shoving my hands into her hair, I grab fist fulls, using my thumbs to rub the sides of her face.

I should be shocked when I see the naughty gleam in her eyes right before she relaxes her throat and hollows out her cheeks to take me further into her mouth.

I pant as she works my cock with her mouth, my eyes nearly rolling back into my head. She grabs my balls and massages them, and that's when I know I'm a goner. If I even stood a chance at denying her anything, that all goes out the window now.

"Dakota," I hiss. She hums around my shaft, and something about it is sexy as hell. "I want to be inside of you, right this second, or I'm going to blow my load." She releases me with a pop, a slight laugh sounding from her chest.

She licks the tip of my king's crown piercing and smirks up at me. "Who am I to deny a king?" She says it so matter-a-factly that I nearly collapse before her.

"If I'm a king, then *you* are my queen." I slide my hands under her ass, scooping her over my shoulder and carrying her to my bed where I plan to ravish her and have her screaming my name until her voice is hoarse.

I drop her on the bed, her body bouncing with the force of it. I slip off her shirt, pulling her nipples into my mouth as they're revealed to me. She moans, and I smile around her breast. Nudging her toward the headboard, I nod my head past her when I speak.

"Hands on the stick, beautiful." She looks behind her to see the hockey sticks decorating the headboard. When she looks back at me, her gaze is hungry. She scoots back, wrapping her hands around the handle, her legs spread wide for me. "Perfect."

I tear her pants off her body, a gasp leaving her mouth as the fabric tears away. She smirks at me as her legs open again for me. Sitting back, I admire her and her perfect pussy that's already wet and swollen for me. I kiss my way up her legs, admiring the tattoos on her thighs as I make my way to my destination.

"I have something I'm incredibly thankful for too," I say.

"What's that?" she asks, her voice breathy.

"You. Your body, your smile, your voice. Everything about you." I kiss her stomach, then between her legs. "You are the girl of my dreams, Dakota Easton. Everything about you is like you were made just for me." I lean over to the bedside table to grab a condom when she protests.

"I want to feel you," she pants. I freeze, my heart pounding. "I'm clean, and I have an IUD."

"I get tested every quarter," I say. "Are you sure?" She nods her head furiously.

"Yes," she says, her voice a plea.

Without wasting another moment, I line myself up with her and press in, slowly, inch by inch. She gasps with the intrusion, but quickly wraps her legs around me, urging me further. I chuckle, leaning into her and kissing her head as I move inside her.

She feels incredible. She tightens around me, and it takes everything in me to keep from coming inside her right now. Using my hand, I play with her clit, and she hisses, her mouth going to my shoulder as I pound into her.

"Oh God," she gasps. "Oh my God."

Her hair is wild as I move above her, her mouth pouty and panting. I watch her, her eyes closed when her body tightens.

"Look at me," I command. "I want to see you come. I want to see your face."

She whimpers, her eyes opening.

I feel her tighten around me, her mouth forming that perfect little o as she shatters around me, panting my name with each thrust. She looks at me, her eyes watery when I let myself shatter too.

My balls tighten, my body tensing as the waves of pleasure rush through me. She watches me the whole time, and the sight makes me feral once more.

Mine.

I collapse beside her, her hands releasing the hockey stick to roam over my chest. She runs circles over the myriad of healing bruises and scars on my chest.

"I worry about you," she says. "I'm so scared that one day I could get a call that you got hurt and I won't be there to help you."

"I won't lie to you and tell you that it's not a possibility. It is." Her eyebrows crease together, and I kiss the space between them. "Hockey is brutal, but that's what I'm good at."

"Just be careful," she says. Her hand stills, her eyes flicking up to mine. "I know your team is playing Toronto soon. I want you to be careful."

"I would do anything for you," I say.

"Anything?" she asks, her eyes swimming with mischief.

"Anything," I confirm. And that's just what I do, over and over again, until we pass out in each other's arms, our pure bliss and happiness radiant.

GOAL Suck

I look worse than I feel.

After almost three weeks of travel and games, I'm aching to be back home with Dakota. Our communication has been short due to my long hours and her business blowing up.

I'm exhausted, but the season is picking up as we approach the new year. Eighty-four games over the course of seven months doesn't seem like a lot, but over time, it adds up.

Our last game was brutal. The team had played dirty, leading to several fights on the ice. I'm not usually one to fight, but even I got several good punches in.

Now as the bus pulls up to the practice rink in Boston, I'm feeling the after-effects of that fight more and more.

There's no time to rest, though. Not really.

As I walk off the bus, we sit in the locker room listening to Coach Hart's lecture before we're dismissed for the Christmas holiday.

Dakota and I are headed to Toronto to see her family. I should be nervous, but I'm zinging with anticipation. Dakota is more nervous than I am, and I can't blame her for it.

I drive back to the condo to find Dakota rummaging through her suitcase, a string of curses slipping from her lips. She doesn't see me, so I stand in the doorway watching her for a moment. When she looks up, a look of relief crosses her face almost immediately.

"Welcome home," she says, standing and walking toward me. Her hands brush across my cheek where there is most definitely bruising.

"Not for long," I say, holding her close to me. "We have a plane to catch."

She groans, burying her face into my chest and breathing deeply.

"Can we just skip it? Do Christmas here with Roman?" She blinks at me several times.

"We promised, plus I'd really like to meet this brother of yours."

She rolls her eyes, walking back to her suitcase and kneeling before it.

"Just remember that I'm cooler than him. And be prepared for all the hockey talk. I'm bringing ear plugs." She shoves a few wrapped gifts into her bag and flips it closed. I take the bag from her, rolling my own behind me.

She grips my hand more tightly as we walk through the building to my car. I can feel her nerves increasing the closer we get.

I'm thankful that she sleeps most of the flight, her head resting on my shoulder. But by the time the plane touches down in Toronto, she's increased her death grip on my hand.

"It's gonna be okay," I say in her ear. "I'll be by your side the entire time."

She nods, her face relaxing a bit.

The light outside has long gone by the time we deboard the plane. When we grab our luggage and pick up our rental car, I see Dakota yawning, her body slumping into the passenger seat.

"Where are we going?" I ask, pulling up the GPS on the screen of the car.

"We're staying with my parents because they wouldn't take no for an answer," she says through a yawn. She types in the address, and leans back into the door.

"They're okay with me being there too?"

"They're going to have to be. I told my mom that either you stay or I'm not coming."

"I bet she loved that."

"Totally." She yawns again.

Twenty minutes later, we drive through a residential neighborhood until I pull into the driveway of a cozy two-story home. It's dark inside, the only light to be seen is the small one on the porch. I take a moment to look over the home that Dakota grew up in. Its light exterior makes it feel inviting. There's snow decorating the outside making it look like something right out of a postcard.

Dakota is slumped in the passenger seat, her breathing shallow as she sleeps. I don't bother waking her as I unload the luggage and run it up to the front door. When I return to the car, I open the passenger door and unbuckle her. She stirs, her eyes fluttering open.

"Mmm, hi," she says. She puckers her lips, and I chuckle before I kiss her.

"Want me to carry you?" She shakes her head, but I don't listen. I scoop her into my arms, and she protests quietly. It lacks its usual conviction, so I move her to my back, and she wraps her arms and legs around me.

"They know we're coming, but it's late. I can look for a key so we don't have to bother them." She squirms on my back, and I tighten my hold.

"I'll do it. Tell me where."

"Put me down, Wyatt," she says, her voice teasing.

"No," I say. "You're staying there."

"Put me down," she says again, trying to escape.

"No." I pinch her side, and she laughs.

"Wyatt," she hisses, and I ignore her. She struggles again when the door opens, a short woman standing in the doorway. A taller man stands behind her. I see a bit of Dakota in each of them. Her father runs a hand through his graying beard when he speaks.

"Ya kids going to stand out here all night?"

"Hi, Daddy," Dakota says from my back. I don't have to look at her to know her face is red. She taps my shoulder, and I drop her from my back. She lands with grace and walks past me, right into her mother's arm. "Hi, Ma." Her mother kisses her head. When she releases her, Dakota walks into her dad's arms. It's an awkward sort of hug, but I smile watching them.

"Ma, Pops, this is Wyatt Lane, my boyfriend."

"Hi, it's nice to meet you," I say, extending my hand.

"Oh honey, we hug here." She pulls me into her arms, and I have to bend to meet her. Her father eyes me curiously. I hadn't expected him to be one to easily approve of me, and by the way he's eyeing me, I know that I have my work cut out for me.

CHAPTER 28
Dakota

Watching Wyatt shake hands with my father is one of the most amusing things I have ever seen.

My father is an intimidating sort of man. He stands over six feet tall, and even though Wyatt is taller than him, I see the way that my father sizes him up like it's no big deal. He huffs when Wyatt greets him, and I can't help the snort that leaves my mouth.

Wyatt's eyes flick to me, and it makes me fully laugh.

I've only brought a few men home to meet my father. Tanner had had an advantage because our parents were friends before we dated. It's only fair that my father gets to intimidate at least one man in his lifetime. I am his only daughter, after all.

"It's nice to meet you, Mr. and Mrs. Easton." Wyatt stands back, grabbing our suitcases and rolling them into the house. As he does it, my mother looks at me from the side, her eyebrows raising.

Tanner wasn't one for chivalry. He wasn't one for anything, really; if it didn't benefit him, he didn't do it.

"Oh please. Call me Everly, and this is Grayson. Everyone calls him Gray, though, and not because he's turning gray." Wyatt chuckles, my father groaning. "Come in, please. It's late, and I'm sure the both of you are tired. We have big plans for Christmas Eve tomorrow."

My father releases another round of gruff noises, and I snort again.

"We can talk more in the morning. I'm sure you both are just itching to grill Wyatt." I see the usually confident mask slip a bit when Wyatt grimaces slightly. It makes me smile for some reason. Maybe because I like knowing that I'm not the only one who's terrified of that conversation.

My mother ushers us down the stairs and to the basement bedroom. It's been converted into an apartment-style living quarter. My father had been tired of my brother living here, so he'd had them convert it so that he would have his own space. He'd finally moved out a few years ago. At that point, I was surprised my parents hadn't just bought him his own place. *Bet you're thankful I moved out at eighteen now, huh?*

"Goodnight, you two," she says from the stairs and closes the door. Wyatt releases a breath, his face relaxing.

"I thought your dad was going to break my hand," he says.

"He won't. He just likes to act tough. Wait until you see him tomorrow. My brother's girlfriend has a kid and he's basically my father's whole world."

"Can't wait," he says, pulling me into his arms. "It's probably inappropriate to suggest sex in your parents' home, huh?" I laugh, hard, my arms tightening around him. "You just look so damn perfect," he breathes. "Your hair a little tousled from the flight. I could mess it up some more if you'd like..."

"Definitely not," I say through a laugh. "I wouldn't be able to look my parents in the eye tomorrow."

"Then don't." He kisses my temple, then pulls back, smirking.

"Next time," I say, shaking my head with a smile.

"Next time, indeed."

Peeling myself from Wyatt's grip, I slide off the bed, turning to look at him before I pad to the bathroom. He'd looked so peaceful; I didn't want to wake him.

I turn on the shower and brush my teeth while I wait for it to warm. When I slip under the stream, the water is steaming and scalding hot, just like I like it.

Running my face under the hot stream, I scrub off the remnants of my makeup from the night before.

When I hear the door click shut, I continue scrubbing, a small smile crossing my face. I feel his presence behind me before his hands grip my sides. He presses his body against mine, and I can feel the hardness already gathering between his legs. I hum lightly when he rubs small circles across my back.

"You're beautiful," he whispers, peppering kisses along my neck. His hands roam, and I shiver under his touch.

"And you're one of the most dedicated men I've ever met."

"Good," he says, slipping a finger inside me. "How quiet can you be?"

"Extremely," I whimper.

"Good girl. Now shh." He pumps his hand inside of me, his thumb playing with my clit. With every movement, I squirm, biting my lip to keep from moaning. I can feel my legs shaking and Wyatt's erection pressing into me. I reach back to grip him and he hisses.

"Shh," I say, and he chuckles into my sopping hair.

"Fuck it. Hands on the wall." I don't hesitate to follow instructions. He braces a hand on my back, lining himself up before he thrusts into me. That delicious scrape of his jewelry inside of me sends my body fluttering.

It feels like barely a minute before I'm shattering, Wyatt following closely behind me. I bite my lip, the waves of pleasure washing over me with such intensity. Sex has always been great, but sex with Wyatt… it's rapturous.

"That will never *ever* get old," he pants. The way that he says it makes my heart swell and my stomach flutter. The confirmation that maybe he's feeling the same way that I am brings a smile to my face.

I let the water wash over me, cascading down my whole body until I'm clean and ready to conquer the day.

When I see Wyatt, dressed in his Christmas sweater and black jeans, it feels like a puzzle piece snaps into place. I won't lie, it scares me. It scares me so much that I have to push down a frown and replace it with a soft smile.

"Ready to meet the family?" I ask. He nods, taking my hand in his.

Walking up the stairs, I hear a series of screaming giggles. Hunter rushes past the basement door right as it opens. My father is crawling on hands and knees at an alarming pace in the same direction. He roars, raising up onto his knees, his wrists bent in front of him like T-rex arms.

I hold my hand to my mouth to muffle the laughter, but the moment my father spots us, the visible parts of his cheeks redden.

"He wanted to play dinosaurs," he says, standing. My brother peeks his head from the kitchen, the corners of his mouth raising when he sees us.

"'Sup, shithead," he says, pulling me into a hug. I laugh. When he releases me, he extends his hand to Wyatt. "Nice to meet you in person, Wyatt."

"Likewise," Wyatt replies.

"This is my girlfriend Casey. And this is her son, Hunter."

Casey walks to his side, Hunter following closely behind. He clings to his mother's legs until he sees me. His little nose wrinkles when he collides with me.

"Hey, bud," I say, lifting him into the air. He hugs me tightly.

"Teekoda," he says, and I laugh.

"Yes! Auntie Koda. You're getting so big, you silly boy. Did you miss me?" I boop his nose, and he giggles, nodding his head furiously. He gestures his hands in Dallas' direction.

"Dada." He claps, his little squeals piercing my ears. I hadn't noticed that everyone was watching this interaction. Everyone is staring at me, and Wyatt is looking at me with such awe that my stomach flutters.

"That's new," my father says.

"What is?"

"Dada," Dallas says, his voice weak. Casey is looking at him the same way Wyatt was watching me earlier. It brings a smile to my face. I release Hunter into Dallas' arms.

"Come, everyone," my mother says from the kitchen. "Breakfast is ready. We have lots to do today."

We shuffle into the dining room, where several plates are set.

Wyatt takes the seat next to me, my mother and father at the heads of the table. Hunter is in a high chair to my left. My father is next to him, trying to feed him scrambled eggs, but Hunter plays with more of his food than he actually eats.

"So Wyatt, where is your family for Christmas this year?" I eye my mom with a serious expression. I feel Wyatt's grip tighten on my leg when he speaks.

"My two best friends are actually the only family I have left," he says. "My family passed when I was young, and my grandparents raised me. They passed almost seven years ago now."

The conversation at the table stills.

"Oh, honey. I'm very sorry to hear that. We are very glad to have you with us here, then."

"Thank you for having me." He releases a breath, taking another bite of his food.

"Why the Yellow Jackets?" my brother blurts. I shoot him a death glare, and Wyatt laughs.

"It's okay, Dakota," he says. "I expected this. I had a choice between three teams during the draft, and I chose the Riders. I'm not going to pretend that I don't know that y'all keep up with hockey, so you must know that my two best friends play for the Yellow Jackets." My brother and father nod in response.

"When I got word of the trade, I saw the upside to leaving my team. I was losing my team but gaining a new one, my two best friends, my niece, and now Dakota. The pros outweighed the cons." He speaks so eloquently and with confidence that my chest tightens with pride. I watch him with a smile on my face as he talks. When I look away, I see my mother watching me. She smiles sweetly, then turns back to the guys.

They continue grilling Wyatt for the remainder of breakfast.

GOAL *Suck*

When we finish, my mother cleans while we set up for the games.

"I don't claim anything that is said after this moment." I wink at Wyatt and sit across from him in the living room. He smirks at me, and I can't wait to wipe that smirk off his pretty face. My father deals the cards to each player, and I grin.

"We're going to start easy with *Bull shit*."

"Mom's a cheater. Watch for her." Dallas punches Wyatt in the arm. "Good luck."

After four rounds of *Bull shit*, we moved on to a trivia game. We've split into teams, girls against boys, and it's getting increasingly violent.

My father's standing, his voice raised as he claims bull shit for the answer my mother just gave.

"It's correct," I say. "She's not wrong."

"She is not. It's a technicality," he seethes. I hold back my laugh.

"Sit down, Dad," I say. "She's right. It was someone pretending to be someone else, so her answer is correct because she said the person who it actually was. We don't actually meet the real him until the end of that book." My dad groans, rubbing his hands over his face.

"I hate this fucking game." He pouts in his chair, and we all laugh.

Looking out the window, I see the sun disappearing in the distance. I hadn't realized that we'd been playing games for so long. Thankfully, there weren't any fights this time.

My mother picks up the cards and shoves them back into their box.

"Go get dressed, everyone. We're going to the Calcalcade before presents." She shoos everyone from the living room. "It's cold out there, so dress warm."

"We will, Mom," Dallas grumbles, and I laugh.

"I see where you get your competitive nature from," Wyatt says from my side.

"It's a sickness." I take his hand as we walk down the stairs. "Thank you for being here."

"I can't imagine being anywhere else."

The moment that Wyatt steps onto the ice, his face changes, softening and smoothing. It's what I imagine pure bliss to look like.

It's still early, and there aren't too many people on the ice like there normally would be. Wyatt runs across the ice and shaves to a stop on the other end. Several people gasp, and I just shake my head.

Looking down, I see Dallas holding both of Hunter's hands as his little feet struggle to balance on the ice with his little sneakers. Wyatt skates across to us, then literally lays down on his chest and slides toward Hunter.

Hunter squeals happily when Wyatt comes to a stop in front of him.

"You're going to get us kicked out," I say, shaking my head.

"No, I won't." He wrinkles his nose at me, and I laugh.

So cocky.

The music starts playing, and several couples make their way onto the ice to dance. My father leads my mom out, and I watch them. My father still looks at her like she's the most beautiful thing he's ever seen. It warms my heart.

We watch from the sidelines until Wyatt extends his hand to me. I look at it for a moment before taking it. When we skate into the center of the rink, he watches me the whole time.

It's quite hard to dance on the ice. I'm not a terrible skater by any means, but something about the slow movements make me unsteady.

GOAL Suck

Wyatt notices, and he steadies me with his arms.

He spins me around a couple of times, and I feel the world disappear around us when his eyes meet mine.

"There's something magical about Christmas," he says. He slips a hand under my chin as he lowers his lips to mine. Under normal circumstances I would shy away from public displays of affection…but these aren't normal circumstances.

Nothing about this is normal. Everything about Wyatt is scary, new, and fascinating. Not only am I learning how to love another person again, but it's weird to admit that I'm learning to love myself again.

He pulls away and looks at me. He doesn't need to speak for me to understand the look on his face. It's one of gratitude and affection. Maybe I was lonely and struggling, but he was too.

He needed me too.

CHAPTER 29
Wyatt

Dakota's in the kitchen with Hunter and Casey. I've been watching her play with them for a while now from the living room.

We'd opened presents this morning, and I was shocked to find that I, too, had presents under the tree.

Afterwards, Gray and Dallas invited me to play cards with them. I have to admit that I've checked out of the game in front of me.

"Wyatt, would you be able to help me with something?" Everly peeks her head from the top of the staircase, and I nod.

Bounding up the stairs I walk into the office where Everly is seated, some decorations piled around her. She waves me over when I stare down at all the empty boxes and knickknacks.

"Please, sit. I wanted a moment to talk with you away from everyone else." She smiles at me sweetly, but a beat of wariness runs through me.

I sit across from her, my legs bending awkwardly in the tiny chair. She shuffles around some of the boxes before she looks at me again.

"I understand that you're leaving us tomorrow?"

"I am. We're playing in Boston tomorrow evening."

"Well, I will definitely be sad to see you go. I've really enjoyed having you here. I think Gray has as well." I blink at her several times, and she laughs. "Not what you expected?"

"No," I say, shaking my head. "Honestly, I'd expected more questions."

"I do have some, but I'll refrain for now. You got enough on Christmas Eve, I'm sure."

"I don't mind." I cross my legs over to get more comfortable in the chair.

"She looks at you differently," she says. "I've never seen my daughter like this. I'm just really glad to have her home, but seeing the two of you together has been an added bonus." She leans forward and places her hand onto my knee. "I wanted to make sure to tell you before you leave that you are always welcome here. It's never good to be alone during the holidays, and we've quite enjoyed your presence. I hope our competitive natures haven't scared you away." She winks at me, and I laugh into my fist.

"I appreciate it," I say. "And no. Dakota is competitive on her own, so I'd expected something."

"I also wanted to tell you that Dakota's ex has been making a spectacle here. He's always been a sweet"—I cringe when she says the word sweet, my jaw clenching—"boy, but lately, he's been different. They have conflicting stories, so no one really knows the truth of what happened between them." She watches me, her head tiling as she does it. "Judging by your reaction, you know more than I do."

"It's not my story to tell," I say, trying to keep my voice light. She nods slowly, her eyes squinted as she observes me.

"I guess it's not," she says, her voice low.

"I'll see you when I get home," Dakota says, her arms wrapped tightly around me. I kiss her, hard, and release her before I have to rush off into the airport.

It's a mad rush the whole way home. The moment the plane lands, I practically run to my car and drive like a bat out of hell to my condo to change for the game.

I walk through the doors of the rink at exactly four-thirty, my maroon suit crisp and without a wrinkle.

"How was your holiday?" I ask when I stand beside Damian. He's got his hair slicked back, a green snakeskin suit complimenting his ginger beard nicely.

"Boring. My family's in Ireland right now, so I just stayed home. The bunnies were nice, though." He raises his eyebrows at me, and I frown.

"Do you ever want to settle down?"

"Why would I? My lifestyle is a little difficult for that."

"Dakota and I make it work," I say, gripping my duffle tighter.

"She's amazing, though, man. The girls I attract aren't like that."

"They could be," I say. He begins to protest again, telling me all the reasons why he can't be in a relationship and why his lifestyle doesn't lend to romance, but Coach Hart walks into the locker room, silencing us.

He runs through his routine that's now familiar to me. Before I know it, we're on the ice celebrating a win that brings us one step closer to the finals.

CHAPTER 30
Dakota

Adjusting my outfit in the mirror, I clasp my necklace and smooth out my top. Sterling appears in the mirror beside me, our outfits coordinating. She's wearing a red power suit, while I am wearing my staple black leather pants and a red-off-the-shoulder top.

We're both wearing gold accents which tie everything together.

"Are you ready to party?" She wiggles, doing a little dance. I laugh, doing a quick spin and grabbing my jacket from the back of the chair.

"You kids have fun," my mother says from the couch. Hunter is asleep in her arms, and I stop to place a kiss on the top of his head.

Dallas pulls the car to the front of the house, allowing Casey to slide into the passenger seat and Sterling and me into the back.

We drive through darkening streets of Toronto until we pull into the parking structure of the club we're visiting.

The sounds of heels clicking on the pavement distract me from the musky smell of the bar. There are so many people here already, several groups crowded around the TV to watch the New Years Eve festivities.

I stop at the bar to grab a soda and bring it to the table where the others are seated.

When I slide into the booth, my brother looks down at his phone several times, glancing between it and the door. I don't think anything of it as I talk with Casey. She tells me about the changes in her job and how quickly Hunter is growing up.

The bar grows louder, the crowd increasing the later it gets. At eleven thirty, I look at my phone to text Wyatt back. He's sent me updates of their win, and I'm beyond excited for them.

> Me: Wish you were here.
> Wyatt: Me too. I'll have to call in my New Year's kiss when you come home tomorrow.
> Me: I'm counting on it.

I look up from my phone when I hear a group of girls screaming. When I see who caused the disturbance, I feel the air in the club drop several degrees. My throat closes when I try to swallow around the rapidly forming lump.

"I want to puke," I say to Sterling, my heart beating quickly. "I want to leave."

He walks through the crowd, many people stopping to speak to him, but he's spotted me. Dallas waves from beside me, and I glare.

"You did this?" I ask, my jaw clenching and my hands shaking. I look at Casey, and she gives me a panicked expression.

"Yeah," he says. "He's my friend." He shrugs, his gaze returning to Tanner.

"God, I can't believe you. If you paid attention for one second, you would know that that man is not your friend." I almost yell it, but I keep my voice calm.

"Don't be a brat, Dakota. That man was only ever nice to you."

I feel my body shake with anger. I glare at him with every bit of disgust I can muster.

"You're a fucking idiot," Sterling says. I look at her, and she holds her hand up. "I won't say anything. I promise." She turns back to Dallas. "Even if he is your friend, it's common fucking courtesy not to invite someone's ex and ambush your little sister."

Dallas looks between us, his eyebrows drawing together. "I don't understand, Dakota. Why are you allowed to have a best friend like Sterling, but I can't? *You* were my best friend, and then you left. Tanner was the closest thing I had."

There's a tightness in my throat now as I register his words. Tanner has always been around, but I didn't know that they had gotten this close. A twinge of guilt rushes through me. I shouldn't be feeling guilty right now. My *brother*, the one safe person in my family, invited my ex to fucking New Year's Eve. This is exactly why they don't know. Tanner has weaved his way so deeply into my family that I can't escape him.

I feel my palms clam up as I search the room for an escape route. Dallas' hand rests on my shoulder, his eyes searching mine. He's a good brother, but sometimes he's really stupid. I squeeze my eyes shut right as he speaks.

"He just wants to talk to you," he says, his voice rough.

"*I* don't want to talk to him. Nothing he could say would ever fix anything he did to me, Dallas. *Nothing.* Not to mention, I'm with Wyatt now, and this is just disgusting." I feel the anger rise up. I don't want to be angry at Dallas, he doesn't know, but I can't help the growing pit of dread in my stomach.

Tanner walks closer, his eyes lighting up when he stops in front of our table.

"Long time no see, baby." He pulls out the chair across the table, and I flinch back. Sterling holds my arm, her body shifting into a defensive position.

"Why are you here?"

"Awe, baby. Don't be like that." His snake-like grin spreads across his face, and I want to gag. He lifts his hand to take the cup from my hand, and it takes everything in me not to flinch again. His fingers brush mine when he takes the glass from me and brings it to his lips. Sterling narrows her eyes at him, anger rolling off her.

"I'd like to leave," I say. I try to stand, but Tanner licks his lips, standing to his full height again. He's big; not as big as Wyatt, but bulkier. Suddenly, I wish that Wyatt was here. I can feel myself breaking inside, but I hold everything inside.

YOU are strong, Dakota.

"I just want to talk. The two of us."

"You're not going *anywhere* alone with her, Tanner." Silver grabs my hand. "Let's go. I'll call us an Uber."

"Why?" I ask him.

"I'm going to be seeing that new boy toy of yours soon. Just wanted to warn him to be careful." He smirks, and I feel my blood boil, the corners of my vision blurring.

"You don't touch him," I say, my voice low and vicious. I step around the table, looking up at him. "I could ruin your life and your career, Tanner. Don't you fucking dare."

"Dakota!" Dallas shouts. "What the fuck?"

"Is that a threat?" He clenches his fists, and for the first time, I don't back away. I look him dead in the face when I speak.

"It's a promise." I look at Sterling, then Dallas. "Let's go. And you"—I point at him—"I don't want to speak to you right now." My eyes grow watery as tears threaten to spill over. "I trusted you to protect me, and right now, I feel very blindsided. You're supposed to be my brother, but you chose *him*." My voice cracks. Dallas looks at me with a pained expression. He looks between Sterling and I, his pained expression shifting back to confusion.

I shake my head.

Sterling ushers me through the bar and out the front door. When the cool air hits my face, I feel the sting of hot tears. There's fresh snow on the ground, and I couldn't care less.

My body shakes when we climb into the back of the Uber. "I want to go home," I say, my voice weak.

I cry on Sterling's shoulder the whole ride home. She runs her fingers through my hair while I sob. When I walk up to my parent's home, I walk inside expecting them to be asleep, but instead my father is seated on the plush chair with Hunter in his arms.

"Your brother called me," he says. "He's very concerned about you. Says you went crazy on Tanner at the bar. What happened?"

I stare at him with a blank expression. "He says I went crazy?" I say, my voice low. It hurts me that this is Dallas' opinion of me. Dallas is supposed to be *safe*.

Looking up at my father, I try to steady my voice as I speak. "Did he tell you what he did to me? That he invited Tanner and didn't tell me? It was practically an ambush."

"They're friends, Dakota. Tanner is a good kid."

I scoff, shaking my head. I can't deal with this right now. It had felt like this trip could have been the time to come clean, to tell them of my pain and struggle with Tanner, but now…I can't burden them with this pain. I can't ruin their perfect image of him. "I'm going home," I say. "Mom said you're coming to watch Tanner play Boston. I'll see you both then, but I can't deal with this right now."

My father gapes at me. I've never stood my ground with him. I've never talked back, and I've always tried to be the perfect daughter. I'm so over it. My whole family has chosen my abuser over me, and I don't have it in me to tell them that. I'd rather remove myself than try to prove what they'll never believe.

I'm their daughter, for Chrissake. Shouldn't they trust me? I feel myself numbing, my emotions shutting off until I can get away from here.

"What's going on?" my mother asks from the top of the stairs.

"I'm leaving, Ma. Sterling and I are going home."

"Oh honey…did something happen?"

"It's nothing. It's not worth talking about." I run up the stairs and kiss her on the cheek. "I love you. I'll see you in Boston." When I pull away, her eyes look sad until she turns to my father and glares. Once again, he gapes and I *almost* laugh. Almost.

I pack quickly, hauling my suitcase up the stairs and out the front door. I make sure to hug my dad on the way out, albeit hesitantly, and kiss Hunter on the head.

We stop at Sterling's hotel and grab her suitcase before we're dropped at the airport curb.

"I'll go check us in. How about you call Wyatt?" Sterling squeezes my shoulder before she disappears into the airport.

My hands shake around the phone, my thumb barely grazing the call button. When I put the phone to my ear, I don't expect him to answer.

When the ringing stops, I think that it's going to voicemail until his groggy voice caresses my ear. I choke around a sob.

"Dakota?" His voice is husky and deep and safe.

"I'm coming home," I say through my tears.

"What happened?" He's more alert now, a note of panic in his voice.

"My brother invited Tanner." I barely get the sentence out before I sob again. There's silence on the other end of the line for a while.

"What did he say?" he finally asks, his voice low and angry.

"He threatened you. Said to be careful."

Wyatt laughs a bitter laugh.

"I told him not to touch you and that I could ruin his career. I'm pretty sure my brother hates me and my father is angry. I just want to go home."

"I'll pick you up. When are you coming in?"

"Three," I say.

"I'll be there."

Hanging up the phone, I step inside, finding Sterling seated near the check-in. Once we make it through security, we sit on the ground near the window.

Sterling cleans up my face and grabs us some snacks, which we both devour.

"I don't deserve you," I say, laying my head on her shoulder.

"Yes, you do. I don't deserve you."

"I love you," I say. "Thank you for coming with me."

"Always. I'll always be here for you. What Dallas did was a really dick move."

I nod my head in agreement. "It was."

We sit like that until we're called to board the plane. When we sit in our seats, buckled and secure, Sterling looks over at me, her lip pulled into her mouth.

"I need to tell you something, but you can't be mad at me."

My eyes widen when I look at her. "Okay?"

"IsleptwithJaiden," she says, her voice muffled by her hand.

"You did what?"

She sighs, her eyes closing.

"IsleptwithJaidenafterThanksgiving."

I laugh quietly when her face goes red. "One more time?"

"Dakota," she hisses. I shrug. "I slept with Jaiden after Thanksgiving. There? You happy?"

"Very," I say. "But why would I be mad?"

"I don't know. Maybe because he's your boyfriend's best friend, and if anything happens between us, it could mess with the dynamic we have going." She shakes her head, looking down. I start to speak when the announcement for take off runs through the speakers. She holds my hand as the plane rushes down the runway and lifts into the air.

"If anything happens, we'll figure it out together," I say finally. She looks at me, and even in the darkened plane, I can see the gratitude on her face.

"So was it good?" I ask, smiling honestly for the first time since we boarded the plane.

She sighs. "So good. I've slept with my fair share of men, but I think I really like him."

I turn to look at her, seeing the way her hand runs over the seatbelt at her waist. My usually aggressively confident friend looks at me with a level of vulnerability.

"He makes me want to lay real roots down. Is that crazy? We're not even really together."

"Not at all. I'm practically living with Wyatt after only a few months. Time is relative, babe. Trust your gut and heart."

"And this is why I love you," she says. Sterling has always been my constant and my bonus sibling.

She lays her head on my shoulder, her eyes closing until her breathing evens. Laying my head back, I let myself succumb to the exhaustion I feel. It isn't until the plane lands in Boston that we stir.

CHAPTER 31
Wyatt

I brought both Sterling and Dakota back to my condo after picking them up from the airport.

Sterling is passed out on the couch, while Dakota is still wrapped in blankets in my bed.

Our bed?

Making as little noise as possible, I sneak out the front door, returning only when I have coffee and donuts for the three of us.

When I walk through the door again, Sterling is seated at the table, her laptop open in front of her. Dakota is nowhere to be seen, but when I hear the water running in the bathroom, I know she's in the shower.

"I got coffee and donuts." I hand Sterling a coffee and open the box of donuts on the table. She takes one and places it onto a napkin.

"Thank you. You're the best." She takes a bite and hums happily.

"Can I ask you what happened? She told me some of it, but I'm wondering whether I need to go beat someone's ass." I pull out the chair at the head of the table and slide into it. She sighs, holding her coffee in her hands.

"Dallas invited Tanner. I honestly think he's just naive and very unobservant. I don't know what he was thinking, but I guess Tanner had been bugging him to talk to Dakota. When he walked in, Dakota panicked, and Tanner, like always, asserted dominance." She rubs her fingers over the cup holder. "Dakota had been itching to run until he threatened you, then she threatened him back. Honestly, it was amazing, but then she told her brother that she didn't want to talk to him for a while, and we ran out of there like our butts were on fire."

"Do you know why she won't tell them?" I look at the wall past Sterling.

She sighs, shrugging.

"I think that she worries that they won't believe her. Tanner is a manipulator. I've only seen glimpses of his behavior, but even then, he's so good at putting up this front."

"I haven't even met him, and I hate him with a passion." I sip my coffee when Dakota walks out into the living room, her hair hanging at her side as she squeezes it with a towel.

"Oh! Donuts." She takes one from the box and kisses me. "Thank you."

"Anything for you," I say. Sterling gags, then laughs.

Dakota adjusts my tie, patting my collar and placing a gentle kiss on my lips.

It's been a couple of weeks since she came home from Toronto, and she's still not fully back to normal. I've seen her retreat slightly, her nerves increasing as time passes.

Toronto is coming here on Valentine's Day. That's still two weeks away, but I feel the same tension she does. Part of me wants to meet this motherfucker, and a part of me hopes I'm benched the entire game so that I don't destroy my career.

I don't fear for myself, and I don't fear for my friends. I fear more for Dakota and what this is doing to her.

We got word this morning that Dallas is coming, against Dakota's wishes. Mr. Easton wouldn't take no for an answer, which is a common theme in their family. I know it's eating her up inside, and I'd do anything to make this pain go away, to ease her mind.

"I'll see you there?" I lift her chin to me, pressing my lips to hers, my tongue swiping against her lips. She moans when I bite lightly, her hand gripping my suit jacket. When I pull away, her lips are swollen and her eyes are hazy.

"Yes. I'll be there." She touches her lips lightly, her cheeks red.

When I turn to walk out the door, Dakota slaps my butt, and I chuckle. "What?" she asks. "I saw an opportunity and I took it."

My mind mulls over her words. Is this an opportunity to tell her, to express the feelings that I've had from the beginning?

I've been telling her without words from the moment we met. Every time I kiss her, or fuck her in *our* bed, I tell her, over and over again. But maybe it's time to use words.

I smile at her, kissing her one last time before I walk out the door.

When I make my way out onto the ice, I skate along the glass until I see Sterling and Dakota. Dakota stands, walking up to the glass and winking at me. Her eyes are gleaming, and I can't believe how lucky I am.

I wait a moment for her to do her thing. It's a thing we started a couple of weeks ago. It's a part of my routine, the little bit of extra luck I need before each game.

She extends her hands out to me, her fist resting on her open palm. I do the same with my gloved hands.

"On three," she says with a smile so radiant that it nearly knocks me off my feet.

I nod.

"One...two...three." She shows scissors and I show rock. Her nose wrinkles, and I laugh.

"Best two out of three," she says quickly. The people around her laugh when I beat her again. She blows me a kiss, and I catch it before I skate out toward center ice.

"Is Sterling here?" Jaiden skates to my side.

"Yeah. Why?"

"Dunno." He pulls his helmet off, shaking out his curly hair and then putting the helmet back on. I look at him sideways, but he doesn't give anything away.

We size up our opponents when they skate out onto the ice. A player I recognize taunts me, and I ignore him. I'm saving my aggression for one person. All of that pent up rage is going to him. I won't waste it now.

The puck drops, and I see Jaiden rush forward. A player moves toward our center and I block them. Jaiden passes the puck and I pass it on until the center has the puck again. Someone rushes toward me, and I spin out of their way.

Cheers ring around us when we score our first goal, then our second. By the time the clock runs out, we've scored a third. Jaiden slides across the ice on his knees. I run onto the ice from the bench, joining the dogpile on the ice.

It feels incredible to win. Each and every time, there is a special feeling that comes with this experience.

The best part about winning is when I get to look over and see the pure pride on Dakota's face. She's not only competitive for herself, but for me too. Sometimes I can make out her yells when I skate by, and it kills me each time.

To think that a couple months ago, that woman wouldn't step foot in a stadium.

Like always, I run through the motions of interviews and postgame workout. My mind is elsewhere. I rush out of the building, my body aching and sore.

Dakota left after the game to drop Sterling off at Lani's place, but for some reason, I don't believe that she'll be at Lani's for long.

I race my own beating heart home, my tie already loosened and shirt unbuttoned. My feet carry me through the front doors and up the stairs to my condo.

When I unlock the door, I find a pair of panties left on the floor. I feel my cock tighten as I bend to pick them up.

I prowl to the bedroom, following the trail left for me.

My breath leaves me when I see Dakota laying on the bed with only my jersey on.

"You know, this is a personal fantasy of mine."

"Well, then, let's make it come true," she says, her voice smooth and filled with promise.

"Yes," I say, ripping my tie from my neck and undoing the button on my pants. "Let's."

CHAPTER 32
Dakota

"Where are you taking me?" I ask while I slip on my heels and a thick overcoat.

"It's a surprise." I feel him behind me, his hands roaming over my body in the way that makes me squirm. "We'll be late. Let's go."

I follow him out to the car, Wyatt opening and closing my door for me. We drive through the city until we pull up to the public library.

He slips his warm hand in mine, heating my cold fingers. The front doors open for us as we walk through the nearly empty library.

I look in awe at the beautiful interior of the library: the incredible portraits on the walls, the architecture, the pillars, and the massive staircases. It's stunning, something that would make any bookworm feel like they're stepping into the scene of their favorite novel.

I almost slip on the marble flooring when we leave the library for the garden. There's a table set in the middle.

I nearly gasp as I see the beautiful setup. My heart thrums in my chest, my eyes threatening to water.

Wyatt pulls my chair from the table, then sits across from me. The heaters leave the air around us feeling warm against the chilly Boston air. It was snowing earlier this week, but somehow the weather had cooperated for Wyatt's special plans.

"Happy early Valentine's Day, love."

I watch him, my smile growing as he stares back. I can't believe that I'm sitting here, across from the most beautiful man I've ever seen.

The waiter comes and goes, bringing drinks and appetizers.

"How did you do this?" I ask, my mouth watering at the sight of the pasta in front of me.

"The manager of this place is a hockey fan," he says with a smirk. "That certainly helped."

"I don't doubt it." I laugh, swirling the pasta on my fork. It smells divine, like roasted tomatoes and cheese. I bend down to sniff, moaning around the bite currently in my mouth. "I fucking love pasta."

Wyatt laughs, taking a sip of his drink. We continue eating, the conversation flowing smoothly until I see Wyatt tense slightly.

"Toronto is coming in tomorrow." His jaw tenses, and I can see the worry cross his face. "Considering your last confrontation, I wanted to see how you're feeling."

"I'm okay. I'm not great, but I'm okay. I'm more nervous for my family tomorrow. The way I left wasn't great."

"You did what you needed to do, Dakota."

"I did, but I've never done anything like that before. I can defend Silver no problem, but myself?" I almost choke over the words. "I can barely say no to my family, and now I'll have to face Dallas…" I hold my napkin tight to my chest.

"You're still hurt," he says. "You've been through so much." His eyebrows press together, his head tilting. "Can I ask why you haven't told them? You said you didn't want to ruin their opinions of Tanner, but is there something else?"

I sigh, laying the napkin on the table. "Just like I made a blanket statement with hockey players, I chose the safe route for myself. Dallas has always thought I was dramatic, and my father often agrees with him." I press my nails into the pads of my fingers to keep the tears from falling. "I really didn't want to drop proof at their feet for them to believe me. I didn't, and sometimes I still don't, have the mental capacity to deal with it."

Wyatt stands and walks around the table to my side. He lifts the leg of his pants a little while he crouches at my side. My face drops when I see the look he's giving me. It's so full of trust and faith that I nearly break.

"I promised you that I would be by your side when you're ready, and I mean that. Even when it comes to your family. I don't want to pressure you, but I think you should think about telling them. Even if it's the bare minimum." He swallows, his hand resting on my legs. "He's an abuser, and he doesn't deserve the friendship of your family."

My eyes bounce between his, my lips pressing into a pout as another tactic to dissuade myself from crying. I don't think I can speak at the moment, so I nod. It's not an agreement, but a promise to *think* about it.

I may not be done hiding, but that doesn't mean I can't try.

The sound of a loud knock on the door sends me flying out of my seat.

I walk through the space between the couch and the love seat, the smell of Mexican food filling up the rather luxurious space of Wyatt's condo.

Wyatt is at the stove cooking the last of the beef for the tacos. He pulls out the pork from the oven right as I open the front door.

My mother is the first one I see, her graying blonde hair pulled back into a short ponytail. She smiles at me, pulling me into her arms.

"Hi, sweetie. I missed you." I breathe her in, missing her apple and cinnamon scent that reminds me so much of apple pie. Releasing me, she walks through the door to greet Wyatt.

My father hugs me, placing a kiss on the top of my head. He smells of cigars and citrus. "We missed you, love. Even your brother."

Said brother is standing awkwardly behind us. He looks at me with apprehension. My father bops my brother on the head when he doesn't immediately move, and I laugh.

Dallas' face relaxes significantly, extending his arms to me before I concede and step into his embrace.

"Yep. Missed you so much." Dallas' voice grumbles against my ear. I can hear the lightness in his tone.

I shake my head in his chest, but I can't help the little snort that slips out.

When I close the door behind them, I see my mother is helping Wyatt move food to the table.

"I hope y'all like tacos." Wyatt sets out the guacamole and salsa next to the bowl of chips. I smile at him, mouthing a *thank you*.

"We love tacos," my father says, shoving a chip full of guac into his mouth.

I slide into the seat next to Wyatt. He scoops some meat onto his tacos, then folds it before he takes a bite. I follow suit, humming through my bite. I do a little happy dance and take another.

"Almost as good as the ones we had in Raleigh," I say with a wink.

"I'll take it," he says.

"These are fantastic. Thank you both for having us for dinner." My mother rubs her hands together, her eyes smiling.

"So, Wyatt, I heard your team is top in the division currently. It's looking good for you right now." My father looks at Wyatt, his napkin pressed lightly to his face.

"We are. I don't want to get too hopeful, but I think we have a shot this year."

"The boys here are rooting for Toronto, but I'll be cheering for you. The fans will probably be brutal tomorrow." Mom reaches across the table to scoop out some guacamole. I see Dallas smirk, and my face falls.

"You'll have to see Wyatt and Damian together. They're terrifying." I glare across the table at Dallas. "Toronto's got some all-star players too, but I don't think they stand a chance against the guys." It's meant to be a joke, a small tease, but I worry that it comes across as anything but.

Dallas ignores me. "Are you getting ice time tomorrow?"

"I hope so. There's going to be some amazing faces out on the ice tomorrow. I'll be honored to share the ice with them."

"You'll be on the ice with my best friend Tanner, then. He's a highly respected player."

Wyatt stills, his taco halfway to his face. He looks over at me, and I glare in Dallas' direction. Out of the corner of my eye, I see my mother tense.

Wyatt's face drops, his taco forgotten in his hand. He looks directly at Dallas, his face more serious than I've seen it before.

"Tanner needs to earn *my* respect."

Dallas blinks several times, his head shaking. "What is that supposed to mean?

"Dakota is my priority, and I respect her too much to answer the question truthfully." Wyatt stands, taking his plate to the sink and pulling out the ice cream. "Dakota, will you help me with the dessert?"

I blink several times before I stand.

The table is quiet when I leave it, but the moment I walk into the kitchen, I hear my mother hiss in my brother's direction.

"What is wrong with you?" she says, her voice low. I clench my jaw waiting for his answer, but it never comes.

I relax when Wyatt walks to my back, running a soothing touch down my arm before sliding me aside to grab the churros from the oven. I visibly relax, reminding myself that I'm safe.

For now.

After dessert, we split across the condo, relaxing in different areas. Wyatt sits with my mom at the table, the two of them talking animatedly. I smile as I watch them.

The couch dips beside me, and I look over to see Dallas pulling a pillow from behind his back before he relaxes beside me.

"So…Wyatt really snapped at me, huh?" He nudges my arm, his eyes full of amusement. "I hope he doesn't talk to you like that."

I scoff, turning to face him fully. "Yeah, no. You were asking for it. And not like it matters to *you*, but Wyatt is the most respectful man I have ever met. He was protecting me, unlike *you*." I nudge him in the side, and he scowls.

"I still don't understand. I get that it wasn't the *best* thing ever to invite Tanner…"

"It sucked, Dallas," I interrupt.

"Okay, it was a shitty thing to do, but he's not a bad dude,

Dakota. He's only ever been kind to me. He might be a cocky bastard sometimes, but I think you're judging him too harshly."

I feel my body and face growing warm. I want to tell him *so* badly, but every time I try to will the words to come, they don't.

I settle for a noncommittal shrug. It feels like the safest option for now. Dallas doesn't need to be burdened with this.

Needing a moment to myself, I rise from the couch, walking into the bedroom and clicking the door closed behind me.

I ignore the second click of the door, assuming that it's Wyatt coming to check on me. I'm surprised to see my mother standing there when I turn.

She sits on the bed, her eyes wandering around the room.

"You're living here now?" It's not quite a question, but I nod anyway.

"I got word that my apartment is ready for me to move into again, but I like being here."

"He's a good man," she says. "He looks at you with this intensity. It's…new and different."

I press my eyebrows together when I stare down at her seated on the bed.

"He's incredible, and I don't deserve him."

"Oh baby. You do. What has ever led you to believe that you don't deserve someone like him?"

I bite my lip. This is an opportunity…I could take it.

"My own insecurities," I lie.

She sighs. "Well, I just wanted to say my goodbyes. I can tell you're socially drained," she says with a smile. "We'll leave you and Wyatt to rest for the evening. I'll see you tomorrow, my love." She gives my hand a firm squeeze, then the door clicks shut behind her.

I feel the tears fall then, the hot liquid streaming down my cheeks.

I'm so afraid of tomorrow, of what it will bring.

Maybe it will surprise me, but maybe all of my fears will come true. It's that possibility that has me crouched on the floor as tears stream down my face.

Strong arms wrap around me, holding me tight as I cry. I hadn't even heard him come in, but I'm thankful for his presence now. He lets me cry into his chest, and for the first time, I let it all free, the pain, the insecurities, and the fear that I've held captive for so long.

I cry until my eyes are heavy. Not once does Wyatt leave my side, not even when my phone rings several times. We ignore it, my heart heavy as I slip into sleep.

CHAPTER 33
Dakota

Walking into the area feels different tonight. Silver's not at my side like usual; instead, my mother walks close to me, her eyes wandering.

The amount of blue I see worries me. They're in our town, yet it feels like the Thunders have an overwhelming amount of support.

I follow the security guard down to our usual seats by the glass. My palms are sweaty when I sit down. I wish I could say that the worry from earlier has eased, but instead it's settled low into my belly, creeping into my chest and throat.

Dallas walks down the steps and sits between my parents, his hands full with snacks and drinks. I'm watching the big screen when Dallas nudges my arm.

"I got you your favorite." I look down at the popcorn. It's got colorful M&Ms in it, and I give him a wary smile.

"Thanks," I say, taking it from his hands and shoving a few pieces into my mouth.

The screen runs through a myriad of funny tweets and little jabs at the Thunders. Before I know it, the players are skating out onto the ice. My heart jumps when Wyatt stops by the glass. He winks at me, his hands raised for rock, paper, scissors.

We go once, and I win with paper covering rock. I waggle my eyebrows at him, and he shakes his head at me. The second time he beats me, crushing my scissors, and the last time, he wins again with paper covering rock. He puts his hand up against the glass, his eyes wary.

I give him the best smile I can muster, but I know he'll see through it.

When he skates away from the glass, my father speaks.

"Little ritual of yours?"

"Yeah. We're competitive, so we kind of made a game out of it."

"That's cute," my mother says.

Yeah. It is.

The players skate around several times, not crossing the red line before the whistle blows. I see Roman and Jaiden skate by, Jaiden fist-pumping along to the music.

I swallow when the players line up at the red line. I don't see Tanner on the ice, which allows my breath to flow more easily.

The first round goes well, Toronto scoring the first point, then Boston scoring almost immediately after.

The players switch out, and I finally get my first glimpse of Tanner. He plays dirty, making some nasty hits and charging at players.

I find myself yelling with the fans around us when Jaiden goes down after scoring a point.

GOAL Suck

My heart pounds when Wyatt skates onto the ice for the third period. I see Tanner's defensive position, and my eyes narrow on the two of them.

The whistle blows and Tanner charges at Wyatt, but Wyatt moves, skating alongside Damian and protecting the puck.

My eyes trail him with an intensity. Roman passes the puck to Damian, who passes it to Wyatt for a setup I recognize. Wyatt skates alongside the glass, the puck ready to be passed across for the center to make a hit toward the net.

The same moment that Wyatt is slammed into the glass, I feel my stomach drop. Tanner skates in the opposite direction when Wyatt hits the ice. Toronto gets the puck, moving it across the ice.

"Get up, Wyatt," I scream. "Get up!"

He does.

He runs across the ice, and I release a breath when Roman moves beside him. He pats him on the shoulder, and I see Wyatt nodding.

Time ticks by, the score tied. My body is wound so tightly that I can barely sit still.

When Wyatt gets the puck again, Tanner goes for him, but Wyatt must see him coming.

Roman hits Tanner from behind, taking the puck and moving it toward the net.

I hear a growl and see everything happen in slow motion. Tanner throws a punch without removing his gloves or dropping his stick.

When Wyatt moves, it only angers Tanner more. Wyatt tosses his stick to the side and lands a punch on Tanner's face through his helmet. It looks like they're speaking, and I wish I knew what was being said.

Tanner fights back, his free arm aiming for punches as he spits angry words back at Wyatt.

I scream as the scene unfolds. Tanner grips the end of his stick, lifting it and hitting Wyatt square in the face.

I stand quickly, the refs skating across the ice to separate them. Damian throws a punch toward Tanner, and the refs move him too.

I can't breathe. I see blood on the ice, but I can't see Wyatt. My father stands, his mouth hanging open.

"Holy shit," my brother says.

"That is *your* friend" I say, my voice angry. "The one you think I'm judging too harshly."

There's more blood as Wyatt is escorted off the ice. I feel my throat closing up and my eyes watering.

"I need to see him," I say, standing. "I need to go." I can't breathe, my mind panicking.

"Why would he do that?" my mother asks, her voice quiet. I glare at her, and she raises her hand to point, and I flinch. I *flinch.*

My father freezes, his pupils nearly disappearing when he looks at me. I swallow, my lip quivering.

I can't stop myself as the tears come. "I need to go," I sob. "I need to get out of here." I step back then, my mother protesting, but I don't listen. Running up the stairs and out of the arena, I follow the path to the press area. The security guard tries to stop me until he recognizes me, then waves me through.

I see Jaiden, and my feet carry me to him. "Is he okay?"

"He's okay. I think his nose is broken, but Coach Hart is pissed. They're blaming Wyatt for instigating."

"Are they going to press charges? That's assault, Jaiden. He assaulted him."

I massage my hand, trying to stay calm, but it's not working.

"That's not how it works. It was dirty, but I doubt they'll be able to charge him."

"He needs to be," I say, my eyes pleading. "That man needs to go away. He—" I bend over, sucking in sharp breaths. My knees hit the ground as I gasp. Jaiden's eyes go wide, his muffled voice trying to reach me, but I can't make out any of his words. I look up at him, but I can't speak.

He shakes his head several times, then mimes taking deep breaths. I follow his directions until I can hear his voice again. He steps away, and when he returns, my mother is with him. She sits down on the floor beside me and holds my hands.

"Is there somewhere we can go? I need to speak with my daughter." The security guard nearby nods, ushering us into a back room.

I sit in the chair across the room, my knees pulled into my chest and my head between my legs. My chest heaves, and I try to catch my breath.

"Dakota," she says. I don't move, I just breathe with my eyes closed. "Dakota!" This time I look up at her.

"What?" A quiet knock sounds at the door before my brother and father walk in. My brother looks pale as he stands across the room. I don't even wait for prompting, I just let the words spill out of my mouth.

"He hit me," I say, my voice quivering. "Every day. He hit me when he lost a game, he hit me when I looked at him wrong, he'd leave bruises on my wrists or pinch me when I didn't behave. He told me that my dreams were stupid and that I'd never make it."

I gasp for air, my body tingling with the anxiety rushing through my body. I have to keep talking. I can't stop; if I do, it'll never come out.

"Dakota," Dallas says, taking a step toward me. I shake my head and he stops. I look at him as I speak, finding some comfort in his gaze. This is Dallas. He's safe.

"Tanner. Hit. Me. He's not the man you think he is. He's manipulative, and you all fell for it. You all love him more than me, and you couldn't even see that he was breaking me. He *broke* me." I feel my lungs constrict. I can't breathe, but I have to keep going.

"Dakota, stop." Dallas walks to me, not stopping when I protest. "You need to stop and breathe. Please." His voice sounds desperate, but I don't care.

I shake my head again, gasping as I stand to my feet. "No. I can't," I wheeze.

"I'm so sorry, Dakota. I'm sorry, but you need to breathe," he says, his eyes pleading. "Breathe." Dallas walks to me, putting an arm on my shoulder, but I shove him away from me.

"NO!" I shake my head again, my hands clenched as my sides. "You *don't* understand. I need to say this. I have to say this now because if I don't, there's a chance I'll never speak of it."

He looks so pained, tears streaming down his face as he stands before me, looking so helpless. It's the first time I've seen him like this, like he has no clue what to do.

My ears ring as I rush to get the words out.

"I wanted to tell you. I wanted to tell you so bad, but how could I? He was your friend," I say, feeling the tears stream down my face. "I couldn't put you all through that. You all liked him *so* much and I—I just couldn't tell you."

I finally pull my eyes away from Dallas, chancing a look at my parents. My mom's eyes are misty, her chest rising and falling. When I look at my father, I feel my chest rip open. He won't look at me, his body turned away from me. I *want* him to look at me.

My voice is broken and pained as I trudge on. "I did the only thing I could do; I patched myself up enough to move away. And then you said he was your best friend, and my heart broke. I love you,

Dallas, and I didn't want you to feel like I abandoned you, but I *had* to. I couldn't stay there."

I wheeze again, my chest heaving as I look down at my feet. Words fail me now. I don't know if there are any left to say.

I cry silently until Dallas pulls me into his arms. His grip is tight, his hand resting on the back of my head as I sob into his shoulder.

"I'm *so* sorry," he says, his voice broken. "I didn't know. I failed you as an older brother, and for that, I'm sorry."

"I just wanted you to believe me," I sob.

"I do," he says into my hair. "I do now."

My face scrunches as I cry. I pull my arms to wrap around him, feeling safe in his arms. He lets me cry, my body shocked from the panic.

When I pull away from him, I look at my mom. She's crying, her eyes downcast.

"I can't believe you had to bear this burden alone," she says. "I'm sorry that we weren't there for you. I *knew* something was wrong, but I didn't know that it was this."

"Does Wyatt know?" Dallas asks, and I nod.

"It's not my story to tell," my mother mumbles. "He's a good man," she says, her voice firm.

"What?"

"I asked him if he knew the story, and he told me that it wasn't his story to tell. He was respecting your wishes. He could've told me, but he didn't."

I don't deserve him. While I'm having a heart-to-heart with my family, Wyatt's dream is being compromised because of me. It's my fault that he's in this position.

My mother's soft sobs fill my ears. I see my father walk to her, pressing her into his arms. I watch him comfort her, and it stings.

He hasn't looked at me once, and I'm glad that he's here to comfort my mom, but I want him to be here for *me*. *I* want his hug and his comfort, the kind of comfort only my dad can give.

I stare at the back wall, my spirit sinking in my chest.

"Can we fix this?"

I look up at Dallas. I know that I've slipped into survival mode now; I feel numb, my body weak and exhausted.

"I don't know, but I want to try."

"Will you come home? I want to fix this, Koda. Let me be here for you."

I don't feel confident enough to speak, so I nod. It feels like a good decision until my dad pulls away from my mom, walking through the door without a single word.

CHAPTER 34
Wyatt

Medical released me an hour after the game ended. We won, but I can't bring myself to be happy about it. Instead, I'm worried.

For the first time in a long time, I'd let my head get in the way of the game. I should've seen the hit coming. I should've thrown another punch or pulled away.

I'd thrown some nasty words at him, but he deserved it.

I'd asked him if that's what he'd done to Dakota, if he'd gotten so wound up that he threw punches before thinking. It was easy to wind him up, to get him so angry that he threw a punch. It was easy to lose my mind in the angry haze that I'd built up over the past few days.

I'd thought I was a better man than that. Hockey is violent. It's painful and rough and that's exactly why I love it, but today…today I hated the game. I hated sharing the ice with a bastard who's so sick.

It was personal. When Coach Hart asked what happened, was the only answer I could come up with; surprisingly, he didn't question it.

Walking through the halls, I stop when the sounds of slamming grow louder and more intense.

The locker room should be empty by now, so my body goes into high alert before I step foot into the space.

I'm taken aback by the sight of Gray opening and closing locker doors with the force of a raging bull.

He briefly turns to look at me, his eyes so blown and his face promising damage. It's not a normal sort of rage. This is a father bear ready to destroy anyone in his path.

"Gray," I say as I approach him cautiously.

"Where is he?" His voice is low and feral. I should turn away, but I can't let him leave like this.

"He's not here." I hold my hands up, walking toward him.

"I need to find him."

I shake my head. "You need to be with your family, Gray."

He slams his fist against a locker, the muscles in his jaw clenching. I walk to the locker beside him, closing it lightly. My head throbs, but it doesn't matter to me right now. Dakota needs her father, and he's bound to make a mistake he'll regret.

"Go be with your family, Gray," I say, my voice more firm this time.

He glares at me as I block his way. He goes to shove me, but stumbles back slightly. He blinks several times, his face filled with surprise.

Gray isn't small, but I'm a trained athlete. I'm taller and stronger than him, and that is the only thing that brings me comfort. If need be, I'll stop him from making this mistake.

"Get out of my way, Wyatt," he growls.

GOAL Suck

"No. Go be with your family."

"Who the *fuck* are you to tell me what to do?"

"I'm the man who's in love with your daughter. I know her, and I know that if she's told you, she's going to need her father. Don't make this mistake tonight, Gray."

He looks at me, shock evident on his face. He heaves a sigh, a bit of guilt replacing the shock. I watch him mull over my words, and see the moment he recognizes my declaration of love. I may have missed it if I blinked, but a look of respect crosses his face before he turns away from the lockers.

"Thank you," is all he says before he walks out of the locker room.

My finger brushes the bruises under my eye in the visor mirror. The bluish-purple skin looks angry, but at least my nose is straight.

I've got a tube shoved up my nose to keep the bone in place, and I feel ridiculous with the string peeking out.

Groaning, I shut the mirror and climb out of my car, heading for the condo.

When I open the door to my condo I see a packed suitcase by the front door. My stomach sinks, a sour taste lingering at the back of my throat.

I kick off my shoes and trudge toward the bedroom. Dakota is shoving things into a backpack. Her hair is pulled back into a tight ponytail, her black leggings and loose sweatshirt drawing my attention to her body.

As if she senses me staring, she looks over at me, her eyes growing sad. She walks toward me, her hands coming to my face gently. "I'm so sorry," she says faintly.

"Where are you going?"

She sighs, her shoulders tensing. "Home. I'm going home."

"To your apartment?"

"Canada." She bites her lip, not looking at me. "I told my family everything. I had to."

I reach for her, but she steps back. That small movement is further confirmation of my suspicions. I swallow, my heart burning for her.

"I know," I say. "Are you okay?"

"No. No, I'm not." She bundles her hands into fists and drops them at her sides. "This happened to you because of me."

"That's not true—"

"It is," she interrupts. "Tanner made you a target because of me. You're benched because of me."

"Temporarily," I interject.

"It doesn't matter, Wyatt. Your dream and your career is compromised because of me. He couldn't have just ruined my life, he had to go and try to ruin yours too."

"He's not ruining my life, Dakota. He broke my nose and got me benched. If anything, his consequences will be worse. They should be worse." I suck in a breath, wincing when I feel my nose stretch over the tube.

"They should, but they won't because he's Tanner Morin and he always gets what he wants."

"Does he?" I ask. "Because from where I'm standing, you're giving up. I already know what you're doing, Dakota. Just say it. Say that you're running away." I take a step closer to her, my hands locking behind her waist. "Well, here's the thing, I love you. I've loved you from the moment you debated knocking on the door to Roman's house that first night. You can push me away and do whatever the hell you need to do, but I'll wait for you. I know that look in your eye; it's the look you get when you feel like you don't deserve something. But I have news for you. You deserve *everything*. You deserve kindness, you deserve love, and you sure as hell deserve me. If anyone isn't deserving, it's me."

Dakota stands there, her eyes swimming beneath the sadness. Her eyes close as she releases a breath.

"I just…I need some time," she says. "I need to heal, and I'd like to fix things with my family if it's salvageable. I realized tonight that I'd been slapping band aids on gaping wounds and expecting them to heal."

"Then do it. Fix things, take your time, but come back to me." It wasn't a request, but a command. I need her too and I think she knows that.

Tears slide down her face as she raises up on her toes to kiss my cheek. "Goodbye, Wyatt."

I don't turn when she leaves. I don't look over my shoulder when Dakota walks away, taking my heart with her.

CHAPTER 35
Wyatt

The alcohol burns my throat as it goes down. I grip the glass of my third—fourth?—drink. The bar is crowded, and there's a woman on my right who's been giving me googly eyes all night.

Does she know who I am? Is that why I haven't given her the time of day?

I take another drink, scrunching my nose when I swallow.

We've got practice tomorrow; I know that I'll probably be hurting from the alcohol consumption, but I don't care.

Right now, I want to drink away my feelings and numb the pain. So that's exactly what I do. I drink, leaving the bar only when I have to.

It's just another night of self-destructive behavior, as Roman calls it. Well, fuck him. He can't fix my broken heart, so I have to fix it myself.

My *fucking* heart. It hurts in a way that I've never experienced before. After only a few months, I'd *known* that she was it for me. Like two pieces of a puzzle, Dakota was my final piece.

I have the hockey dream and everything it entails. I've got a home and friends that put all others to shame.

I hadn't *needed* a partner, but when I found one, it changed everything. All of my plans had changed, and now my heart is paying the price.

Admitting that I'm afraid is the hardest part of this. But the truth is that I am very afraid. I'm afraid that she won't be able to move past this and that one day I'll wake up and realize that she's never coming back.

I walk through the streets of downtown Boston, looking at all the lights. My eyes squint, causing the lights to splinter off in two directions. Sighing, I rub my face.

Did I push her too hard? The media can be cruel, and now I'm second guessing myself. I've learned to live with the attention, but with attention comes criticism and insecurity. I've been a victim of it myself; it isn't fun.

I would have given it all up for her. Every single bit of it.

My hands fumble to pull my phone from my pocket. I scroll through my contacts and type out several words before deleting them all. I can't text her now. Not like this.

Stumbling through the doors of Roman's home, I walk through the hallway and dump myself onto his couch.

I don't remember falling asleep, but when a pair of little hands walk across my back, I groan, tossing a pillow over my head.

"What's wrong with Uncle Wyatt?" Lily whisper-yells.

I crack an eye open and peek from underneath the pillow.

My mouth tastes like ass, the leftover alcohol not sitting well in my stomach. My head pounds when someone moves around dishes in the kitchen. It sounds like someone's starting a rock band, and I curse them.

"He's got a broken heart, Bug."

"Did Dakota break his heart?"

I sit up then, shooting Roman a glare.

"I miss Dakota." She sighs.

I miss her too.

"Let's leave Uncle Wyatt alone, Bug. I'm sure he wants to sleep some more." He walks over and lifts Lily from the floor where she'd slid off the couch. Watching them leave, I see pure sadness crossing Lily's face.

I hate myself for being in this position. I shouldn't be hungover on Roman's couch with my niece here.

It's time that I get my shit together again. If not for Lily, for myself and for Dakota. She'd been so strong through this whole process, then when she leaves, I'm suddenly a sack of shit.

Peeling myself from the couch, I write an apology to Roman, and slip out the front door. It's time that I pull myself out of this slump.

"You look wrecked, man." Jaiden tosses a handful of popcorn into his mouth, chewing it rather obnoxiously.

"Wow, thanks, jackass." I lift the weights over my chest, looking up at the ceiling. "Why are you eating popcorn in the gym?" I huff a breath when I extend the bar over my head and back down to my chest.

"Because I came to get my daily dose of entertainment." He sits on the bench beside me, still chewing away at his popcorn. I grind my teeth as he chews, the sound making my ears bleed.

I breathe through the next couple reps, pushing my body past its limit until my arms are shaking. Racking the weights, I sit up and stretch my arms above my head to get the blood flowing. When I swing to the right, I get a glimpse of my face in the mirror. The once purple and blue bruises have now turned an ugly yellow-green color. It's been six weeks and the bruises are still there.

It probably doesn't help that I feel like shit. Every day is the same when we're not traveling. I go to practice, then work out in the gym until I can't feel my arms or legs. After my workout, I run on the treadmill to get out all the soreness, then hit the ice bath before the showers.

The end of my day is spent at the condo that feels empty. It's not home without her.

The first week that she was gone, I found a pair of her shorts stuffed in one of my drawers. Every reminder of our time together hurts, like a wound reopening.

Jaiden peeks at his phone, then frowns as he shoves it back into this pocket with buttery fingers.

"What was that?"

"A mistake," he says, rolling his eyes, but I can tell there's something else there.

"Care to elaborate?" I look at him from the bench.

He sighs, dropping his head into his hands. "I've been sleeping with Sterling."

Roman looks at me from where he's standing. His eyebrow is raised in question, and I shake my head. I hadn't known either.

"Why is that a mistake?"

"I don't *do* relationships, man, and she's getting clingy." The way he says it tells me that he's lying. He's scared.

"Do you like her?" Roman asks from over my shoulder.

"Does it matter? I'll ruin her."

"It does matter, Jaiden. She's best friends with Dakota, I don't know where we stand, but I can't protect you if you screw this up. What are you afraid of?"

He shakes his head, running a hand through his curls. "Ever since my ma died, y'all know I've been a mess. People I love get hurt, and I told her from the start this was just fun."

"What changed?" Roman sits on the bench beside me so we're both facing Jaiden.

"I dunno. I guess she caught feelings. I ghosted her during the anniversary of my Ma's death, and I haven't said anything since."

Roman's face grows angry. "You can't do that to her. You owe her respect. Would you want someone doing that to Lily?"

Jaiden shakes his head furiously.

"Then treat Sterling with respect, man. Set a good example for your niece. You owe Sterling at least that much. If you can't be in a relationship with her, at least do her the decency of having a conversation. It'll hurt like hell, but at least you can say you were decent about it."

Jaiden nods, his eyes wandering to the back of the gym.

"You're coming over tonight?" Roman asks from my side.

Great. The attention is back on me.

"Naw. I'm busy."

"Doing what, Wyatt? Sulking like you have been for over a month? No. Lily misses you, and so do we. It's time you pulled you head out of your ass."

Damn. Roman's pulling all the punches by throwing Lily around today.

GOAL *Suck*

I narrow my eyes at him, my face angry. Everything in my body screams to snap at him, but I can't bring myself to do it. He's right.

"Fine." I toss my towel over my shoulder and walk to the showers. The guys slowly follow me, and I just *know* they're exchanging that look—the look of pity. I don't want their pity.

I shower in silence, not speaking to any members of my team. I trade the increasing tension for the silence of my car as quickly as possible.

Pulling out my phone, I scroll through the notifications. I haven't heard from her in weeks, and I'm beginning to question if I ever will.

I'd fucking poured my heart out to her. I'd told her that I loved her, and here we are. The worst part about it all is that I *still* love her. I love her so much that it hurts to breathe. I have to get up and play hockey like everything is normal. It's not. Nothing is fucking normal.

A notification for an article slides across my screen, and my heart clenches. It's the article that Dakota did a few months ago.

Women in Charge: Boss Babes and Their Claim to Fame

I read through the article against my better judgment. It talks about our *relationship* and something that Tanner had said which pissed both of us off.

I fucking hate him.

Staring straight ahead, I breathe through the place that my mind takes me. I breathe and breathe, a frustrated cry ripping from my throat.

I miss her so goddamn much. Everything about Dakota is perfect. She's motivated, intelligent, competitive, and she understands me. I've never felt like this with anyone. There was a future there, a story that had yet to be written, and I wanted every chapter of it.

The more I think about it, the more that I feel that the future I had begun to see is fading away. She tried to tell me that hockey was my dream, but she missed one very important thing.

She is my dream too.

CHAPTER 36
Dakota

My face is squished against a pillow in my room at Sterling's Toronto home. I've been hiding myself away in this place for Lord knows how long. The place smells stale, like I really need to open up a window, but I can't be bothered.

When was the last time I showered?

I roll over in my bed to see a text from Aida from Boss Babes. She outlines the release and the success of the article.

I don't know why it's such a hit. I'm not much of a success now. I've hidden away from Wyatt for over a month and I haven't talked to my family much either, outside of Dallas.

I slide my arm across the bed, wrapping my arm around the teddy bears he's brought me. That's only one bit of it. The fridge is filled with casserole that he's *made himself* and my favorite juices from our childhood. Not to mention the baskets upon baskets of candy and treats littering the living room. It doesn't *stop*, and a piece of me is glad for it, but another piece of me wants to wallow in self-pity *alone*.

As if my thoughts have conjured him, a knock sounds at the door. He's here every other day, and it's highly laughable.

I pull myself from bed, padding down the hallway and to the front door. I don't even bother looking at him before I turn away and flop onto the couch cushions.

"That bad, huh?" Dallas closes the door behind him, his tone telling me he's hiding his laughter.

I nod my head into the couch, groaning when he sits at my feet that are sprawled up the back of the cushions.

"Can we talk?"

I sigh loudly into the cushion, and he laughs this time. Rolling my eyes, I wiggle into a child's pose before sitting up and pressing my back into the couch so I can see him.

I wave my hand at him, indicating he should talk, and he snorts.

"I know that I've apologized many times, but I wanted to say it again. I was talking with Casey, and she advised that I just let you talk. I feel like there is a lot that we haven't talked about since you moved away."

"There is," I confirm.

"You said something that night. You said you wanted me to believe you." His hands rest in his lap almost like he's trying to keep from fiddling. "Why did you think I wouldn't?"

I twist my mouth to the side, my eyes threatening tears. "Honestly, I felt a little like you and Dad thought I was annoying," I say with a sigh. "I always felt like I needed to be tough and more tomboyish to fit in. You were my idol and I wanted to be more like you. Dad called me dramatic once, and it just switched something in me."

"I didn't know you felt like that," he says, his eyes down.

"Yeah, well, how could you? I didn't communicate. Everything you did, Mom and Dad praised like you were shitting gold, I swear. I just felt like I had to work harder for them to like me, which now that I say it feels ridiculous, but it's the truth. You were the older child, but I almost felt like you had the luxury of being the younger sibling, like I had to fit myself into this mold to fit into my own family. This stuff with Tanner was so out of that box that I got so worried you, out of all people, wouldn't trust me. He was your friend, and it felt like Mom and Dad practically worshiped him. And then I told Dad I wanted to be a tattoo artist, and it felt like he was looking at me with…disappointment? I don't even know. So I worked extra hard to be this successful businesswoman, and look at where we are now. He can't even look at me because I've failed him so bad."

He reaches over, grabbing my hand in his. He laughs lightly and I look over at him. "Dad loves you. When you moved away, you're all he would talk about. Every single milestone, he'd find news articles and announcements for your business and paste them on the fridge like they were trophies. He's so proud of you, and I'm fucking sorry that *I'm* the one telling you this and not him."

I'm silent, taking in his words. *My dad is proud of me?*

"You know that I'd trust you with my life? And my son's life too. I'm sorry that you felt that way, and I hope that, with time, I can fix it."

"I'd like that," I say. "I missed you, Dal. I'm sorry you felt like I left you. I was just…"

"Broken?" he supplies, and I nod my head. "I get it."

"Just…can I request something of you?"

He nods.

"If you have more kids with Casey, can you change the dynamic?

I don't want your kids feeling this way. If you have a baby girl later, I wouldn't want her to experience this. You're too good for that."

"I promise, Dakota."

"Good. Now leave me alone. I fucking love you, but I want some damn space." I slump into the couch. "Oh, and your casserole sucks. No one died, I'm not your neighbor, and I don't understand why people even want casseroles in those situations. If you want to bring me food, fly to the states and get me some damn In-N-Out."

Dallas' deep laugh fills me with joy. "Okay, fine. No more casserole."

"I love you," I say. "But get the fuck out."

He laughs again, harder this time. "I love you too. I'm leaving." He stands, smiling at me before he walks through the door, locking it behind him.

I press my face harder into the couch cushions, feeling the heaviness settle back into my chest. I let my thoughts wander, running through the events of the last couple weeks.

When I first ran away from Wyatt, I'd come to Canada thinking that I could fix things with my family. Thank God Dallas and I are okay *now*, but things with my mom and dad are still rocky after weeks of being here. It's been anything but easy to tame the sour taste in my mouth every time I've been faced with looking at them.

It doesn't help that my heart is splintered. I wake up, night after night, unable to breathe as the tears stream down my face.

Wyatt.

I can't stop my brain from thinking of him, and each time I do, I feel myself break a little more. It feels like pouring rubbing alcohol into an open wound. That broken part of me aches, but I'm too afraid to assign a feeling to that yet.

Did I ruin everything? Did I run away for nothing? I wanted to heal and fix this broken part of me, but I hadn't predicted that leaving him would break me more.

Gasping for breath, I cry into the cushion, the pain almost unbearable. It feels like a piece of myself is missing. *I did this to myself. I ran away.*

I swallow around the knot in my throat, my eyes puffy and swollen from the tears that have fallen in the past few minutes. Evening my breathing, I let myself succumb to sleep.

When I wake, it's much of the same.

I feel trapped, like my body won't let me move even when my mind fights to survive.

The tears fall again. There are several different kinds of tears these days, and these are tears reserved for Wyatt alone.

I love you.

How dare he admit that to me? How dare he be a human who makes me feel worthy of a love like that from him when I can't even love myself? I've spent this life as a shell of myself, and for the first time in a long time, I feel like Dakota. Just Dakota.

I move back to my bed, staying there until I can't anymore.

Light peeks through the small window, and I assume it's early morning. The days all run together.

A light tap sounds on the bedroom door before I see Sterling's face peek through the small crack. She shuffles in, Lani following close behind.

"So this is Canada," Lani says. "It smells like sadness." Sterling jabs her and she laughs. "What?

"Hey, babe," she says, her hand running over my probably greasy hair. I look up at her then hide my face in my pillow again. "Awe, we came all the way from Boston to see you and you won't even look at me?"

"Go away," I moan. "Let me wallow in peace."

"Not how it works, love. Now come on. The least you need to do is shower, and then we'll feed you." I look up at the mention of food.

"Ice cream?"

"Ice cream," she confirms.

"Fine." I groan, sliding my legs out from under the covers with my head still pasted to the pillows. "There better be toppings." I trudge to the bathroom, turning on the shower and letting the room fill with steam.

Once I'm showered and clean, I hate to admit that I feel better. My hair is no longer in knots, and those pesky eye bags are not as dark.

I dress in leggings and a baggy t-shirt before I walk down the stairs to the source of the voices.

"I'm so frustrated," Sterling says, tossing her phone onto the cushion. When she turns, we lock eyes.

"What's going on?" I ask, sitting on the couch. I run my fingers through my wet hair before I braid it aside.

"Oh, today isn't about me. I don't want to bother you with this."

"Silver," I say, narrowing my eyes at her.

She rolls her eyes. "Fine. Jaiden just stopped talking to me. I've texted him a million times, but something's wrong. I've never stayed the night there, and then after I do, it's like something shifted."

"Are you sure he just stopped talking to you?"

She nods. "He's still active on social media and shit. I sound crazy, but I thought it was my phone or something." She slumps a little, her eyes shooting to the corner of the room to avoid eye contact. "I was starting to fall for him. He was good for me. I even got a job with the team. I was tired of traveling around, and I thought I was ready to settle down a bit."

"Wait, you got a job with the Yellow Jackets?" I say, my eyes going wide. "Silver! That is amazing! What the fuck?"

"Holy shit," Lani says. "Congratulations, love!" Lani and I exchange looks for a moment.

"Yeah, well, it was. But if this shit continues and I'll have to see him every day at work, it'll be horrible."

I pull my legs into a criss-cross before I look at her again. "Sterling, this is amazing news. You *deserve* this, and you deserve to be treated like the damn queen you are. I don't give a fuck that Jaiden is Wyatt's best friend, you're deserving of so much more. Maybe you can fix it, but on the chance you can't, it should be because you know your worth. Don't let him treat you like that."

"I couldn't have said it any better," Lani says. "Jaiden ghosting is a douche move. Maybe there's something going on. I think a conversation is the best way to go, but if that can't happen, fuck him."

"Fuck him," I repeat.

Sterling sighs, slouching as she sits on the couch closest to the loveseat. "You're right. I do deserve better." Her voice is low and sad.

"Damn right. So, Lani, are you having relationship problems too?"

She laughs almost bitterly. "You could call it that," she says. "He's just so *absent*. But it's fine. I'm used to it at this point."

"If it makes you feel better, I don't know if Wyatt will still want me when I go back home." For the first time, I admit my fear out loud.

"Looks like we all needed a bit of therapy," Sterling says, her voice humorous to distract from the seriousness of the last several minutes.

"I think we need ice-cream-and-movie therapy too."

Both Lani and Sterling nod. We pile onto the couch, flipping through the movies until we find something with hot men and action.

I fall asleep holding on to both of my best friends, feeling safe and content.

It's been several days since Dallas has been here. I hadn't expected to see him for a while, but when the knock at the door sounded, I was *almost* glad to see him—until I saw my mom standing behind him. My mom and I are *okay*, I guess, but I wasn't prepared for this today.

Now I'm sitting on the kitchen stool as everyone else sits in the living room. It feels safer here.

My brother sits on a chair next to Sterling. Lani is on the opposite side next to my mother.

My mom watches me with this look of pity and sadness.

"Don't look at me like that," I say, my voice pleading.

She tilts her head, her shoulders dropping when she stands.

There's silence as she walks toward me and pulls me into her arms. I stay seated, but hold on to her like she's going to disappear.

I've been pushing them away for so long. A part of me doesn't want to let them back in, to allow myself to trust them, but as I stand here in my mom's arms, I feel a sense of rightness washing over me. I'm tired of living in sadness and fear. It's time for me to fix my problems, and for my family to fix theirs.

"I want a hug too," my brother says from his chair.

"Awe, is Dallas jealous?" I say loud enough for him to hear.

"Yeah. I am, butthead," he says with a laugh.

I smile, releasing my mom and leaning back into my chair.

The sound of the front door closing has everyone's eyes shooting that direction.

My father walks through the front door, his eyes sadder than I've ever seen them. When I watch him walk through the room, I can see the slight slump to his shoulders, his graying hair more prominent.

"Hi, Daddy," I say, my voice quiet. I don't expect him to acknowledge me, but he looks over at me and blinks several times. I see his face shift, and all at once, a sharp sob racks through his body. I'm unsure of how to react, so I watch him, my eyebrows pulled together.

"Hi, baby," he chokes out. It pains me to see him this way. It's the first time he's barely said a word to me and I want to know why.

"Why are you doing that?" I ask.

"What?" he asks, his emotions settling.

"Why are you caring now? You could barely look at me for weeks, and I don't understand what I did wrong."

His face falls again, a fat tear falling down his face. "Oh baby. I'm so sorry I made you feel that way. You did nothing wrong—nothing, you hear me?" In three big strides, he's standing in front of me, his hands raising like he wants to touch me but he's afraid to.

A lump forms in my throat as I look at him.

"Then why couldn't you look at me?"

He purses his lips. "I couldn't look at you and see that pain in your eyes. It was like a knife to the heart seeing you so hurt. I never knew, and I was *so* angry. I felt like I failed you as a father. I was angry at myself, and at Tanner, and I just didn't know what to say to you."

He pulls me into him and holds me for the first time in weeks. His voice is low as he speaks into my hair. "You're so selfless, baby. You're always thinking about everyone else. This is what you do, you care *so* much, and it was selfish of me to not look at you, but I just couldn't. I see how wrong I was, though. I'm sorry I couldn't protect you like a father should."

"It's okay. You didn't know, Daddy. You couldn't have."

"But I could have," he interrupts. "I should've seen it. It's my job to see it. Even Wyatt knew. He had to stop me from doing something

I'd regret, and for that I'll be forever thankful to him."

"Wait, what?" My heart pounds at hearing his name.

"I went looking for Tanner that night, and Wyatt stopped me. I could've murdered someone in my rage. I even shoved Wyatt, and he had the balls to stand up to me and tell me no. I earned a whole lot of respect for him that night. If any man is going to choose you first and protect you above all else, it's Wyatt."

I'm stunned. My father had gone looking for Tanner the night I told them everything? And Wyatt had stopped him…

My heart pounds in my chest. I love him—that's what this feeling is. It's why my heart has been fractured since the moment I left. I *love* Wyatt, and I walked away from him.

Fuck.

I'd believed my father was disappointed in me for weeks now. I'd thought that he was disappointed that I hadn't told him. Instead, he'd been angry at himself.

I gasp in deep breaths, tears blocking my vision. My dad grips me tightly, his hand rubbing soothing circles across my back. Trying to calm my breathing, I count out each breath. When I can finally speak, I feel my lips quiver as I choke out the words.

"I thought you were upset with me. I won't lie that I'm still upset with all of you. It'll take longer than a few weeks for me to get over years of feeling like an outcast in my own family, but seeing as we all still can't communicate, I think it's time we do exactly that."

"Koda, there is absolutely nothing that you have done that has disappointed me. You are a successful business owner, for Chrissake. You chase your dreams despite the opinions of others, and look where you are now! And that damn boy you found? He looked at you like you held the moon and stars in your hands. I never saw Tanner look at you like that. I'm so sorry that it took me this long to say it out loud to you." My father releases me and turns to Dallas. "I may be a man of few words, but you two are the best children I could ever ask for."

"Excuse me, what about me?" Sterling waves from the couch beside me, and I smile.

"Yeah, you're great too, kiddo. And Lani, you're a part of this family as well. Don't forget that."

"Awe. Thanks, Gray."

"Did he really look at me like that?" I ask.

My mother smiles at me thoughtfully.

"We actually have something for you." She winks at Sterling, the room falling into a comfortable silence.

The silence only lasts a few moments. Sterling pulls something from behind a pillow nearby and hands it to me. She nods her head toward the door right before the doorbell rings.

I leave the package on my seat and open the door to reveal a large vase with flowers. My throat tightens as I swallow and bend to pick up the flowers.

My mind rages as I stare at the vase on the coffee table. There's a note attached, and I can't quite bring myself to open it.

"Open the package first," Sterling says. Grabbing it, I hold it in my hands for an obscene amount of time. The beautiful paper wrapping feels smooth in my hands, and I'm so afraid of what I'll find inside.

Taking a breath, I rip, the paper coming off in one clean tear. My teeth bite into my lip when I look down at a printed piece of my article rested on top of a book.

> "Dakota Easton is the most incredible woman I've ever met," Wyatt Lane details his relationship with Dakota. When I asked him one of his favorite things about her, he replied with a simple statement: "What started as a

competition with her grew into so much more. Dakota fights, even when the odds are against her. That's what I love most about her."

I read the words over and over again until I slip them off the book to reveal another bound fanfiction. It's the one that was the hardest to find and the one that started my love of reading. It's the story that made me want to be the woman that I am.

I fumble to grab the note from the flowers when I'm suddenly aware of my friends and family watching me.

Opening the note, I see the tears splotching the ink on the note.

I'm so proud of you. Don't give up.
xo Wyatt

"I'll stand by your side through anything, Dakota. I need you to know that." Sterling watches me, her eyes wet with tears.

"Where do I go from here?" I set my things down and sit on the couch between them. They both wrap their arms around me, making me feel warm and loved.

"We fight. We fight until we win," Lani says.

"You're a damn lioness, Koda. It's time you act like one again." My father winks at me, his words making me smile.

"Do you love him?" Sterling asks.

I know the answer immediately, but the words taste like ash on my tongue. I don't feel deserving of those words when it comes to him. I think I could learn, though.

"I do. So much."

"Then fight. Not only for you, but for him. It's time. Actually it's way past time, but that's fine."

"He won't get away with this, love."

"You're right. He won't." It's Dallas that says it, and I turn to look at him. "I owe Wyatt an apology, but first, we owe it to Tanner to ruin all that he is for what he did to you."

"I shouldn't condone violence, but I support this fully," my father says with a raised hand. I laugh, hearing others join in with the laughter. For the first time, I feel like healing is truly possible. I've still got a long road ahead of me, but I'm ready to take the leap.

I sit between my friends, letting them cuddle me. Things are finally looking up for me.

CHAPTER 37
Dakota

"Thank you for meeting me," I say to the man across from me. He's dressed in a suit with his hair slicked back.

I look around the spacious office, taking in all the details to ease my mind. The desk is wide and tall to accommodate the long legs of the ex-hockey player that sits in front of me. The walls are decorated with Thunders merchandise and photos of all the players. When I look closely, I see a photo of Tanner on that wall.

"It seemed rather urgent. I doubted I had much room to refuse," the man says, his tone curt and cold. I'd expected nothing less from the general manager of the team.

"It is. I assure you."

My brother sits in the seat next to me, his comforting presence grounding me.

"What can I do for you?"

"I'm here to make you aware of something." I slap a folder down on his desk, the force of it disturbing some of the other papers resting there. He frowns, his eyes narrowing on the folder.

"What is this?" He flips it open, and his face shifts from annoyance to disgust and rage. His hands rummage through the myriad of photos I'd taken of myself during my relationship with Tanner. The photos depict a happy couple until the photos of the bloody wounds and bruises.

"I was going to press charges against a player of yours, but seeing as the law system sucks and it'll probably take years for me to get anywhere, I was going to take this"—I tap the folder—"to the media. I don't think that would look great for your team, so I came to speak with you first."

"What do you want?" He folds his arms in front of himself, his face now passive.

"I want Tanner to be expelled and blacklisted from the NHL. He assaulted someone I love. There are many other players I care for, and I won't see him hurting them."

"He did all of this to you?" He points down at the photos.

I nod. "He did."

"I trusted him around my family and he's around the families of the other players. This is completely unacceptable."

"He's sick and he needs help, but he won't get any until he has no other options," my brother says from my side. When my eyes find him, I see him staring intently at Raphael. "I've met you before, Raphael. Tanner was my best friend, and I was always here supporting him. I can't sit back knowing what he did to my sister, and if you care for your players, your family, or for hockey in general, you will do this."

I hadn't expected much from this meeting, but when he nods,

ushering us from the office, I leave feeling hopeful. It's not a prison sentence or a court proceeding, but it's something, and that's powerful.

For any victim of abuse, this is a step in the right direction. It's not perfect, but it's progress. I can't expect perfection from myself anymore. All I can hope for is progress.

This is only half the battle.

Dallas and I walk through the halls of the Thunders' business center in silence. It's not an uncomfortable kind of silence, though; it's a companionable silence, one that I'd hoped I could have with my other brother from the moment I was old enough to admire him.

I look over at him and smile, looping my arm through his and leaning my head against him.

"I'm proud of you," he says, clearing his throat. I hide my smile when I hear the slight choke of emotions in his voice.

"I couldn't have done it without you."

"There's something else I need you to do." He stops when we walk through the double doors. His hands go to my shoulders, his grip firm. "After we finish everything here, I want you to go home and to talk to Wyatt."

"What?" My heart races, my body feeling cold.

"You need to go back to Wyatt. I've never seen you as happy as you were with him. I don't know if soul mates exist, but I swear to the Lord above that you two are made for each other. The fact that he plays fucking rock paper scissors with you before his games…Dakota…"

"He told me he loved me." I swallow, unable to move.

"I know."

My eyebrows press together, and he clarifies, "Even before Sterling told me, I would've known. He stood his ground against me when I goaded him. He *chose* you, and he still does, seeing as he bought you a bound copy of those stupid fanfictions you read." He raises an eyebrow at me, and I laugh.

"They're not stupid. They're perfect."

"I wouldn't know," he says, shaking his head. "Go home, Dakota. You deserve to be happy."

"So do you, brother. Are you ever going to marry Casey? Her son literally calls you dada."

"Stop changing the subject. I'm serious, Dakota. It's been too long since I've seen you like that, and of course I had to be a jerk and ruin it, but it's the truth." He continues walking, the sound of his car engine rolling over. I can see his breath in the cool air, and it makes me shiver. "And since you asked, yes."

"Yes what?" I smirk at him, and he elbows me before we climb into the car.

"Yes, I'm going to marry her, you boob."

"Oh, I'm gonna miss you, brother."

"I'll miss you too, butthead." He laughs, his car thrown into reverse. I laugh too, a real laugh that shakes my whole body. When I look over at Dallas, I'm smiling. I think that everything is going to be okay.

My phone rings, and I panic slightly before I answer it.

"Roman, thank you for calling me back," I say, my voice shaking slightly.

He sighs, and the sound of it calms me.

"Things may be weird right now, but I'm glad you reached out. What can I do for you?"

I almost cry with relief as I process his words.

"I need a favor. Wait, I'm sorry. Maybe two favors. Can you get me on the phone with your coach? I spoke with the general manager of the Thunders, and there could be some fallout that I'd like to warn him about."

"Is this about Tanner?"

"It is. I don't know how much you heard that night, but I've been taking action against him, and I don't want it to impact Wyatt."

"Yeah. I can get you a meeting if you want." He pauses. "What's the second favor?"

"Can you get me into the last home game?"

"Absolutely." I can hear the smile in his voice. It sends my body into a fit of anxiety, but not the nervous kind. My senses are heightened, my body almost shaking with anticipation.

I'm coming home.

"Nice to see you again, Miss Easton—and with your feet firmly on the ground." Coach Hart smiles at me from across the table in a small cafe. "I'm assuming this is important, considering Roman practically rushed me from the Thunders' stadium to meet you here."

"Nice to see you too, Coach Hart. It is quite important. I needed to speak with you before the game this evening."

"Please call me Ryan."

I chuckle. "Okay…Ryan. I met with Raphael last week to discuss a matter regarding Tanner Morin. I don't know how much Wyatt shared with you the night that Tanner broke his nose, but everything that happened on the ice that night was because of me." I sigh, looking down at my coffee and sandwich that rest before me. "I dated Tanner in the past, and he abused me. I'll spare you the details, but Tanner attacked Wyatt because of our history. After years of letting it go, I finally took action. The Thunders will be releasing a statement soon. They've decided to end their relationship with Tanner. I also took out a restraining order on Tanner, which will include any contact with Wyatt as long as he chooses to remain in a relationship with me. I'm unsure of how they'll proceed, but I'm assuming that this will put your team in the hot seat."

"Why are you sharing all of this with me?"

He looks at me curiously, and I blink several times.

"I thought I made that clear," I say. "I'd rather you have a heads up before things go public."

Ryan shakes his head several times. "I'm aware of the press release, Miss Easton. Raphael contacted me a few days ago and warned me, so there's really no need for this conversation. I want to know why *you* felt the need to tell me this now."

I narrow my eyes at him, but I see no traces of annoyance there.

"I want to protect him," I admit. "I don't know if he's still on probation, and I really don't want Wyatt to sacrifice his dream for something that isn't his fault."

Ryan smiles, his face softening. "Funny. He said something similar to me just a few days ago."

"What do you mean?" My heart stutters as I wait for his response.

"Wyatt came poking around my office asking about potential careers outside of pro hockey. He's looking into being a scout. He called it a backup plan. Wyatt wants to protect you as well. He chose to ride the bench this upcoming game, even when I insisted that wasn't necessary." He waves his hand flippantly, his eyes dancing with intrigue. "He worked with our team attorneys to draft up restraining orders against Morin, including your protection as well. It's really quite humorous to see the both of you protecting each other without telling the other."

"He's looking into jobs outside of hockey?"

"I have no doubt in my mind that he would give up his dream for you if it meant you were comfortable. I'm sorry that Morin did that to you, and be aware that I gave Wyatt full permission to deck that fucker if he comes near either of you again." He smiles before taking a huge bite from his sandwich. Chewing thoughtfully, he nods several times. I stare at him, my mouth agape. "Is there anything else I can help you with, Miss Easton?"

"Dakota, please," I say when I finally regain my composure. "That's all…"

"Perfect. I suppose I'll be seeing you in a couple of weeks. Take care, Dakota." He nods at me, shoving another bite of his sandwich into his mouth and strolling away from the table.

I was not expecting that. Not one bit.

April 15th, 2021

WHAT HAPPENED TO TANNER MORIN?

In Tuesday's special of Pucked Up News, the GM for Toronto Thunders released a statement detailing abuse allegations against former player Tanner Morin.

After the team severed ties with the former bad-boy all-star, many speculations were made regarding the circumstances around the split. For several weeks, the team has remained silent when questioned about the nature of their split.

Morin has been unable to obtain a contract with other teams within his conference, which has left people shocked

GOAL Suck

and confused. Fans have been outraged at the lack of information surrounding the situation, stirring protests.

After two weeks of madness, Raphael Côté, the general manager for the team, has finally come forward, clearing the air of confusion.

It appears that Morin was accused of domestic abuse, but due to the nature of the law system, they decided to end their relationship with the player to protect the victim and future players.

Morin was suspended during a game in February when he broke Boston Yellow Jacket's Wyatt Lane's nose with the back of his hockey stick in the final period of the game.

Since then, Wyatt Lane has been mostly quiet about his relationship with Dakota Easton. When we reached out for a comment, he refused to answer any questions.

It has been a wild week for hockey fans across the world. I'd like to say that I'll be sad to see Morin go, but after learning some of the truth, I can't in my right mind support a player like that.

If you would like to see the full statement by Mr. Côte, you can find it on the official Thunders website along with a press release.

As always, skate on. Let's puck some shit up!

xo Brandi Wilder with Pucked Up News

CHAPTER 38
Wyatt

"This is it, men." Coach Hart paces the locker room, his hands tucked neatly into the pockets of his slacks. "This is our chance to clinch a spot in the finals. You all have played amazing this season, and I'm thankful to be your coach. Whatever happens, it'll be worth it to stand alongside some incredible players."

The team hoots and hollers as Coach Hart nods his head several times at all of us. He leaves the room, allowing us to run through our routines.

Like always, I watch Damian lace up that bead onto his skates and secure it with a knot. Jaiden kisses his skates a few times and wraps his stick exactly twenty-seven times.

I pull over my jersey, acknowledging my lucky underwear that don't exactly feel so lucky anymore.

GOAL Suck

This game leads us into the postseason, and everything is riding on our ability to crush our division title.

Lacing up my skates, I feel the frown already taking over my face. This had once been my dream to be here, and it still is, but something about it feels wrong. There's been a sense of wrongness since the moment that Dakota walked out of my condo.

A few weeks ago, I'd stopped drinking, deciding that it wasn't worth destroying my liver and ruining my relationship with my niece.

Things are going back to normal, but there's still that one piece missing.

Jaiden taps me on the shoulder with his stick, his eyes mischievous. "How ya feeling?"

"Kinda like I want to puke," I admit.

"Me too. That's normal, though."

"You pussies ready to go?" Damian walks to Jaiden's side, slinging an arm over his shoulder. I watch the two of them, wondering when Damian finally clicked with my friends.

"I heard they're doing something different with the big screens today. I'm looking forward to watching from the ice during warmup." Jaiden raises an eyebrow at Damian before they both look at me.

The players start shuffling out of the locker room, so I ignore them to follow after the others as they walk through the tunnel.

The cheers are deafening as we skate onto the ice. I take a loop, looking along the glass for someone that I know I won't see.

Running drills with Roman, I do my best to ignore the crowd, attempting to focus my wandering brain. I turn my head when I hear my name. I look around, but go back to the drills when I can't find the source.

"Wyatt," someone chants to my left. I wave, thinking it's fans trying to get my attention, then several people shake their heads, pointing up. Damian points at the screen above our heads, and I skate into a position where it's more visible.

The breath leaves me when I see Dakota's face on the screen. She's waving and trying to get down to the glass, but a security guard has stopped her. I panic, skating to the glass and yelling for the security guard.

"Hey! She's with me," I say through the noise. She gives the security guard the sassiest look, and I laugh, my heart stuttering when she locks eyes with me. I search for any bit of panic within them. After everything that she's been through, I'd expected her to be fearful to step foot in this place, but when I turn to look into the big screen, I see nothing but radiating confidence.

She's just as beautiful as I remember, if not more. There's this new confidence in her that sends me soaring. I want to touch her, to hold her, make sure that this is real and not a dream.

She sprints down the stairs and right to the glass. Not wasting a moment, her hand rests against the glass, her eyes hesitant.

I pull off my glove, placing my hand against the glass. I can see her sigh, her body relaxing. She pulls her hand away, clenching it into a fist and resting it on her palm. I shake my head with a smile.

"On three," she says, her voice shaking. I nod.

"One…two…three."

Jaiden slides across the ice, his arms raised above his head as the crowd cheers. We all spill out of the side, rushing him.

"The Boston Yellow Jackets have clinched their division," the announcer yells over the cheers. My ears ring as players crash into my back in a dog pile.

GOAL *Suck*

"We're going to the finals," Damian yells at my side.

Everyone is screaming, but there is only one place I want to be right now, some business I need to take care of.

Damian looks at me, nudging his head toward the tunnel. "Go. I'll cover for you."

I nod, skating away from my team and toward the tunnel. I rush into the locker room.

When I reach into my cubby for my towel, a note falls out onto the floor near my feet, and I hold it between my fingers.

Meet me at the place you first knew.

I smile into my hand, my body burning to be rid of this gear and out of this place.

Leaving before the others shuffle into the locker room was a feat all on its own. I slipped out and into the darkness of the spring night to find Jaiden leaning against my car.

"You're going to need this," Jaiden says, extending my phone to me. My eyes narrow when I take it from him. "I was on strict orders. Before you leave, look at the first article I sent you." He winks, righting himself before he walks through the doors of the stadium once more.

The leather seats of my car allow me to slip in effortlessly. When I'm seated inside, my car warming already, I unlock my phone and read through the article.

As I read, I find myself sitting up a little straighter, the smile on my face widening. Not waiting another moment, I toss my car into reverse and drive to the arcade downtown.

It's empty when I walk through the doors. At first I question myself, thinking maybe I got it wrong, but then I spot Dakota at the basketball machine, tossing balls into the hoop quite effortlessly.

My first instinct is to rest my hands on her waist, but I think better of it until she reaches her hand behind and pulls me against her.

Pressing back into me, she stays there while I wrap my arms around her waist and breathe in the fruity scent of her hair.

"You came," she says.

"Of course. Did you think I wouldn't?"

She turns around to face me. Her eyes are watery, and I kiss her cheek before wiping away the stray tear.

"I was worried that you'd moved on." Her face falls to the floor. I slip a finger under her chin and lift it to face me.

"I would wait for you forever if I had to." I tilt my head to look at her more closely. There's no trace of the fear that had once been there before. This woman standing before me is different. "You look better," I say. She blinks at me several times, then smiles.

"Did Jaiden send you the article?" She raises her eyebrows questioningly.

"He did." I pause, placing my hands on her shoulders. "I'm so damn proud of you. How did you even do it?" She snorts, shaking her head.

"I may have threatened media attention, and Dallas pulled the family card. It worked though; he can't hurt you now. I filed for a restraining order, which means he can't hurt you either. But I'm told that you've been making some things happen on your end too."

"Whatever do you mean?"

She shakes her head at me, her eyes smiling.

"A lot's happened then, huh?"

She nods. "Yes. And that actually leads me to why we're here." She gestures to the arcade around us. Taking a deep breath, she looks at me intently before she speaks. "Wyatt, you told me before I left that you loved me. At first I didn't feel worthy of love from you. I'd been broken, and I still have some healing to do, but I'm on the right track. While I was gone, I realized that I needed to forgive myself first before I could love someone else. But during my time away, I realized that"—she grabs my hands, squeezing them tightly—"I couldn't imagine my life without you. I love you too, Wyatt. I think that I've known it for a while, but I was too afraid to admit it. This whole time that we've been together, you've made it abundantly clear how you feel through your actions. It's the little things, like the bound fan fiction and the way that you look at me, that should've tipped me off."

"I'm not great at hiding my feelings," I say.

She laughs, her face scrunching.

"See. You're perfect. So all of that being said, I wanted to do something for you. Please don't laugh." She pushes me backward a few steps until she drops to one knee. I raise an eyebrow at her, and snort when she glares at me. "Stop it. You're going to ruin the moment."

"Keep going," I urge her. She pulls out a small packet from her pocket and unwraps it, holding it out to me.

"I got you this ring pop because I don't know your ring size." I snort, and amusement scrunches her face. "I want to spend my life with you, Wyatt Alexander Lane. It doesn't have to be right now—or even soon—I just want you to know that I want you, Wyatt. I want you forever. I want to be a part of your family and you mine. I want you to come to Christmas with me and I want to have Thanksgiving with your family. I want to play rock paper scissors with you before every game, and I don't even care if I lose every time. I just want you to be mine. So, Wyatt, will you marry me someday in the future?"

"You know that's my job, right?"

"Shut up and answer the question, Wyatt. My knees hurt." She shakes her head, and I laugh a full belly laugh. "If you really want to, you can do some elaborate proposal, but let me have this."

"Fine." I lift her off the ground and into the air. She wraps her legs around my waist, and it feels like this is exactly what I've been missing. "Dakota Easton, I will absolutely marry you. Now shut up and let me kiss you."

Her laughs echo through the small arcade as I press my lips into her.

"Take me home, Wyatt," she breathes, and I don't have it in me to deny my fiancée anything for another minute.

CHAPTER 39
Dakota

L ips brush my neck as I buckle the harness across my chest. Wyatt's hands glide down my sides, and I shiver into his touch.

It's my first day back to work in months. I'd worked when I was up to it, but I know that there will be so much for me to catch up on. My stomach has been in knots and my body tense in anticipation of today.

"Do you want me to come with you?" He places a light kiss against my hair, and I lean back into him.

"I'll be okay. You're coming for lunch though?"

"Wouldn't miss it for the world." He looks into the mirror at me, and I see the softness in his eyes.

"I'm scared," I say, my voice low.

"You are the most talented woman I know, Koda. Being scared is normal, but trust me when I say that you have nothing to be afraid of."

Releasing a deep breath, I look at myself in the mirror one last time. I'd chosen an outfit that makes me feel feminine and powerful.

Healing isn't linear, and it's a journey. I know that this is another piece of my healing journey. My business is important to me. I'm incredibly proud of it, and it's time that I give it some extra special attention.

"I love you," Wyatt says, bending to place a kiss on my lips as I walk out the door.

"I love you too. I'll see you at lunch." He nods as I leave with a smile on my face. This is just a taste of what our lives could be, and I can't help but relish in the feeling of it.

As I walk through the doors of my shop, Lani and Silver are standing in the doorway with coffee and treats.

"Welcome back!" They both take a step toward me, pulling me into their arms.

"God, I can't tell you both enough how thankful I am for you."

"Holding down the fort wasn't that hard, you know. You're an incredible boss, and this is hardly work." Lani gives me a wide smile, and I return it.

"Well, we've got lots to do today. I won't lie to you and say that I'm not stressed about it."

"We got this!" Silver says, handing me a scone.

"Oh my God, it's blueberry!" I shove the scone into my mouth, taking a big bite. I nearly moan around the sugary goodness. *So damn good.*

Several hours later, I finished my second-to-last appointment before lunch. I hadn't expected today to go perfectly smoothly, but when thing after thing continued to go wrong, I found myself taking a break to wipe frustrated tears from my face. It's been a damn day, and it's only half over.

I sit, hunched over my iPad with Lani at my side. We've been rescheduling appointments all morning to get people back onto my books, but when there was an error in my system, every new appointment disappeared in seconds.

I take a deep breath, clenching my hands into fists as I stare at the screen in frustration.

"All of that damn work, just to have it disappear?" I say, my voice tense.

"I'm going to hop on the phone with IT. I'll be back." Lani holds her phone to her cheek as she walks upstairs.

The front door to my shop slams open, and I stand abruptly, my body shuddering at the impact.

"You!" Seeing Tanner walk through the doors of my shop sends my body into a panic. He holds his finger out in front of him as he points at me aggressively. "You *bitch!* You're ruining my life."

He walks toward the front desk, ignoring the other people in my shop. Several people gasp, but I can't bring myself to care. As if today couldn't get any worse…

I hear someone walk down the stairs, Sterling appearing in my peripheral vision. She peeks her head out, then rushes back up the stairs.

I sigh, keeping my voice calm. "I didn't ruin your life, Tanner. You did that yourself."

"Oh, is that what you think? You're such a fucking cunt, you know that? You deserved this. I just gave you exactly what you deserved. Who cares if I knocked you around a bit?" He throws his hands up as he walks toward me. I step back, feeling my back press into the wall behind me.

"Is that what you have to tell yourself so that you can sleep at night? You're not supposed to be here, Tanner."

"I don't fucking *care*, Dakota," he shouts, his breath nearly hitting my face as he approaches me.

"I dare you, Tanner. Do it," I say, taunting him. If he touches me, I promise all hell will break loose. He growls, his eyes so far gone that I can't even see a single trace of the man I once cared for.

He slams his fist against the wall behind me, flecks of paint chipping off and causing me to flinch. His face comes closer to mine, and I hold his eye contact. *You can't scare me anymore.* My dad thinks that I'm a lioness, so I better start roaring like one.

When his hand comes down to my shoulder, his grip tight, I hiss. His nails dig into my flesh, and it takes everything in me not to react.

"Fuck you," I spit. "You can't hurt me anymore."

His face is red with anger, his eyes murderous.

Suddenly, Tanner is ripped from my face, his body flying backward.

"You don't *touch* her," Wyatt spits, his teeth bared as he growls at Tanner. "I promised you that if you laid one finger on her, that I would end you. But guess what? I don't have to even do anything. You've done that yourself."

By now, everyone in my shop has moved to the side, their phones out and cameras rolling.

Tanner moves away from him, standing. "You want to fight? Let's fight." He charges at Wyatt right as he moves to the side and out of the way.

"Outside," he says, his voice full of authority.

"This is *your* fault too. You two sluts are working together to ruin my life."

I laugh, unable to stop myself. They both look over at me, and I can see the smirk on Wyatt's face.

"It's everyone's fault but your own, huh?" I shake my head at him as he scoffs.

"Fight me," he yells. "Fight me!" He swings, and Wyatt grips his fist, stopping it mid punch. He looks at me, almost as if he's asking for permission. I snort, nodding my head.

He punches Tanner in the face, landing another in his gut. Tanner hunches, blood spilling from his mouth. When he returns upright, he smiles at me, his expression almost mad. He spits at me, and Wyatt punches him again, a sharp grunt leaving his mouth this time.

"That's all you got?" Tanner asks, his tone taunting.

"Unlike you, I don't normally resort to violence. Plus, it looks like your ride is here."

As if on cue, several police vehicles pull up to the front of my shop, several officers charging into the shop.

I stop hearing their voices as Wyatt walks over to me, pulling me into his arms.

"Are you okay?" His eyes roam over my body as his hands run an inspection as well. I laugh, my eyes looking over his worried face.

"Surprisingly, I feel perfectly fine. Did Sterling call you?"

"Oh, she called me, all right. I can't tell you how fast I ran here." He bends, resting his forehead against mine. I close my eyes as I breathe.

"He violated his restraining order…I didn't think he would do that."

Wyatt opens his mouth to speak, but I'm pulled away by several officers. They ask routine questions, gathering all of the information needed. Multiple people offer their videos to the officers, and they accept.

After an hour, my shop is empty once more, only my staff and Wyatt remaining. Sterling stands across from me, her eyes full of glee.

"What happens now?"

"We're pressing charges. He'll go to court and go from there. Our state takes these things pretty seriously, so I believe we've got a shot at something serious. Best-case scenario, jail time and a fine with entry into a program." My friends nod. I can't help but smile. I hate that he came to my shop and put my people at risk, but I am incredibly proud of myself. I may have felt some fear, but something in me shifted today. That is what I'm most proud of. He didn't hold that same power over me.

"I can't believe he spoke to you like that," Lani says.

"I can, but after all of that, I'm glad that there's no way in hell that he could deny it now. There's proof, and that's more than I could ever ask for." Wyatt tucks me under his arm, kissing the top of my head.

"Lunch on me," he says. "We have cause for celebration." He looks down at me, his eyes gleaming. I have no doubts that he can see the shift in me.

"Yeah, we do," Silver says. "Justice is served."

EPILOGUE
Wyatt

FIVE MONTHS LATER

My hands tangle in Dakota's hair as my tongue runs across her lips. She gasps, and I take the opportunity to swipe my tongue into her mouth, tasting the sweetness of the fruit she'd been eating.

She bites my lip and I groan into her, her legs wrapping tightly around me.

"Happy birthday to me," she says, her voice breathy.

"Oh, we're celebrating much more than that," I say, kissing her neck. I vaguely register the sound of footsteps before someone shrieks.

"Ick! Guys, get a room." Sterling laughs, shaking her head as I help Dakota slide off the kitchen counter. "The party is waiting for you. And not on Roman's counter."

"They can wait," I say, nipping at Dakota's ear lobe. Her face reddens just the way I knew it would.

"Let's get this over with," she says, laughing. "I hate being the center of attention."

"You'll be fine. Just smile and look pretty." Sterling smirks as Dakota laughs.

"Easy for you to say," she says, her arm looping through mine. Sterling walks ahead of us as we walk through the house and out the back door. Several people cheer as we appear in the back yard together.

There are several balloons, some saying happy birthday and some saying congratulations. I'm surrounded by greens and golds, the apparent theme of the party.

"Congratulations," several people yell. I look over to see everyone who's here to celebrate with us. Many of my team members are scattered across the lawn, Jaiden staying far away from Sterling. Dallas and his wife and child stand by the food table, while Dakota's parents stand with their hands clasped to our right. Gray winks at me, his cool demeanor from Christmas completely gone now.

I look forward to every step in our journey, every moment that I'll be able to share with her.

Our family is here with us to celebrate the engagement that we'd kept secret for months. Dakota had made it official, buying me a real ring that rests on my left hand.

I catch her playing with it often, the other rings on my fingers quickly forgotten. Even now, as she stands beside me, she twists the two-toned gray and gold band around my finger.

Jaiden grabs the inflatable diamond ring from the fence. He's got a big goofy grin on his face as he walks across the lawn toward us. Stopping in front of Roman, he gets down on one knee, extending the giant ring toward Roman.

"Roman, my love. Will you marry me? Make me the happiest

man alive!"

"Oh fuck off," I say to Jaiden, shaking my head with a smile.

"What?" he asks from the ground. "I'm just taking a page out of Dakota's book."

I release Dakota, walking toward him ready to get him in a headlock and give him a noogie.

He stands abruptly, shrieking loudly as he rushes away from me.

"You're going to make such a beautiful bride, Wyatt," he yells over his shoulder. I growl, tackling him to the grass.

His deep laugh echoes through the backyard as I put him in a headlock.

"Boys, it's a party, not a wrestling match," Sterling calls from the dessert table.

We right ourselves quickly. I walk back to Dakota's side and Jaiden walks far, *far* left. There's been tension between Jaiden and Sterling since the end of the season. They're nearly always at each other's throats when not acting like the other doesn't exist. It's frankly exhausting for everyone around them. I know it's taking a toll on Dakota. She loves this found family so much, and she takes the troubles of others onto herself.

This one isn't her problem to fix.

Roman's knife clinks on his champagne glass from across the room. Lily stands on a chair beside him in her emerald dress that matches the decor of the backyard.

"Lily and I have a few words we would like to say to the happy couple. Go ahead, baby girl."

Lily clears her throat. "Uncle Wyatt, I'm glad your heart isn't broken anymore because I like you better when you're not sad."

I bend over laughing, and Dakota looks over at me, her hand on my back. She winks and I stand upright again.

"Did you tell her to say that?"

"Me? Never." She grips my hand. We look up as Roman continues after Lily.

"When I first met Dakota, I have to admit that I thought about dating her myself until Wyatt practically growled at me from across the table." He laughs into his arm as the crowd laughs too. "But as I've seen the two of you together, I can't imagine a better pair. You're both competitive as hell, and some of the most talented people I know. Being a hockey player isn't easy, but I've witnessed them both take it in stride. Finding a partner while you're already in the career is hard. I know, because I've failed myself. I'm happy for you, bro. Dakota, you've become one of my best friends through this process. Thank you for being a part of our family and for taking so nicely to Lily. If soul mates exist, I can confidently say that I believe the two of you are exactly that. Not only did you win the Stanley Cup this year, you won this beautiful lady beside you. Congratulations to the both of you, and happy birthday, Dakota."

"Hear, Hear." Voices sound off around the room, Dakota holding her champagne glass in her hand as everyone cheers.

"Let's eat cake," I say, over the cheering.

As we make our rounds, I'm overly aware of raised voices at the back of the lawn. Several heads look in that direction and I see Sterling and Jaiden at each other's throats.

"The cake," Dakota says, her voice low. I grip her hand, weaving us through the crowd to the back.

"How *dare* you say that to me, Jaiden? This is your doing. I had the audacity to get a job? I was pursuing my *dream*, you asshole."

"I *never* said that, and you know it. Why do you have to be so dramatic?" Jaiden yells at her, his hands squeezed into fists and his knuckles white. Sterling screams, her head thrown back.

Everyone stops what they're doing to watch. My throat bobs and I swallow back anger.

"Maybe it was a mistake to invite them," I mumble, and Dakota nods.

"You know what? I *fucking* hate you, Jaiden Thomas. I hate you so much. I am *not* dramatic." She looks around her, and I see Dakota lunge for her the moment it happens.

Sterling shoves her hand into the cake, taking a handful and shoving it into Jaiden's face. He stumbles backward with the force, cake hanging out his mouth.

Sterling shakes off her hand, flinging cake at Dakota, who had stopped in front of them. Her eyes go wide when Dakota stares down at her dress now sprinkled with cake.

"Oh my gosh, I'm so sorry," Sterling says, her eyes going wide when she realizes that everyone is staring.

"You two," Dakota says, her voice low and feral. "Inside. Now." She points to the house. Both Sterling and Jaiden walk with their tails between their legs inside the house, Dakota following after them.

"Carry on," I say, waving Roman over to follow us. Damian stops flirting with one of Dakota's friends to follow us inside.

I can feel the rage pouring off of her, and not because Sterling and Jaiden almost ruined her party.

This has been a battle for months. The two of them can't seem to get along after Jaiden royally fucked up.

After the four of us walk inside, I close the slider door to the backyard, giving us privacy.

Sterling stands by the pantry, her arms crossed over her chest, while Jaiden stands opposite her with his hands shoved so deep into his pockets you'd think he was trying to disappear inside of them.

"Can the two of you help me with something?" Dakota's voice is sweet, but I see the mischief swirling behind her eyes.

Sterling frowns, her eyes narrowing. "Uh, sure."

Jaiden shrugs, following after her.

"Great. Since the two of you ruined my cake, I'm going to need a new one. Can you grab the cake mix and frosting, please?"

"Sure…" They walk inside the pantry and Dakota slams the pantry door shut behind them.

"Chair, please," she says, waving her hand at me. I snort, grabbing a chair from the table and handing it to her.

"Dakota!" Sterling yells. "Don't do this. You can't!"

"I can and I will," she yells back. "You two are making everyone around you miserable, and today is my last straw. This is supposed to be a party, and it's my fucking birthday. Until the two of you can work out your shit and agree to behave, I'm not letting you out of there. And before you complain, there's enough food and water in there for weeks, and an emergency bucket. I'm tired of your shit."

"Dakota," Jaiden whines with a groan.

"Don't you dare. Enjoy the pantry. Come, *fiancé*, we have a party to attend." She extends her hand to me, and I take it. As if I thought I couldn't love her anymore, this proves that I will love her more and more every day.

"Sorry about your pantry, Roman," I say over my shoulder.

Damian snorts. "I like her."

Me too, bud. Me too.

"Perfectly fine. That was the best thing I've ever seen." Roman strolls out the back door, leaving it open for us.

"I love you," I say, bending to kiss her.

"I love you too. I can't wait to marry you."

"Soon, love. Soon."

The End...

The series will be continued in book two of the PuckHeads Series, Dirty Dangles.

ACKNOWLEDGEMENTS

Wow. Thank you so very much for being here. This book means so much to me. I have loved every moment of writing Dakota and Wyatt's story. I love both of them so much and I truly hope you love them too.

First things first, gotta thank God because my faith is something I value and I truly believe this talent of writing comes from him.

This book would absolutely not exist without the help of several of my friends. I've got a list, don't worry.

Jess, thank you so freaking much for believing in me so much to practically bully me into writing this. You knew my love for hockey and had faith that I could write something amazing. I hope you love it.

Ash, thank you for being my sounding board. You've read basically every stage of this book, and for that I am incredibly thankful.

Britt, you are my playlist Queen. The aesthetics and songs are only in existence because of your amazing brain, so thank you!

Lexi, you are a goddess. Thank you for encouraging me to create and with all of your help inspiring me to make my own dang covers. Yeah. I did that.

Leez, thank you for hyping me up so much! I'm so freaking happy to have you be a part of this journey. Thanks for telling me my writing doesn't suck, hehe.

Courtney, Gah! So much of this story---the concepts, the freaking name, the Canadian aspects---those things would not have been possible without you. Thank you for everything you've done to make this story great.

Colby (Bae) I fucking love you. Thank you for loving these characters as much as I do. You have been so supportive and loving throughout this whole process and I'll never be able to thank you enough. This story is what it is because of you. I'm keeping you forever.

Hazel, girllllll, Thank you for reading for me when the lizard brain was getting heavy. Your reactions and commentary gave me life and encouragement as I was finishing up touches on this story. Thank you for talking things through with me and for cheering me on! YE YE!

Reva, my other Canadian bestie. Thank you for all of your help and for helping me with Canadian terminology and for teaching me photoshop because your girl was struggling.

To my human and his family! For anonymity purposes, I appreciate you and your support through all of this!

To my family, I love all of you and thank you for your support. Thanks for putting up with my crazy.

Dad, thank you for being my biggest supporter. I obviously wouldn't be alive without you so it's true to say the cliché 'I wouldn't be here without you,' but for real, I wouldn't be a writer without your encouragement. I told you I was writing a book and I received nothing but support from you. Thank you for always encouraging me to do what I love. You're the best dad a girl could ask for. Love you!

Last but not least, to all of my readers, thank you for taking that chance on me. I am incredibly thankful for every single one of you. You are the ones who truly make me an author. Being able to converse with you is some of the best experiences of my life, so thank you.

xx
Gabbie D.

CPSIA information can be obtained
at www.ICGtesting.com
Printed in the USA
BVHW091332040123
655465BV00014B/685